THE GUILTY TWIN

HOLLY RIORDAN

THOUGHT CATALOG Books

THOUGHTCATALOG.COM

THOUGHT CATALOG Books

Copyright © 2023 Holly Riordan.

All rights reserved. No part of this book may be reproduced or transmitted in any form or any means, electronic or mechanical, without prior written consent and permission from Thought Catalog.

Published by Thought Catalog Books, an imprint of Thought Catalog, a digital magazine owned and operated by The Thought & Expression Co. Inc., an independent media organization founded in 2010 and based in the United States of America. For stocking inquiries, contact stockists@shopcatalog.com.

Produced by Chris Lavergne and Noelle Beams
Art direction and design by KJ Parish
Circulation management by Isidoros Karamitopoulos

thoughtcatalog.com | shopcatalog.com

First Edition, Limited Edition Pressing
Printed in the United States of America.

ISBN 978-1-949759-75-4

CHAPTER 1

EVAN

I twirl my butter knife between my fingers, wondering whether the blade is sharp enough to slit my throat. I would rather bleed out than waste another second in this tacky neon diner. What was Brooke thinking, asking me to meet at a dump with wailing children and claw machines by the bathrooms? This time last year, I was lounging on mountain-view balconies, gossiping over champagne and charcuterie boards.

I guess karma finally caught up with me.

My phone buzzes across the scarred wooden table where I've been waiting for fifteen—no, twenty—minutes. I expect an apology text from my date about running late or canceling plans completely, but it's an email. An order placed for a customized shot glass. After shipping and material costs, the sale won't bring in much money, but it's better than nothing. Until the divorce is finalized, every cent counts.

I'm tapping at my screen, approving the order, when a husky voice calls over my shoulder. "Evan? Is that you?"

I crane my head, scanning the woman towering over me. Wiry. Tan. A different hair color than her profile photos, the beachy blonde swapped for a sandy brown chopped to her chin. I fake-advertised on the app too, so I don't have a right to complain. Besides, she looks good. Butterflies-batting-around-my-stomach good.

"You found me," I say, rising to wrap her in a hug. The sleeves of her sweater dress are tight against her arms, but floral tattoos spiral around her bare thighs like vines.

"It's nice to finally meet you in person," she says, even though we've only been messaging for three days. "I was worried you were a catfish with those photos. You looked unreal."

I snort, flipping my platinum curls. "You don't have to lay it on that thick. Full disclosure, I haven't been on a date in forever."

"I've been on way too many, so it'll even out." She settles into the seat opposite me, her face sinking. "Shit. Maybe I shouldn't have admitted that. But, you should know, studies say women fall in love seven times before finding their person."

"Seven?" I whistle. "I'm only on two. Unless dogs count. Then it's somewhere in the hundreds."

"I would have sworn you were a cat person."

"It's the glasses."

"And the slow blink. I feel like you're staring straight into my soul."

My lips twitch, but before I can bounce back a reply, a server putters over to the table. The hunched, middle-aged woman recites the daily specials, then veers into a rant about the torn disc in her back. I zone out as she rambles, hoping she gets the hint to hurry it up. Since I moved back to Long Island, I've been surviving on home-cooked meals and pizza deliveries to avoid mingling with the neighbors. I almost forgot how chatty everyone in this town gets while snipping hair or scanning groceries. It's like their self-awareness gene is missing.

If Brooke is bothered by the interruption, she masks it better than me, nodding along like she actually cares. It takes five excruciating minutes for her to order a cheeseburger, hold the onions. I make it two and add hard drinks.

As the waitress hobbles away with our oversized menus, I skim the paper placemats hidden beneath. They're eyesores, cluttered with advertisements for car rentals and dry cleaners and cafés. And in the corner, a posting about the ten-year anniversary of the Faith Flynn disappearance.

I swallow, my collar suddenly tight and scratchy against my neck. It feels like the thermostat has been cranked up to one-hundred, but it's the dead of winter and the door is propped open. I chug the rest of my water, hoping to cool myself down.

No luck.

I plant my glass over Faith's face, but I already got a good view of her picture. They went with her school portrait, senior year, a white gown covering her real clothes. Her makeup must have taken an hour—lined lips, heavy blush, eyeshadows in glittery golds and browns. She looks sweet, not like the type of girl who would burn her sister with a sparkler, leaving a permanent scar. Who would plant a joint in my work locker, trying to get me fired.

"Are you going?" Brooke asks, tapping her mat. "To the memorial dinner? I keep hearing about it."

"Oh, no, I don't want anything to do with that crap."

Her forehead puckers.

"That came out wrong. I'm not heartless, I swear. I just don't want to be around their family. It's too depressing."

"Uh oh," she sing-songs. "Does gore freak you out? Because, fair warning, I'm super into crime docs."

"No worries. The stuff usually doesn't faze me—but I went to school with this girl."

I purposely leave out how many nights I spent in her bedroom. It's not like we were on speaking terms. She would grumble whenever I passed through the door, move her blankets to the couch whenever I spent the night. She wasn't my favorite person, either. I would shoulder right past her, beelining for the mattress across from hers, where her sister was sleeping.

"No way, you knew the twins?" Brooke asks, popping a piece of bread onto her tongue. "Were you close?"

"Not with Faith. But we both worked at the theater, so we saw a lot of each other."

"Flynn Family Films? I was there a few days ago."

"You're kidding. I figured the place would be converted into a junkyard by now. It's really still standing?"

It's a throwaway question. A while back, I set up a Google alert to monitor the cinema, so I already know the answer. But it's not like there's anything more exciting to discuss. First dates are meant for surface-level fluff. It's more about subtext and testing chemistry than caring about the specific topic. She could be yammering about birdwatching or baseball cards and I would pretend to eat it up.

"Yeah, the place is gorgeous," she says, spreading butter onto more bread. "It's just as nice as any of those bigger theater chains."

"Then they must have gotten rid of that corny-ass crystal ball."

She cocks her head. "A crystal ball? Like, that sees into the future?"

"Yup. It was bizarre. You would slip some coins into this giant glowing orb and a fortune would spit out. They were super vague like *you're going to find your soulmate soon, as long as you keep your eyes wide* or *be careful because those who love you don't always love your success*. The one time I tried it, it told me: *You're never alone, no matter how far into the shadows you crawl.* It was supposed to be inspirational, but it sounded like a warning that ghosts were out to get me."

Brooke fake-shivers. "I'm surprised you didn't quit on the spot."

"Believe it or not, it was my longest job. I started when I was fifteen and stayed until the end of high school. It was fun. For a while."

"Until the murder."

"Kidnapping."

"Right. Kidnapping."

Silence descends over our table, harsh as a gavel. Luckily, our server shuffles over with plates crowded with burgers, coleslaw, pickles, and fries. I slather the latter in ketchup, smearing it like blood across the plate, trying to think about anything other than that final night at the theater. The drinking games. The stale cigarettes. The horror film I barely watched, too distracted by my own drama to care about the killer stabbing horny teens on screen.

The next morning, the police interviewed me in a musty room swinging with a single bulb. Like we were in a damn noir film. I swore I didn't know anything about Faith's vanishing act, lied when they asked whether anyone had reason to harm her. A better question was, *was anyone actually upset she was gone?*

"Enough about the Flynns. Tell me about your family," Brooke says, cradling her chin.

Over the next hour, she asks a million questions and peppers in her own info—she's an Aries, a marathon runner, a certified yoga instructor. She's swam with sharks in Australia, bungee jumped in Nepal, ziplined in Costa Rica. She's like a walking, talking bucket list.

"I'm not following," I say midway through the meal. "If you've seen half the world, why move to the most boring, nothing town on the east coast?"

She shrugs. "It seemed like a nice enough place to settle down. But we'll see. It might not stick."

A pang hits my chest, but there's no guarantee she'll want a second date, anyway. There's tension on my end, but it's hard to gauge her interest. On my first date with my ex-husband, he whisked me back to his apartment without dessert because he was so desperate to unzip my jeans. Meanwhile, Brooke has gone quiet, picking at her second course—a double chocolate cheesecake—while repeatedly checking her phone.

I bite back my complaints, but my face must give me away. "Sorry," she says, baring bleached white teeth. "I'm not ignoring you on purpose. The sitter is texting me. Apparently, my daughter is acting out. We're not used to being apart for long."

"You never mentioned a kid."

"I know, I hope that's okay. I'm not really comfortable posting about her online. There are so many creeps out there. I don't want to attract the wrong type of attention."

"I can't blame you," I say, but I take a longer drag from my drink, draining the glass.

A surprise daughter rules out going back to her place tonight. And my place isn't an option, not with a flimsy sheetrock wall between me and my parents. I already feel like a leech, relying on my mother to wash my underwear and my father to shop for tampons and toilet paper. I'm not interested in sneaking a stranger into my bedroom and muffling moans with pillows.

Brooke peeks at her phone again, chewing her lip. "Do you mind if we take a rain check? I swear I'm not making up some emergency to ditch you. I'm having a surprisingly good time. Surprising because of my track record. Not because of you."

I flick my wrist. "No problem. I'll call you."

"No," she says, a little too fast. "If we don't set up something now, we never will. I've been single long enough to know how this whole thing works. There's this new bar that opened a few towns over. Come with me Thursday night."

I hesitate, but my schedule isn't exactly packed and there's no reason to play it cool with her. She's being forward enough for the both of us. "Lucky for you, I never say no to a drink."

"Perfect. I'll text you the address," she says, then presses a kiss against my cheek and saunters out the exit.

Looks like dinner is on me.

I toss down a credit card and five singles. As I sign the receipt, Faith catches my eye again, a water ring disfiguring her face. With a groan, I ball up the placemat and chuck it onto our greasy stack of plates. Then I snap open my wallet and swap the five for a twenty. As if I might actually be able to reverse all that bad karma.

CHAPTER 2

FIONA

"Have a nice day. Drive safe," I chirp as guests shimmy around me, trickling out of the theater. Some exchange polite smiles and nods. Most ignore my presence completely. I don't mind. I prefer being invisible. However, I would prefer if they *didn't* litter the aisles with popcorn kernels and candy wrappers.

On a slower morning, I would enjoy sweeping while orchestral music swelled from the speakers, but it's only a few minutes until our next showing and we're dangerously low on employees. Colds have taken out half the staff, and I never want to pressure them to put a minimum wage job ahead of their health.

Not that I follow the advice myself.

I head toward the lobby doors, dragging a trashcan in my wake. The hall is narrow, but the coast was clear a moment ago, so I shuffle backward without checking over my shoulder. I'm almost to the exit when a customer bumps into me, my back colliding with his chest.

"I'm so sorry," I say, wheeling the can aside to make room. "Excuse me, sir."

The man holds up his oversized soda and nacho tray. "Don't worry about it, sweetheart. You didn't get a drop on me."

"You must be lucky. Because I'm certainly not."

He chuckles and I make the mistake of rotating toward him, revealing my face. The transition is instantaneous. One moment, he's smiling with gums. The next, he's cradling his snacks closer to his chest. As if I might swat them from his hands.

"You're that twin. From the papers," he says. "I'm surprised they still let you work here."

"Actually, sir, I run the place now. If you've ever visited us before, you would have seen me. I'm always zipping around, putting out fires. I'm guessing you're new to town."

"I'm not telling you where I live."

My smile goes slack. I never *asked* for his address, but there's no sense in arguing with someone who has already decided to hate me. I excuse myself, slipping out of the theater with my heart pounding harder than the bass in the floors.

I've grown intimately familiar with passing whispers and glares. Or worse. Once, a woman hawked spit in my eyes. Another woman slashed my tires, then bragged about it on social media. My father banned them both, but new skeptics pop up every year.

The dirty looks tend to calm down in summer, when my sister recedes to the back of everyone's minds, but they ramp up again in winter. The memorial dinner is to blame. Posters are littered across town, plastered on grocery store bulletin boards and stapled to telephone poles, inviting the whole town to join in *celebrating the life of Faith Flynn*.

I tried talking my mother out of hosting the get-together this year, but she insists on repeating tradition. She claims honoring Faith is the least she can do, but I know the truth. She's holding out hope she's alive, that a concerned citizen will step forward with magic information to make our family whole again.

Technically, my sister *could* still be out there somewhere. Her bones were never discovered. Her body was never plucked from the water or the woods. But it's been ten years. What would she have been doing during such a long stretch of time? Starving to death in a cracked, concrete basement? Being tortured and abused until her organs give out?

Despite what my parents tell themselves, everyone else is convinced she was murdered. And an alarming amount believe I'm the one responsible.

Evan and her friends sparked the rumor. They never admitted to leaking quotes to the tabloids, but no one else would've come forward to say: "*The girls weren't exactly close. To tell you the truth, Faith was actively avoiding Fiona the last few months. If not years. Twins can feel each other's emotions, can't they? I bet Faith sensed something was wrong with her sister. But knowing wasn't enough to save herself.*"

The police couldn't scrape together any evidence to use against me, but that didn't stop everyone in town from coming to their own conclusions. They decided they knew better than the officers who had trained in their field and had actual, classified information on the case.

Evan and her friends were interrogated too, but no one seems to care they were among the last to see her alive. We were all at the theater that night, drinking until we were on the verge of blacking out. I was the only one who thought it was strange their group disbanded so shortly after the kidnapping. Raven and Seth broke up. Cameron dropped out of school. Evan fled town. And they all quit the theater.

A quiet part of me wanted to quit too, to move away and start fresh somewhere where no one knew my history. But I didn't have the heart to abandon my parents. I tried to convince them to come with me, to sell the house in exchange for a new one down south where they could raise horses and pigs and goats, but they insisted on staying put. So Faith would know where to find them when she returned.

The walkie on my hip crackles. A line has formed at the concession stand, winding toward the ticket booth and blocking our only bathroom. Until the weather gets warm enough for beaches and barbecues, plopping kids in front of a movie screen is the best way to keep them entertained.

Good news: We should be packed for the next few weeks.

Bad news: My cashier needs backup, which means more human interaction.

I hop on an empty register, manning the touch-screen computers I hand-picked during renovations. I hoped the makeover would smother some of the memories, but my sister's ghost lingers in every corner. Whenever I pass the concession stand, I see us at age eight, sneaking fistfuls of popcorn. In the break room, we're twelve, silently scribbling on homework packets. And in every single theater, we're teenagers tiptoeing around each other, requesting separate shifts. I can't pinpoint when the change happened, when we switched from best friends to strangers sharing a last name.

"Thanks for the help," the girl on a neighboring register says as the rush ends. "Hey, have you seen *Hydra Scales* yet, that animated musical with the dragons?"

I stiffen. My parents keep encouraging me to be more involved with the crew, but I can't shake the feeling they're only nice because I'm their boss, the hand who signs their paychecks. They're probably counting down the seconds until I leave so they can chat with their real friends.

"I watched a few minutes during my lunch break yesterday," I say, switching my weight from foot to foot. "But I haven't seen the whole thing. Why?"

"A few of us were thinking we could all watch it together? We can order pizza and serve drinks to anyone over twenty-one. It would be good for morale, don't you think? It would give everyone a chance to talk off-hours."

My face falls. We used to hold employee movie nights when I was younger, but I can't stomach a repeat of them. Not when my sister went missing during our final showing.

"Unfortunately, it's against company policy for management to mingle with part-time crew members," I say, my pitch a little too high. "But you're entitled to free movies, either way. Bring your friends by whenever you want. I'm sure you'll have a better time without your bosses breathing over your shoulder."

Before she can reply, I do us both a favor and remove myself. I cross the lobby, disappear into the office, and slice open boxes. Some promotional materials were delivered earlier this morning, posters and banners and cardboard cutouts. I tuck the posters under my arm, then roam toward the ticket area near the entrance. The line has died down, only one couple lingering, debating what to watch.

I unlock the plastic display boxes along the walls, tearing down a sign for a romance movie with a couple kissing in front of badly photoshopped fireworks. The replacement, *It's Always Bloody*, is a slasher movie with two men wielding dripping machetes. I would've been the first in line to see it when I was younger, but I lost my taste for horror when my sister vanished. My brain always replaces the actresses with her. Running. Shrieking. Bleeding out on cabin floorboards.

Onto the next poster. An action movie with a muscular, tattooed woman driving a muddy sports car. I start to tear it down, but movement in my peripherals distracts me. I whip toward the window and catch a flash of long black hair and pale, almost translucent skin. A little girl who looks exactly like me.

Like Faith.

I bolt to the entrance, bursting through the door. A bell chimes overhead as my head snaps left, to the nail salon. Right, to a bookshop. The sidewalk connecting the strip of stores is empty, aside from a single brunette and a man tugging his toddler by the wrist. No one is in the parking lot, either, climbing into their car with groceries or dry-cleaning.

The wind bites at my cheeks, stings my eyes. I step backward and let the door fall closed.

The little girl was probably my warped reflection. The illusion of my sister.

Incidents like this happened every few days when she first disappeared, when we were close to identical. I would walk into the room and my mother would gasp or my father would do a double-take. They couldn't hide their disappointment when they realized it was me.

"Are you okay?" the kid manning the ticket booth asks, creeping out from his desk. "Is something going on outside?"

"Nothing exciting. I was just checking if the sidewalk was clear," I tell him, throwing up the second poster. It's lopsided, but I'll fix it later. "There's still some snow. I better get a shovel. Don't want anyone slipping."

I hurry away, passing a supply closet stocked with shovels and ice melt to sneak into our all-gender bathrooms. I need a minute to myself.

After locking myself in the furthest stall, I sag against the wall and reel out my phone. My only notifications are emails, reminding me to pay my car insurance and alerting me of BOGO deals across town. My text messages are empty. No one cares enough to check up on me. Correction. No one knows I need checking up on.

I tap open Instagram and scroll through sonograms and wedding photos, bachelorette parties and pregnancy announcements. It seems like everyone is celebrating for one reason or another. Raven's hair salon was mentioned in a local magazine spread. Cameron's drummer is dropping hints about an upcoming album. Newborn baby. Promotion. Engagement. Vacation. A feed filled with humblebrags.

Meanwhile, the clock on my phone ticks up and up. More movies will be letting out soon. I pocket my cell and unlock the stall.

Then I lock it again.
Unlock.
Lock.
Unlock.
Lock.

I suck in a deep breath and pinch my eyes closed, promising myself nothing bad is going to happen when my rituals go uncompleted. My house isn't going to burn down. My parents aren't going to drop dead. I'm not going to get into a car accident or have a heart attack or slip and bash my head—

A fist bangs on the stall door. I start, clutching my chest.

"Move it, Monk. Get out of there before I tear you out."

My shoulders lower. It's only Jonah.

"I told you," I call out. "Monk is inaccurate. I'm not a germaphobe."

"Are you more comfortable with Sheldon?"

"I don't count, either."

Sometimes, I wish I had a specific number to reach—knock twice, check the oven three times—because at least there would be an endpoint in sight. Instead, I repeat the behavior until it feels *right*. I don't know why my brain is wired this way, and neither does my therapist. My parents don't share my OCD symptoms, so we're not convinced there's a genetic link, and it wasn't caused by a traumatic event either. I've dealt with it before my sister went missing, and I'll deal with it until the day I die.

I step out of the stall to face Jonah, who's towering over me with his broad shoulders, moody brown eyes, and Clooney jawline. He's older than the rest of the crew, nearing the end of his twenties like me. He probably should have advanced to another job by now, but he's comfortable working here. And I'm comfortable having him here. I promoted him to supervisor as an incentive not to leave me.

"Are you still seeing that shrink on Thursdays?" he asks while wiping down counters, drying water that has sloshed up from the sinks. "Or do you want to do something fun for a change?"

"You know I don't drink," I say, rinsing my hands.

"Who mentioned drinking? Maybe I'm inviting you to a Bible study. Or a book club."

"I'm not sure whether it's harder picturing you in a church or a library."

"Don't dodge the question."

I punch the dryer and slide my hands under.

"Don't drown me out, either. I know this week is going to be brutal for you. And I'm sick of only seeing you during work hours. There's more to life than a paycheck. You have to *spend* that paycheck, too."

"I'm not skipping therapy."

"I didn't know it was an all-day event."

"I feel emotionally drained after. I like to head straight home to decompress. Snuggle with the cat. Drink some tea."

He adjusts the cap smushing his bangs. "Isn't that what you do every other day?"

"So what? It's a nice routine."

"Routines are meant to be broken."

"That's not the saying."

"It should be. You need to mix things up every once in a while, or what's the point in existing?"

I exhale. Aside from theater-related events and Sunday dinners with my parents, I can't remember the last time plans were scribbled on my calendar.

"Fine," I say, shuffling toward the exit. "I guess I can meet up with you after my session, but only for a little while. I don't want to be out too late."

"Am I hearing you right? Is that a yes?"

"It's an, *if you insist*."

"Perfect." He splits into a grin, roping his arm around my shoulders. "I'm going to break you out of that shell if it kills me."

CHAPTER 3

EVAN

I miss my goddamn house. There's a split second each morning, before my brain registers the popcorn ceilings and puke green walls, when I can pretend I'm upstate again. For those few bittersweet moments, I'm convinced I could spring from the covers and bound down the spiral staircase, into the marble kitchen where my vanilla bean coffee is steaming.

That house wasn't a mansion, it wasn't even my dream house, but my fingerprints were all over it. The halls were strung with my canvases. The cupboards were stocked with my mugs. The yard was overflowing with strawberries and watermelons planted with my own two hands. And now some other family has infested it, staining my sink and tracking mud across my hardwood floors.

My eyes mist, but the walls of my childhood home are too thin to break into sobs. I scrub the runaway tears with a sleeve, swing off my rock-hard mattress, and unzip some suitcases to swap my sweatpants for real pants. Anything to feel more human.

I refuse to unpack, to admit this move is permanent, so it takes a while to assemble an outfit. Tight, ripped jeans. A slouchy, off-the shoulder-sweater. And my browline glasses, so I can see more than two feet in front of me.

Then it's over to my flimsy plastic desk, which is smushed against the window I used to climb out after curfew. My parents knew about my late-night rendezvous, but they never called me out on them. In the beginning, I thought their silence was a subtle psychological trick, that they were waiting for me to confess to the crime myself. But apparently, it was easier to act oblivious than to work out a fitting punishment for me. They were the type of parents who masqueraded as friends, who slipped condoms and wine coolers into my stocking each Christmas.

It worked, my mother used to tease. *Look where it got you, Evan.*

I shake my head and get to work on the order sent to my inbox yesterday. A birthday shot glass with glittering pink letters spelling out FIRST LEGAL DRINK. When I'm finished, I swaddle the product with bubble wrap and seal it in a puffy orange envelope.

In my old home, an entire room was dedicated to crafting supplies. A hand-carved mahogany table carried packaging peanuts and shipping tape and address labels. Boxes upon boxes sat beneath, filled with blank keychains and t-shirts ready to be personalized. Now, I'm stuffed into a corner with barely enough room to stretch my arms. A poster of a scantily clad girl band hangs to my right, its corners curling. A corkboard is nailed to my left, pinned with photographs of my parents posing in cheesy, coordinated Halloween costumes and my friends sneaking through the woods, playing manhunt.

I ignore the Polaroid tacked to the corner of the board. It's creased down the center, hiding the brunette in frame with me. Fiona Flynn. It was taken the night we played dress-up and snapped paparazzi pictures like we were walking the red carpet. Or going to prom.

Fiona wasn't big on fashion, but she surprised me with a catwalk in her living room after my hamster died, showering me with neon wigs and chunky costume jewelry. Her sister stood on the opposite side of the camera as we posed, directing us. *Angle toward each other. Lean a little closer. Position your hand higher on her waist. Perfect!*

I almost forget there were any half-decent memories of Faith. I guess they were overwritten by the louder moments—prying the twins apart during one-sided screaming matches, talking Fiona down from panic attacks after another pointless spat. Whether they were at odds over whose turn it was to fold the laundry or who used up all the hot water, the cycle was the same. Faith would start drama. And I would end it. It's why she hated me so much. I was her sister's closest thing to a backbone.

She'd be thrilled to know Fiona currently hates my guts.

I swivel my chair back toward my workstation. Part of me is tempted to delete the webpage and shut down the shop for good. I have enough materials to last a while, but once they run out, I won't have enough cash to replenish them. I need a steady gig if I'm ever going to escape this town.

Speaking of which…I tug my phone from its charger to check my email. No news from the dozens of job applications I sent in—for administration positions at the local high school and dental clinic and hospital, whoever was hiring for more than minimum wage.

I keep scrolling, clicking through the order forms that have pinged into my account overnight. The first up is a customized bar necklace in rose gold. Men usually buy them as last-minute holiday gifts for their wives or mothers, so they order the pre-set options. I LOVE YOU or FOREVER YOURS.

This customer gets creativity points for requesting: RESURRECT YOURSELF. It's on the lengthier side, but it should fit. Unlike my shot glasses and mugs, I don't have to worry about spacing the letters myself. A machine does the work for me. I bought it for close to 2k, back when money was an afterthought.

The necklace is good to go five minutes later, and honestly, it came out better than expected. I'm not religious—I stopped going to church when they pressured me to confess sins I would rather keep to myself—but I appreciate the sentiment. Nothing wrong with a fresh start.

I tuck the jewelry into a cotton-lined box, slap a branded sticker onto the lid, and pluck an envelope from my pile. Then I click back to the order form to copy down the contact information. The address is nearby, in the same state, the same town. My parents must've been advertising for me again.

I jot down the address, then scroll further, to the name of the buyer.

I blink. Blink harder, thinking I misread. But no. A name I never wanted to see again peers back at me.

FAITH FLYNN.

"How the hell?" I murmur, a shiver rolling through me.

Why would a customer list a dead girl on the slip? Was this some kind of joke, a nasty *welcome back to the neighborhood*? I can name a handful of people who have reason to resent me—classmates who overheard me talking trash about them, teachers who caught me stealing answer sheets—but I can't come up with a single one who would take it this far.

I grope for my laptop to type the address into a search engine. A grainy picture appears. A one-story home. Lopsided shutters. Loose siding. Rust-coated railings. The image tickles my memory. I've been to that house before, but I can't recall when or why.

I shove away from my desk and roam into the living room. My mother is engrossed in a phone game, pawing at rainbow bubbles soaring across the screen. My father is watching a ghost-hunting show, snoring over the narrator.

I tap my mom on the shoulder, flashing the package at her. "Do you know who lives in this house? The street sounds familiar, but I can't remember who was in that area."

"You're too young to have memory problems," she says without sparing a glance at me. She continues tapping bubbles, finishing the round. "You should stop pouring so much sweetener in your coffee. The radio says it's bad for you. Maybe start doing some crosswords, too. They're supposed to keep your brain strong."

"My brain is fine, thank you. I've purposely purged this place from my mind as much as humanly possible. I'm surprised I know where I am right now."

"Oh, hush. Don't talk like you're better than us. You're one of us again." She sets down the game and sticks out her index finger, imitating an alien. "One. Of. Us."

"I'm sure you'll get a casting call for SNL any day now. Now, can you please take a look at this?"

She lowers wiry glasses onto her nose and squints at the packaging, wetting her chapped lips. "Oh, you know where this street is. Over near the trailer park. Wasn't that where one of your friends used to live? One of the boys from the movie theater? We picked him up once or twice when he needed a ride to work. I haven't seen him since the funeral."

Right. That explains why the house only seemed vaguely familiar. I've never stepped through the threshold. I've only parked against the chipped curb, blasting pop-punk and beeping until he hauled his ass into my backseat.

"Cameron lived by those trailers," I say. "He was only a road away."

"He ordered something from your shop? That's sweet of him."

I don't want to correct her. I don't want to mention Faith Flynn.

After she went missing, my parents made a temporary switch to *overprotective mode.* My mother lectured me about sticking in large groups after dark. My father bought me pepper spray to clip onto my keychain. They were worried sick about Faith, but it wasn't because they cared about her, specifically. It had more to do with the fact she was my age. She went to school with me. She worked with me. If someone was snatching up girls on their way home, it easily could've been my photo on the news.

They both underestimated how hard her death hit me. Sure, her sister was my best friend, but they knew *we* weren't tight. I never brought up the weird rivalry between us. Or our intense conversation on the night she disappeared. Sometimes, secrets are the only thing stopping your loved ones from leaving you.

"…right, honey?"

My head cranes. I didn't realize she was still speaking.

"Yeah, of course," I say, hoping the answer tracks.

My mother frowns, the lines around her mouth deepening. She strokes my cheek with her knuckles. "Are you sure you're getting enough sleep, sweetheart? Maybe we should buy you a new mattress. The one you've been sleeping on is almost as old as you are. It can't be good for your back."

"Relax. You don't need to baby me. I'm a big girl."

"But there's no reason for you to be uncomfortable."

"I'm fine. Seriously. I need a hit of coffee, then I should be good to go."

"If you're sure," she says, then calls after me, "Remember, no sweetener."

I circle the corner, turning into a kitchen in dire need of an update. The counters are cluttered with cheap decorations. Salt and pepper shakers shaped like mushrooms. Tea towels printed with owls. A beehive cookie jar stuffed with receipts instead of actual cookies. Anyone who steps foot into the room would guess my mother teaches children.

She's been at the same elementary school for so long some of her students have soared past me in age. And reputation. She'll call me at random, gushing about ex-students who won awards or popped out newborns or received acceptance letters to prestigious universities. It's silly to be jealous. If anything, I should be relieved. They take away some of my only-child-burden to make her proud.

Lukewarm coffee is waiting near the microwave. I could brew a fresh pot, but I don't want to waste grounds my parents paid for with their money. I pour the dregs into a mug I designed for my mother last year, a black cup printed with: FROM MY ~~ONLY~~ FAVORITE DAUGHTER. She unwrapped it in my living room as we gathered around an eight-foot tree draped in dark reds and golds. That was before divorce was on the table, before discovering a second cell phone filled with nudes and sexts, before contacting lawyers and packing my shit—but it still felt like a milestone Christmas. The last one without children.

I chug my cup and hit the bathroom, then print out the order form for the necklace. I lug the package with me to the car, a ruby Mustang with tinted windows. I'll have to downgrade when the lease is up, but I might as well enjoy the heated seats and surround sound speakers before they're ripped away like everything else.

Cameron's house is a few blocks away, a five-minute drive, tops. But the stark transition from my town to his makes it feel like we live in separate cities. With each spin of the wheel, the houses shrink. The lawns fade from bright, artificial green to a brittle brown with lumps of dirty, old snow. My parents aren't exactly rich, but they at least keep the shrubs trimmed and the walkways shoveled.

Once I reach the right block, I ease my foot off the gas, scanning houses. Half of the address numbers are discolored or dangling off the mailboxes. I have to work out which place is his based on memory alone. I'm pretty sure it's not the one with a Husky tethered to a pole. Or the one with a broken basketball hoop screwed onto the garage.

I pull up to the tiniest building on the road, a squat, muddy brown house. Bingo.

Two beat-up trucks with missing wheels are hogging the pebbled driveway, so I park on the curb. I tuck my designer sunglasses, e-reader, and anything else valuable under the seats. Then I poke my keys between my fingers, letting them stick out near my knuckles in case anyone comes searching for trouble.

The car locks with a chirp. Children scream on the opposite end of the block, charging toward each other with hockey sticks. A cat screeches. A dog howls.

I hurry across moss-covered stepping stones leading to the screen door, then climb a set of stubby porch steps. I smack a doorbell with its paint flaked off, but I don't hear a buzz. Either the system is busted, or everyone is ignoring me. Either way, I'm not leaving until Cameron vomits out an explanation. I pound the door with loud, heavy knocks and wait.

The blinds twitch. A heartbeat later, Cameron swings open the door wearing a tank top and loose, low-hanging jeans. His eyes are bloodshot, his cheeks are sallow, and his waistline is smaller than mine. The wind could knock him over. He was always a stringbean, though. He survived on personalized pizzas and chicken tenders smuggled from the concession stand. There was no one at home to cook for him. His parents were too busy selling drugs or chasing their own high.

"Cameron. Good to see you," I say, flashing a smile. I was hoping our bond had held up over the years, even though we cut contact, but now I'm not so sure. He's eying me like an intruder, panic etched into every feature. He whips his head both ways, checking behind the overgrown bushes surrounding the stoop. His chest heaves while he scans, practically panting.

I'm worried he's going to tear out a shotgun and chase me off the property, but he latches onto my arm and drags me into the house. With quick squirrelly movements, he slams the door behind us, double locks it, and peeks out the blinds again. They hang lopsided on the railing, barely holding on.

"Did you come here on your own? Is anybody with you?" he asks.

I shake my head slowly. No sudden moves. "It's only me. Why? Are you expecting someone?"

"Nah. Nah, I just wanted to make sure there weren't any surprise visitors," he says, stepping away from the window. His hunched shoulders start to lower. The muscles in his jaw relax. When he turns toward me again, his face softens like he's seeing me for the first time. "Jesus, Evan. I can't believe you're here. This is wild."

"Am I the same sweet young girl you remember?" I ask, batting my fake lashes.

"No way. That girl was cool and all, but you're much hotter. How'd you age so good? Plastic surgery?"

"It's not Botox. It's bitch face. If you never smile, it keeps the wrinkles away."

He belches out a laugh. Then he spreads his arms, trapping me in a warm, sweaty hug. He stinks of weed, but the scent is calming, familiar. I just hope he hasn't graduated to harder drugs.

"I didn't know you were still living with your parents," I say once we peel apart. "Are they home?"

"Nah, you didn't hear? They died a while back."

My face drops. I forgot my parents mentioned a funeral a few years ago. I was planning on sending flowers or at least a condolence card, but then life got in the way. It's not like his mom and dad held some special place in my heart. I only met them once and they were too high to hold a coherent conversation. But I should've been there for Cameron. Judging by the state of his yard, he could use all the help he could get.

"I'm sorry," I say, massaging my neck. "I'm such an asshole."

"You don't have to apologize. If you didn't bring it up, I wouldn't have known you weren't there. It was a shitshow. People sobbing on my shoulder and slipping me money and leaving meals on the stoop. I didn't have to cook for weeks. It was a weird perk."

"What about the house? They left this to you?"

"Yeah. And the rats in the walls."

I frown. "You're not happy here?"

"Hate the town. Hate the neighbors. But selling it wouldn't make me much money when there's so much that needs fixing, so there was no reason to leave. Not until my career takes off. We're making a new album. I think this could be the one. It's got a real unique sound."

"I bet. You always crushed it."

I picture him headbanging on stage, strumming with guitar picks printed with Bible verses, his hair as long as Jesus himself. It was like he thought public displays of worship would make up for all the trouble he got into in private.

"I'll send you a copy when it's done," he says, flapping a bony arm. "Come on. I'm freezing my ass off. The heater's in the other room."

I follow him through the cramped, one-wall kitchen. Bottles piled high in the sink. Water rings staining the counters. Dirt crusted in the floor tile. The living room is sparkling clean in comparison, but that's mostly because there's nothing to stain. The room is empty aside from a sagging couch, a bong, and an array of acoustic guitars. I wonder whether he sold the rest of the furniture to keep the electricity on.

"So, why did you stop by?" he asks, plopping onto sunken cushions. "I heard you were back in town, but I never expected you to come over. It's been forever since we've seen each other. All of us. You're not the only one who went M.I.A."

"It wouldn't have been smart for us to stay in touch. I missed you guys, but life moves on, right? I tried to put this town behind me. But it dragged me back, kicking and screaming. Anyway..." I lift the package, jiggling it over his head. "I stopped by because you ordered something from my shop. I was wondering why, so I figured I would save myself some stamps and deliver it to you personally."

"You have a shop? Where is it?"

"Online. At least, for now. I might splurge on a physical location eventually, but no one leaves their house anymore, so an online storefront is a lot more cost-efficient and customer-friendly until I'm ready to take the next step."

I trail off toward the end, clearing my throat. I'm not sure why the lie spilled out so easily. That was the spiel I rehearsed for my old friends in my old town when I lived my old life. There's no chance a self-run business is in the cards now. I'm going to be stuck at a mind-numbing desk job for the foreseeable future. And that's if I'm lucky, if I can overcome unemployment.

"Ah. That's cool," Cameron says, tapping out a tune on his armrest. "But I don't trust the internet. I buy groceries in person. Pay my bills through the mail. I don't want to get scammed or tracked by the government. Or by somebody worse. The mess that got my parents killed... It probably wouldn't have gone down if they stayed off the grid. I definitely didn't order anything from you, not even if I was too wasted to remember."

"I'm not completely surprised. I didn't think you wore jewelry." My eyes drop to his chest. Several rope necklaces dangle over his sweat-stained shirt. He has the bracelets to match. "Well, not in this style."

I dip into the bag, pull out the little white box, and remove the lid, exposing the necklace nestled inside. Cameron leans forward to read the message engraved onto the metal. RESURRECT YOURSELF. There's no expression on his face, except maybe boredom.

"I would take it for the next girl who spends the night, but I don't vibe with it. No offense. It's nice and all, but I'm not religious anymore."

"I don't think that's what they meant, Cam."

"What else would they mean?"

I pass him the order form.

His forehead crimps as he scans the page. Slowly, the color drains from his concave cheeks. "Are you screwing with me? Is this supposed to be funny?"

"I was planning on asking you the same thing. I never would've guessed you would use her name, but the form led me to this house. To you."

He shoves the paper into my hands, crinkling the page. "That doesn't make any sense. It wasn't me."

"Does anyone else live with you? Do you have roommates?"

"No. Unless I'm on stage or recording, I keep to myself."

I swallow. "Could it have been one of the others, then?"

"Beats me. I haven't had contact with anybody. Not Seth. Not Raven. Nobody. I shouldn't be involved in whatever this is."

"You've lived in the same town for ten years. You must have seen them at some point."

"We avoid each other. I'm serious." He springs from the couch and staggers toward the kitchen. "I haven't seen Seth since he stopped by the wake for Mom and Pop, but that was only for two minutes, max. We barely spoke. He gave me a card with a little bit of cash and booked it. Sure, sometimes Raven will show up at my gigs, but it's never on purpose. There are only a few places to hang out on weekends, so we're bound to run into each other. It's not like we ever stop to chat. We'll smile or wave, and that's the end of it."

"Okay. Fine. Then do you think this has anything to do with—"

He fumbles with the locks, like he can't kick me out fast enough. "You've got to leave. I don't want to be a part of this."

"You think I do? I just want to know where it came from. It was a creepy-ass order, and it's even creepier knowing it directed me to you. Someone must've planned it this way on purpose. They knew what they were doing. I'm worried about what else they know."

"It's just a prank. Someone is screwing with you because they're pissed you're back in town."

"Why would they be pissed at me?"

"I don't know. It's not like you're everyone's favorite person, Evan."

I stiffen, balling my fists. "In case you didn't notice, you're included in this as much as me. Your address is on the form. That couldn't have happened by accident."

"I don't know why my stuff is on there. And I don't care. I don't want to think about her. I'm just going to forget about it, okay? You should, too."

I drag in a breath, letting the cold air flood my lungs. Arguing with him is pointless. If he doesn't know who ordered the necklace, he can't help me.

I linger near his open doorway. A part of me is tempted to smooth things over, to forget about Faith and talk about the good old days—when we did jello shots at Jones Beach or stole six-packs from the gas station or shared joints on the school roof.

But we stopped talking for a reason. I'll only bring up bad memories for him. I don't need to give him more excuses to drink himself to death.

"Fine," I say, stepping out the door. "If you want me to go, I'm already gone."

I march toward my car and shove the key in the ignition, blasting myself with warm air. Before shifting into drive, I lay the order form against the wheel, smoothing out the wrinkles. I skim the small print once more, hoping to find a hint concealed in the margins. Of course, there's nothing. The fields for the phone number and email address are blank, and the affiliated credit card isn't available for me to view. If Cameron isn't the one who ordered the necklace, I don't have a clue who's to blame.

But it must be someone who knows we lied about Faith.

CHAPTER 4

FIONA

I zip my coat up to my throat, as high as the zipper can tug. I'm encased in three layers—a puffy coat on top of a flannel on top of my normal button-down blouse—but the air still stings. The heater in my Thunderbird puttered out a week or two ago. I have money for the repairs, but I've been too swamped with work to schedule an appointment. Tonight would've been a good night to visit the shop, but I promised Jonah we would meet up after my therapy session.

If I need to cancel, that will be my excuse.

My grip tightens as I merge onto the congested highway. I hate driving. Even short distances. I flinch whenever a car weaves too close. Or when there's a motorcycle or a semi-truck or a helmetless biker. Studies show driving is more dangerous than boarding a plane or parachuting out of one.

Behind the wheel, all I do is overthink—about the present *and* past. Around this time of year, my thoughts are always pulled to the night my sister went missing.

It was the first Friday of the month, the date my parents reserved for free employee movies. They usually caught up on work as we watched, balancing books in their office or organizing boxes piled around the projection room. But that night was different. They trusted us alone. Me. My sister. Evan. And all our other teenage coworkers.

We were unsupervised until one in the morning. After the credits rolled, I locked up the building myself. I circled the theater twice, calling for Faith, but she wasn't throwing up in the bathrooms or sneaking munchies from the concession stand. She must have left without me, so I trudged home alone. It didn't feel like a big deal in the moment. We only lived a few blocks from the theater. The walk took ten minutes.

When I slipped into the house, I shut the door with a soft click. My parents were already sound asleep. It was their one night to relax without us interrupting. I didn't want to ruin it. Judging by the upside-down wine glasses in the sink, they had the romantic date they deserved.

I crept into the bedroom, tiptoeing to avoid the whining floorboards. Faith wasn't in the bed parallel to mine, but the bathroom door across the hall was sealed. We usually left it cracked when it was empty, so I assumed she was inside, scrubbing away her makeup or brushing the taste of liquor off her teeth. If I was sober, I would've checked on her after a few minutes, but the drinking wore me out. I dozed off before I had the chance to change into pajamas.

The next morning, I wandered into the kitchen in the same wrinkled outfit. My mother was whipping pancake batter and pouring it into a pan. My father was long gone, working an opening shift at the theater, but traces of him were scattered across the room. His half-drunk coffee mug. A newspaper, flipped to the business section.

"Did you have fun last night?" my mother asked without turning from the stovetop.

"Yeah, the movie was good. Five stars."

"What about the staff? There wasn't any drama? You know how much I worry, leaving a group of teenagers unsupervised."

I shook my head, but *of course* there was drama. Evan and I had a heart-to-heart, making up from another ridiculous fight. There was some weird tension between Raven and Seth. And Cameron was stumbling through the hallways, high as a kite. At one point, he lit a joint directly in front of me. I had to lecture him about smoking indoors. If the seats stunk, my parents would never leave us alone again.

"There weren't any issues," I said. "We behaved ourselves. And cleaned up after ourselves. You shouldn't find a single kernel on the floor."

"Good. Your father keeps saying we need to give you girls more freedom, and I don't need either of you taking advantage of it. Speaking of which, where did your sister run off to? I've told you a million times, you need to leave a note stating an emergency number and when you'll be back."

I yawned. "Don't ask me. I just climbed out of bed."

"She didn't tell you she had plans this morning? She was already gone when I woke up."

"I haven't talked to her. Not since yesterday morning."

She'd screamed at me for hogging our only bathroom, even though my showers took five minutes and hers took twenty. It had been like that a lot lately, her finding more and more reasons to pick fights with me. I chewed too loudly. I walked too slowly. I moved our toothbrushes to the wrong side of the sink. I couldn't win with her.

And my parents weren't much help. Whenever I tattled on her, they would lecture me about fighting my own battles. None of the groundings got through to her anyway. When she disobeyed them, they punished her with extra shifts at the theater, extra chores, extra-long scoldings. Nothing worked.

"What do you mean?" my mother asked, wheeling toward me, batter flying from her spatula. "She was supposed to see the movie with you last night."

"She did. But there were a bunch of us. I was hanging out with other people. Faith sat a couple of seats away, so it was hard to hear each other."

"What about on the way home? You walked in silence?"

I chewed my lip, studying the ground.

"Fiona, don't you dare tell me you walked home separately. You were supposed to stay together. What were you thinking?"

"I couldn't help it. She left before me. I thought she got home first."

"And did she?"

I swallowed, struggling to picture the last time I saw her. Early in the night, when we were gathered in the lobby, she complimented Seth's shirt, running a hand down his arm until he pried her fingers away. She bumped into Raven a little later, accidentally sloshing alcohol onto the crotch of her jeans. And Cameron was always flitting from person to person, so they must've spoken once or twice, too. But the second half of the night was fuzzy, clouded by alcohol.

"I'm not sure," I whispered to my mother. "I thought she was in the bathroom."

"You never saw her? You can't tell me for sure she came home last night?"

My head rattled, my throat too parched to speak.

"Oh my God, Fiona. Get me the phone."

That was the beginning of the end. My mother relayed the situation to my father, who sent the crew to inspect every theater in case she was still on the property. Then she rang Faith again and again, redialing as soon as she reached voicemail. I did the same, texting until my fingers stung.

Then came the cops. The questioning. The guilt and grief and regret. My parents blamed themselves for leaving us alone, but I blamed myself more. I could have called Faith when I was locking up the theater to make sure she arrived home safe, but I was frustrated with her for disappearing on me. I thought she was trying to spite me because I spent most of the night with Evan. The two of them never *admitted* to having a problem with each other, but they never lingered in the same space for long. One would enter the room and the other would leave, like a revolving door. And that was on their good days.

Toward the end, Faith was actively trying to get Evan fired. She complained to our parents about Evan showing up late and taking extended breaks—even though *she* was the one always disappearing into theaters to watch movies with Perry, her rich friend from the Hamptons. When that didn't work, she blamed Evan for stealing revenue from the registers. My parents recounted the drawers and came up short, then noticed a stash of twenties hidden in our dresser. Faith was grounded for a month.

The memories dissolve as I switch on my blinker. I turn into a long, winding driveway lined with shrubs. A few years ago, my therapist stopped holding sessions in her concrete office building and moved them into her sprawling, two-story house. The house she shares with Seth.

When I learned she was dating him—let alone marrying him—we nearly parted ways, but she assured me that she took a confidentiality oath, that my secrets would remain a secret from everyone, family included. And I trusted her.

I shift the car into park and unclick my seatbelt, mentally preparing myself for the session. This one is sure to revolve around my sister. What else would we talk about for forty-five minutes? How uneasy a night out with Jonah makes me when there's bound to be alcohol involved? How many hours I've been putting into the theater because I'm the only daughter remaining to make my parents proud? It all circles back to her.

I blink hard, hoping to clear my mind, but I'm slammed with an onslaught of images. Brain matter and bone marrow and warm, pooling blood. My sister flashes in front of me, her hair matted and her mouth lolled open, stuck in a scream. I picture the same thing happening to my mother, my father, my cat.

I click my seatbelt back into its slot.

Unclick.

Click.

Unclick.

Click.

Stop it, I murmur to myself, *you need to stop*. But recognizing my actions are irrational doesn't mean I suddenly have the power to stop them. I click a few more times, then close the car door and scale the stone driveway.

The office is as warm and welcoming as a bearhug. A heater hums in the corner. Candles flicker on a coffee table. An area rug with wide, colorful spirals covers the floor.

I settle into a horseshoe-shaped sofa peppered with throw pillows. Angel nods a stiff greeting from her armchair, readjusting her crocheted shawl, then her hoop earrings. Maybe I'm imagining things, but her brown eyes look glassy, her shoulders hunched and head low. I shouldn't read too far into her body language, though. She has two young children. She has a right to be exhausted. I can't expect her to perk up whenever she sees me.

"How are you feeling today, Fiona?"

I unzip my coat, letting it fall around my waist like snakeskin. "I'm good. It's freezing out, but otherwise, I can't complain."

Her peach mouth puckers. She knows it's not my real answer.

"Sorry. I guess… I'm not the greatest. My OCD has been pretty overwhelming. I thought it was getting better, but it's much worse than last week."

"These things ebb and flow. Have you been keeping track of your compulsions like I've asked?"

I nod. I have a pocket-sized notebook in my center console and another on my bedside table. They work the same way as a habit tracker or food journal, except I jot down all of the moments when my anxiety spikes. I write the time of day in one column and the source of my stress in the next. Sometimes, the rows remain empty for weeks on end. But the book has been filling up more and more the last few days.

I list examples off the top of my head, including the moment in the car and the other day in the theater bathrooms.

Angel scribbles notes onto her clipboard. "Interesting. And were you able to pinpoint what caused those moments? Remember, it's important to note when they pop up so you can either avoid triggers or learn methods for coping with them."

I don't want to bring up the flash of black hair outside the theater. Or the little girl at the grocery store this morning who made me do a triple take. She floated down the aisle, her back facing me, her hair cascading behind her in soft curls. The way my sister styled it. I abandoned my grocery cart to scurry after her, nearly toppling a display of crackers, but ended up losing her. The store was packed with mothers and daughters, but I couldn't spot anyone with her thick black hair.

I'm not sure what could be causing those visions. Angel would be able to work out an answer with me, but I can't risk confiding in her. It might lead to a hospital stay.

The last thing I want is to get committed again. The weeks after my sister went missing were a waking nightmare. Stale food. Nosy roommates. Constant paranoia I would say or do something that would get me locked up even longer. The concern from my parents was the worst part. They were already juggling enough, between the police investigation and the theater and the bills. Making them worry about me on top of my sister felt selfish. It's why I learned how to manage my OCD better. Or hide it better.

"Fiona. Usually, you report worse symptoms during periods of extreme stress. Have you been stressed about anything specific?"

I fidget with my bracelet, rolling it around my wrist. "I mean, yeah, of course. I'm usually thinking about my sister when it gets bad. But she's always on my mind, so it's hard to tell whether that's what's causing the compulsions. I just…I feel like I should be done mourning by now. It's been ten years."

"You never really get over the loss of a loved one."

"I know, but isn't it supposed to get easier?"

"Some days, it is easier. You've told me that yourself. But healing isn't linear. You need to be gentle with yourself, Fiona. Remember you've been here before. Anniversaries are difficult. It's perfectly normal for your mental state to take a hit at this time of year." She scribbles some more, flips a page. "Since you can't stop yourself from thinking about your sister, welcome the thoughts in. But let's try to make them positive. Can you give me a warm memory?"

I hesitate, chewing my nails. The bad times were front and center, either because they were fresher or because they made existing without her easier. I take a second to fish for happier memories, then tell Angel about the red velvet cupcakes we used to bake together, the dance parties in the living room where we twirled around to All American Reject songs. Even when we were teenagers, we would have mini movie marathons in our pajamas, rarely speaking but sharing popcorn and trail mix. She was my twin. Even when I didn't like her, I loved her.

During our remaining time, we discuss how much pressure I'm under to keep the theater running and how much I'm dreading the memorial dinner at the end of the week. Usually, our sessions run over unless Angel has another patient scheduled, but today she rises as soon as her phone dings.

"It looks like our session is up," she says. "I'll see you next week, okay?"

I pass her my co-payment and slither into my coat. Then I head outside with my chin tucked into my collar. A gust of wind slams into me, stinging my cheeks and whipping my ponytail sideways. It isn't snowing yet, but clouds swirl in the distance. The ground could be covered by morning.

I study my sneakers to avoid slipping on ice patches, so I don't realize anyone else is in the driveway with me. Not until we're a few feet apart.

"Fiona," Seth says as our paths cross, nodding a greeting. He's lugging a brightly colored trashcan back from the street. Slippers cover his bare feet, but he's wearing a tweed jacket and tie. It feels strangely intimate, like I've walked in on him dressing.

I return his nod and continue forward. I'm not used to running into him here. My sessions are scheduled at the same time every week, when he's busy at his accounting office downtown. I'm not sure whether Angel purposely lined up our schedules to avoid intersecting or whether it was a happy accident.

Either way, it worked out for the best. Even when we were teenagers, our interactions were limited to the basics. *Will you restock the ice for me? Will you hop on register two until the rush ends?* Otherwise, he only glimpsed me long enough to determine which twin I was.

But now, his garbage can scrapes to a stop. He abandons it in the middle of the driveway, jogging toward me.

"How are you doing?" I ask, not wanting to be rude. "Do you have the day off?"

"Work never stops. I decided to operate virtually for the day. I'm on my break."

"Oh. Okay. I don't want to keep you, then."

I shuffle down the drive with my arms crossed, but he charges forward, shortening the gap between us. My breath catches. I expect him to reach out and grab me, but instead of scrambling for safety, my body locks up. I freeze, mid-step.

"Fiona. Did my wife mention anything about her bookings to you?"

"Her bookings?"

"Her appointment schedule."

"I'm not exactly sure what you're asking."

"Right. I didn't think she would," he mumbles, stroking his clean-shaven chin. A nick dissects his neck, like the razor slipped. "Fiona, my wife has tried her hardest to help you for years. She treats you with the utmost kindness and respect, so I would appreciate it if you did the same for her. Otherwise, you should consider alternative options for therapy."

"I don't understand. I didn't do anything to her. Is she upset with me?"

"Please. Don't insult my intelligence. I know all about the *new client* who tried to set up an appointment using your sister's name. Are you going to pretend you don't know anything about that?"

My heart grinds to a stop.

"This person requested your slot. The exact day. Exact time. And the reasoning they gave behind wanting therapy… Well, I don't need to explain something to you that you already know. It's clear you were behind it. My wife won't tell me what kind of illnesses you're diagnosed with or whether you're dangerous because she takes her doctor-patient confidentiality seriously, but the incident disturbed her. If she's not going to say it, then I will. Your behavior is completely unacceptable. She might tolerate it, but I certainly won't."

My lashes beat, once, twice, at a loss. I want to ask why he would suspect me, of all people, to smear my sister's name.

"I'm not comfortable with you coming to the house where my children sleep. I never have been, but my wife insisted I was overreacting. However, these antics of yours prove I had a right to be worried. So to make myself abundantly clear, I'm going to be here, outside, watching you, every time you visit my home. Until you stop visiting."

I open my mouth to defend myself, but my throat squeezes shut. I can't choke out a sound, let alone a coherent sentence.

He must take my silence as a win because he storms away. Unless he's hurrying inside so Angel doesn't realize he's harassing a patient. I'm positive she wouldn't approve of his behavior, but it doesn't change the fact he's going to make my life a living nightmare if I step foot on his property again.

And just like that, my safe place suddenly feels a lot less safe.

CHAPTER 5

EVAN

Interrogating Cameron was a bust, so I book it back home. My pulse is still pounding as I hop out of the car and cut across the lawn, stomping over my tiny, ten-year-old handprint embedded in the porch steps. On my right, violets I planted in elementary school buckle in the wind. To my left, a wire reindeer we've had since my first Christmas peeks out from the snow. I hoped my old home would feel like this someday, a time capsule with a million little moments frozen in amber.

Screw me, right?

"You're back quicker than I thought," my mother says, startling me. I didn't expect my parents to be lazing around the kitchen. I was hoping to slip into my room, undetected. "How was Cameron?"

"Cameron," my father echoes, flipping through a car magazine. "Which one was he?"

My mother answers for me. "The guitarist. We went to the services for his parents, remember? They were buried a few years ago."

"You could've mentioned that fun fact earlier," I murmur, scuffing my boots against a welcome mat of a t-rex in oven mitts. "What happened to them anyway? How did they die?"

"They said it was a heart attack."

"Both of them died from a heart attack? On the same day?"

"It's called a sympathy death," my father says, licking his thumb. "One dies and then the next dies of a broken heart."

"You buy that?"

My mother rests her crossword on the table, folding her hands over the booklet. "It's impolite to ask those sorts of questions. Remember when your uncle died from an overdose? Only close family knew the real reason. Everyone else was told it was a medical condition. It's easier that way."

"So you think they overdosed together?"

"Honey, you're rather gossipy for someone who doesn't want the town gossiping about you."

I salute. "Got it. It's none of my business. We're not even friends anymore."

"Oh, hush. I'm sure Cameron was delighted to see you. He ordered from your shop. That has to count for something."

I suck in my cheeks. I don't want to explain the mix-up. Best to remove myself from the situation.

"I'm going to hang out in my room until dinner," I say. "Just a head's up, I have plans. So you might want to put a pin in any family game nights."

My mother perks up. "You're going on another date? With the same woman?"

"Yeah. Can you believe she's willing to put up with me twice in a week? That's probably a red flag."

"No. We call that a miracle, honey."

I putter to my room, collapse onto my stale mattress, and peel open my laptop. For some reason, the lie about Cameron's parents is bugging me. Them dying of an overdose is easier to believe than them suffering from back-to-back heart attacks, but it still doesn't line up with what he told me. He implied *the internet* killed them. He claimed it was the reason he went off the grid.

It could've been another lie, an excuse to trick me into believing he wasn't the one who ordered the necklace. But if he was serious, if he *wasn't* the one screwing with me, someone else from our group could be to blame. Who else would guess the mention of Faith would scare us shitless?

I log onto Facebook to do some light stalking. Seth is my first victim. I type his name into the search bar at the center of the screen. His account pops up, but there's not a single photo of him. His profile picture shows his wavy-haired sons in matching striped sweaters. They can't be older than two or three, maybe four.

I keep scrolling, clicking through snapshots. A golden retriever runs along a white sand beach. Flutes of wine perch on a boat edge. Crayon drawings hang from a smart fridge. There are a few photos of his wife, too. She looks happy enough, flashing a toothpaste commercial smile, but it could be a front. Either way, I'm not convinced he would give up everything he's earned—the house, the money, the kids—to drudge up the past. He cares about appearances.

As advertised, Cameron doesn't have a social media page. Not even one for his band, which explains why he's having so much trouble making a name for himself. There's zero trace of him.

Next comes Raven. Her profile photo is a fun, full-length shot of her posing outside a hair salon with her name on the sign. Below, there's a candid photo of her chopping hair, followed by a collection of customer photos with cornrows and box braids and Bantu knots. Unfortunately, our town is mostly populated with red-pepper-is-too-spicy Caucasians, so she's mastered the art of mullets and undercuts, too.

Finally, I hop over to Faith's profile, which is spammed with RIP posts. They're all bullshit, calling her *stylish* and *confident* and *strong* instead of *obnoxious* and *vain*. The only believable goodbye is from a deactivated account under the name Perry Pierce. "You were a bitch, but you were my bitch," it says. "I miss making trouble together. Don't cause too much hell until I'm down there with you. Love you forever and always."

Scrolling all the way down to her status updates would slow my computer, so I click through her photos instead. Her selfie album is packed with two hundred pictures of her rocking duck lips, neon bra straps showing. I click on a smaller album, filled with tagged shots posted by *friends*. I start from the back, moving up in time, but it's mostly posed family photos with her mouth in a straight line.

The only shot where she's caught with a genuine smile is candid. She's leaning beside a freckled girl in a yellow-and-blue school uniform, complete with a loose tie and thigh highs. Like a *Gossip Girl* reject. I vaguely remember her visiting the theater, flipping through fashion magazines with Faith on her lunch break. That must have been Perry.

The album ends with a group shot of the theater kids, captured the night Faith went missing. Before the Flynns wished us goodnight, they gathered us together for a photo and uploaded it using their desktop computer.

I pinch the trackpad to zoom in on the photograph. I don't remember half the people who worked with us. Their faces are familiar, but I can't conjure up a name or voice to go along with the features. I do recall them whispering about me being a snob, though. If I was trapped on shift with someone outside my friend group, I would bring a comic to skim or sneak out my phone to text instead of humoring them with small talk. I didn't want to hear about their odd dream last night or their trip down south to visit their grandparents. Sue me.

I ignore the no-names for now and inspect the recognizable faces. Raven has her lips puckered and her head angled sideways to capture her razor-sharp cheekbones. Cameron is crouched with his knees spread, throwing a peace sign to the camera. Seth has that blank, no-smile stare teenage boys think is cool. And Faith is all the way on the end, almost out of frame, like they had to pull her into the photo.

Then there's me, standing a little too close to Fiona, my arm draped over her shoulder and her head tilted against mine. This must've been snapped moments after we made up from our fight. Earlier in the week, we had yet another argument about her being excluded from hangouts with my other friends. Same shit, different day.

I almost click away, then remember to examine the others. Just because they're irrelevant to me doesn't mean the feeling is mutual. Most of the coworkers staggered in between us are tagged, but all their pages are private. It's impossible for me to see anything other than birthdays and relationship statuses. I could add them as friends, but I would need to wait for them to accept the request.

I'm impatient, and I don't want their noses in my business, so I pull out my cell and scroll through my contact list. I never went through and decluttered it, so there are countless numbers teenage-me programmed in case I needed someone to cover a shift. I sift through them. DAVID THEATER. KARA THEATER. REDHEAD THEATER. DOUCHE BEARD THEATER. I dial the first name on the list. After two rings, it sends me to voicemail. They must have declined the call, and I can't blame them. I would do the same.

I try the second name and receive an out-of-service message. On my third attempt, a man answers.

"Hello?" he says in a raspy baritone. It rings zero bells. I'm going to have to wing it.

"Hey. This is Evan. We used to work at Flynn Family Films together."

"Ah. Let me guess. You're involved in some multi-level marketing scheme. You want me to join up with you."

I wince. "Not even close. I don't want your money."

"You wouldn't call unless you needed *something*."

"I'm looking for information. On Faith Flynn."

"For what?"

I suck in my cheeks. I should've planned out a script. Straight-up asking whether he's the prankster won't get me far.

"For the memorial dinner," I improvise. "I'm trying to collect fun stories. Or see if anyone has any interesting takes on what happened to her. Were you there the night she went missing?"

"Are you serious?"

"Yeah. I thought it would be nice to—"

"We hung out that night. Me and you took shots together."

"I guess I overdid it with the vodka. My memory is a little fuzzy."

"Oh, yeah? You don't remember the fortune teller prank? You don't remember me nearly pissing my pants?"

I screw up my face, primed to ask what the hell he means, when the memory comes whooshing back. Our group tampered with the crystal ball. Seth figured out a way to crack open the back, so we could plant fake fortunes in the compartment. It was harmless fun, like when we dared each other to creep into the woods by the dumpsters after watching a campy horror movie. We made up absurd fortunes like YOU ARE NOT GOING TO LIVE THROUGH TONIGHT and THE REAPER IS COMING and THEY WON'T MAKE IT MUCH LONGER.

We didn't think anyone would actually believe them, but the youngest boy on the crew, who was only fifteen with a fresh work permit, spiraled into a panic attack. One of his siblings had been in the hospital, recovering from intensive surgery. He wasn't sure whether his brother would pull through, so when he read the fortune, his eyes welled. His breathing went heavy. He called his parents to pick him up early.

It must be him on the phone. Of fucking course.

"We didn't think it would be a big deal," I say, scratching my neck. "It was supposed to be funny. We couldn't have known what it would do to you."

"You could have. If you pulled your head out of your ass and paid attention when other people talked. I was moping about my brother for weeks. Management made everyone sign a sympathy card. Your name was on it."

"Look. I'm sorry. That was years ago and I was—"

"The same. You haven't changed, Evan. It's great you're trying to redeem yourself by doing good deeds around the neighborhood, but no one wants to rehash the past. Especially with you."

The line goes dead.

I steeple my fingers, taking a second to compose myself before moving onto the next number on the list. Every call follows the same choreography. Someone answers, already skeptical, ready to hang up. They give me a chance to speak, but the second I namedrop Faith, they excuse themselves, or insist there's nothing important they have to add.

I'm about to dial the final number when an incoming call comes through. Brooke's name spans the screen. I shove away from the desk and answer, pacing my cramped room.

"Good, you picked up," she says, her voice giving me instant goosebumps.

"What, did you think I was going to ghost you?"

"I wasn't sure. We've never spoken on the phone. Some people only text."

I smirk against my cell. "Does that make me old fashioned?"

"I hope not. I'm not looking for a sweaty apple."

"Uhh. Is that a sex thing?"

"Oh my God. No." She bursts out laughing. "It's a nerdy history joke. About an old courting ritual. Women would tuck a peeled apple under their armpit while dancing, then give it to their crush at the end of the night. If they liked her back, they would eat it. To prove… loyalty? Attraction, maybe. I can't remember the details."

"Hate to break it to you, but I don't think we've reached the apple phase yet. Can I fight for you in a duel instead?"

"That won't be necessary," she snorts. "But if we're together long enough, you'll be dragged to Medieval Times at least once. Plus, a renaissance fair or two."

"What about tonight?"

"We're sticking to a bar. But you can still wear a corset."

"Keep dreaming, Milady."

Once she gives me the address, we agree to take separate Ubers and meet there. I hang up with a goofy smile—but am *not* happy about it. Getting attached wasn't part of the plan. I was originally looking for a hookup, a casual rebound to power me through the divorce, but I already agreed to the date. I might as well enjoy it. Besides, if his history is any indication, my ex is probably screwing a replacement-me against our old headboard right about now.

After months of moping, I deserve some romance. Or at least an orgasm.

CHAPTER 6

FIONA

Seth's accusation rings through my mind during the whole drive back to my apartment. *A new client tried to set up an appointment under your sister's name. Are you going to pretend you don't know anything about that?* He might have gone rogue by threatening me, but there's a chance Angel believes I'm responsible, too. I don't want her to hate me over a misunderstanding.

I tap-tap-tap my fingers against the wheel, worried I'm going to be forced to find a new therapist. I want to correct the issue before it snowballs, but I'm not sure who contacted her, impersonating my sister. Honestly, it could be anyone.

"Stop thinking about it," I murmur to myself. "You can worry about it later but not tonight. Tonight is supposed to be fun. You're supposed to have fun."

The universe isn't making it easy for me. A truck loiters in my parking space, number 26, which is situated directly in front of the staircase door. The spots aren't reserved, but we have an unspoken rule about parking in the same place every single day out of courtesy to our neighbors. I circle the lot twice, searching for an opening marked with another even number. 13 and 37 are available, but they feel like bad luck. I doubt the world will end if I park in the *wrong* space, but why chance it?

I end up parking on the opposite side of the apartment complex, so I'm half-popsicle by the time I make it up to my apartment. My cat, Hunter, greets me with a chorus of meows. I crouch to scrub between his ears, then spoon soft food into his dish and refill his water bowl. He's a pound or two chubbier than a Russian Blue should be, but I can't resist spoiling him rotten.

"All right, Hunter, what do you think I should wear? Want to pick out my outfit?"

His tail swishes, nibbling his dinner.

"I'll figure it out on my own, then."

I pad through my cramped kitchen, into a bedroom with bare walls and a single curtained window. My accordion closet is already unrolled, revealing dozens of gray hangers. I usually recycle the same clothes, fishing them out of the laundry basket without bothering to hang them. That won't cut it tonight, though. I slip into a loose, long-sleeved dress with the price tag still attached. Then I throw on a pair of boots and rose gold earrings to match my bracelet. I'm pleasantly surprised by my reflection.

Then the second-guessing starts. There's a decent amount of cleavage. And my legs are exposed, from my ankles to my knees. If I wear such a high-effort outfit, Jonah might think we're on a date. I don't want to give him the wrong impression, but he's not the type to assume showing skin entitles him to touch it. Still, I feel funny now, so I start from scratch, squeezing into tight, black denim jeans with a silky button-down top. It's still cute, but it's not first-date-cute.

I don't have enough time to do my hair, but I'm more comfortable with it pulled back anyway. After smoothing down flyaways, I copy and paste the address Jonah texted me into my GPS. He wants to meet at some bar outside of town called Cider Shack.

My phone claims the destination is thirty minutes away, so I scurry to my car and switch on an audiobook to stop my mind from drifting. I make it three chapters into a fluffy, escapist romance before reaching a hand-painted wooden sign with a sloppy arrow pointing right. I turn into a packed parking lot, parking beneath a row of apple trees.

Jonah paces outside the steel building, rubbing his palms to keep warm. I almost brush past him on my way to the entrance. I'm used to seeing him in all-black with our branded theater hats. Now, he has on ripped jeans and a blue flannel with the sleeves rolled up veiny forearms. Almost every woman does a double-take as we step through the entrance, but he holds his focus on me.

"You didn't have to wait outside," I say, freezing just looking at him. "You're lucky you didn't get frostbite. The temperature is supposed to be under twenty all week. We'll probably get more snow soon."

"Ehh, losing a toe was worth the risk. You're not a fan of crowds. I didn't want to give you a reason to turn your car around. I know you're probably looking for any excuse you can to run home and cuddle your cat. And no, that's unfortunately not a euphemism."

"Believe it or not, I'm happy to be out of the house tonight."

"Wow. Therapy must have gone well. Sign me up."

I smile as he steers me around the room, hunting for a free table. The wide-open, warehouse-like space is overrun with people in their twenties and thirties. Jonah was right. Crowds of this size normally make me nervous. However, we're too far from town for anyone to recognize me without context. There aren't any nasty looks or passing whispers. I'm just another stranger buzzing around in the background of their lives.

I'm loving the atmosphere, too. It's much calmer than most nightlife spots. There's no dance floor pulsing with partiers or loud, live music to scream over. It feels more like a restaurant than a bar, except there are only snacks available for purchase and all of the tables are standing tables. There are mocktails though, so at least I won't be stuck sipping water.

Jonah excuses himself to order drinks. I flutter around our table, fiddling with the flap on my wallet. I made sure to bring cash so we could split the bill.

"Put that thing away," he says when he returns, jerking his head. "Has it been that long since you've gone out? I pay for one round. You pay for the next."

"Oh. Right. We can do it that way."

I cradle my drink, a tall, skinny glass sloshing with purple liquid. A strawberry slice balances on the rim. I take a test sip.

"What's the verdict?" he asks.

"Better than expected."

"I sure hope so. It's almost as pricey as mine even though there's not a drop of tequila." He gulps from a wide-rimmed glass swimming with amber liquid. "Tell me again why you don't drink? You're not an alcoholic, so what's the deal?"

"You don't need to get addicted to something to realize it's a bad idea for you to keep doing it."

"So you had one bad experience and gave it up for good? I had a hundred bad experiences and am still going strong. I've been through bar fights, sloppy hookups, drunk texts, you name it."

"Whatever makes you happy," I say, spinning my straw. "I'm not going to pressure you to go cold turkey and join a convent as long as you don't pressure me to take a sip of *that*. It looks like pee."

"You think I'm sharing my margarita? This baby cost twelve bucks. I'm savoring every drop." He slurps some more, moaning against the glass. "I'm just trying to understand where you're coming from. You never had any fun drinking? Ever?"

"Sure. When I was a teenager. The tipsy stage was nice, but everything that comes after is awful. It's tricky to stop at the right point."

Especially when my OCD was telling me to drink another. And another. The night my sister went missing, I overdid it. I was worried something bad would happen if I stopped on an odd number of drinks. The theater could burst into flames, burning us to a crisp. A serial killer could break inside strapped with guns, mowing us down. Whenever someone encouraged me to take a shot, I would have to take two. I forced myself to stop after seven, when the room started spinning and my eyesight went fuzzy.

And look what happened.

My smile slips. That night is the last thing I want to think about right now. I'm out to get her *off* my mind. But I can't fault Jonah for bringing up the topic. He doesn't realize he's struck a nerve. He moved to town a few years ago, so he missed the height of the search, when there were hounds and helicopters sent to retrieve her, when reporters pounded on our door with questions and rang our phone at all hours of the night.

"Was it a mistake to bring you here?" he asks, face falling. "I could've taken you to a paint night or bowling alley. But they have drinks, too. Shit. I figured this place was far out of town and—"

"It's fine," I say. "Being around alcohol doesn't bother me. Let's just talk about something else. I want to know what's been going on with you?"

It's a diversion tactic, sure, but it's also true. We might see each other six days a week, but most of our conversations revolve around the theater. All I know is that he prefers ushering and portering—so he can sneak into theaters and watch movies—over manning the registers or working the backroom. He's a movie buff, a wannabe filmmaker who grew up with a single mother and a boatload of sisters, a few who are still in single digits.

Over the next hour, he tells me about his rescue puppy with a limp, his freezer stocked with coconut ice cream, and his tradition of belting Elvis songs at karaoke bars. If there was a machine set up at the Cider Shack, he would be gyrating on stage by now.

I'm happy I didn't cancel on him. It's nice being surrounded by strangers who are giggling and flirting and lost in their own little worlds. I scan the room, admiring couples with arms wrapped around waists, friends clustered in tight circles, crushes standing a little too close and staring a little too long.

Then my eyes snag on one woman in particular. Evan O'Connor.

Platinum blonde hair tumbles down her chest. Trendy, oversized glasses perch high on her nose. A striped romper covers her long, lean legs with a golden belt cinching the waist. Forever fashionable, like she was peeled off the pages of a style magazine. She's in the middle of an animated conversation with a tattooed woman, their heads bent together like swans.

I've grown used to spotting the others around town. I might run into Raven at the cafe, ordering iced cappuccinos to sip in between beauty appointments. I might pass Cameron perched on a street corner with his guitar case propped open, accepting requests in exchange for cash. I might come across Seth at the park, guiding his sons down the slide.

But Evan? I haven't seen so much as a social media post from her in a decade. I'm not sure whether she blocked me because she hates my guts—or because she considers me a nobody who isn't worth her trouble.

It's hard to believe we were once close enough for her to come over without a warning text, a knock on the door. She would bound straight up our porch, raid our freezer for ice pops, and plop on our couch to play *Mario Party* or *Animal Crossing*. I did the same at her house. Her parents never batted an eye, just nodded hello and set out an extra plate.

Now, I watch her strut toward the bar with two empty glasses. Jonah must mistake my staring for attraction, either to her or the men standing at the bar beside her, because he says, "I need to piss. Can you get us the next round?"

Before I can protest, he bounds into the bathroom. He *did* buy the last set of drinks. It's only right for me to return the favor, so I reluctantly approach the U-shaped bar. Customers swarm around every server without forming a formal line, so I squeeze into the crowd and wait for a worker to notice me.

Evan spots me first. Her neck snaps back like a bolt of electricity struck her, her mouth falling open. I say a silent prayer that she's going to pretend she never saw me, but her gray, catlike eyes scan me up and down. She wades through the crowd, shoving strangers aside, her lips ticking upward.

"Long time, no see," she says once she reaches my side.

I rack my brain for something short and sweet. Nothing rude. Nothing overly friendly, either. I settle on: "It has been a while, yes."

"You must have missed me."

"What gives you that idea?"

"Your jewelry. It's from my shop. It's nice to know you still have good taste."

I glance down. My sleeves have ridden up, revealing my bracelet. Rose gold with an inscription of my initials. "It was a present," I say, focusing on my breathing.

"So you've never bought anything from my shop?"

"I've never seen your shop."

"You don't have to lie to me. It's flattering, really."

"I'm not lying. I haven't kept tabs on you, Evan."

"I find that hard to believe."

My nails dig into my palm, scraping the flesh. I can't tell whether she's teasing me or interrogating me. Either way, I should be the one questioning *her*. Not the other way around. How does she have the nerve to walk over and start a casual conversation like everything is fine when *she's* the one who ended our friendship? We've been estranged for years. She could start with an apology. An explanation. *Anything*.

I whip away from her, heat spreading through my body. A spot has opened on my right, so I shimmy sideways.

She shadows my movements. "Who gave it to you, then? A boyfriend?"

"A friend."

"What friend?"

"You wouldn't know him."

"It's kind of weird you aren't saying the name."

"It's not weird. You've never met. You moved out of town, remember? You ditched everyone because you thought you were too good for this place."

Her nose wrinkles. "I mean, you're not wrong. This place was bad news for me, so I got myself out."

"I hope it made you happy."

"It did. I got married. Got a big house. Got most of my goals crossed off my bucket list, which is more than most people can say."

"But then you lost it all."

She blinks. "Excuse me?"

"That's why you're back, right? Because you were able to create a nice life, but you weren't able to make it last?"

She sets her jaw, like the comment struck a nerve. Good. She could've walked over and said she was sorry for ignoring my texts for ten years and I would've been civil with her. She set the tone.

I'm about to storm away—who cares about the drinks?—when Jonah strolls over. He inserts himself between us, thrumming his long fingers on the counter. "Hey, are you Evan?" he asks, beaming his startlingly white smile at her.

She issues a small, almost imperceptible nod. As if she's too stubborn to admit he's right.

"Your mom works with mine," he says, extending a hand. "They have standing dates in the break room to talk trash about their third graders."

"Right. Nice to meet you." She pumps his hand once, then reels it away. I'm surprised she doesn't scrub his germs on her pant leg. "I'm glad she has good company."

"You should be. Because of her, I splurged at your shop last Christmas. Ordered some jewelry for my mom and aunts and sisters. And Fiona, obviously."

"Ah. You're the *friend*. I appreciate the sales."

"No problem. It's a nice site. Smooth. Easy to navigate. I recognize you from the pictures. That's good branding right there. If crafting doesn't work out, you could get into web design."

"Maybe," she says, but it comes out like a *no*. I expect her to get bored and leave, but then she asks him, "How long have you two been dating?"

"We're not dating. Not trying to piss off HR."

"You work at the theater, then?"

He nods, puffing his chest. "You're looking at the Flynn Family Films employee of the month for six months running."

"Did you work there when you were younger, too? I'm bad with faces."

"Nah, Fiona hired me a couple years ago. She looked past my criminal record and took a real chance on me."

I chuckle, but Evan's mouth remains slack, expressionless.

"That was a joke," he clarifies. "Don't go calling the cops on me. I couldn't keep my trap shut long enough to get away with littering, let alone a federal offense. Anyway, it was nice to meet you. Tell your mom I'm waiting on more of her cupcakes."

With a wink, he slips his arm around my shoulders and leads me to the opposite side of the bar. We lost our table since no one was around to guard it, but I'm not sure how much longer I'm staying anyway.

"She's nothing like her mom," Jonah mutters once we're out of earshot. "That woman is a saint. I guess kids don't always turn out exactly like their parents, but her apple is nowhere near their tree. It's rolling around in the rose bushes next door."

"I think you lost the metaphor. But thank you for rescuing me."

"Lucky for you, there was no urinal line. After I zipped up, I noticed you looking white as cream. Figured you could use some help." He waves over a bartender in a crop top. She pours our drinks and swipes my card. "So what was her problem, anyway? Do you two have some long-lost history I don't know about?"

"I don't know. Kind of. I guess so."

"That's a strong yes. Go ahead. Spill. I'm too drunk to remember tomorrow anyway."

"Off *one* margarita? You liar," I say. But it might be nice to get it off my chest. "We were best friends in elementary school. And middle school. Most of high school, too. She used to come over to our house to play games and watch movies. Typical teenage stuff."

"What happened?"

"You would have to ask her. She stopped talking to me out of nowhere."

"You didn't do anything to deserve it? You didn't sleep with her boyfriend or run over her Barbies?"

I shrug. "I've gone over it in my head a million times, but it's still a mystery. If anything, I should've been the one to end the friendship with her."

"What do you mean? Was she always this snobby?"

"She was fun one-on-one, but she would ditch me whenever her other friends invited her out. She never let me tag along with them, even though we all knew each other from the theater. It really bothered me, but she never cared."

"Why did you put up with her for so long?"

I cup my chin, taking a second to answer. "I guess... I wasn't involved in any sports or clubs since my parents wanted us working at the theater most nights, so I never met many people who *got* me. When Evan was actually around, she was great. She listened to my stories and remembered little things about me and calmed me down when my OCD got bad. And whenever my sister made a mean comment, something small I would usually let slide, Evan would stick up for me. She made me feel like I mattered, like I was worth an argument. We even kissed once."

"Oh?" He leans forward, interested.

"It's not that scandalous. It was during a spin the bottle game at the theater, so everyone was doing it. It didn't mean anything."

Unless it did. Faith always teased me about Evan being in love with me, calling her my *girlfriend* to get under my skin. At the time, it never even crossed my mind that the crush might be real—but dating wasn't really on my radar. I was a late bloomer. My first non-game kiss was at nineteen. I lost my virginity at twenty-two. There had been relationships here and there, but I always got dumped before the six-month mark. Somehow, it was always my fault. *I worked too much. I worried too much. I was too set in my ways.* Despite my love of rom-coms, staying single was easier.

"Can we please change the subject?" I say. "I don't want anything to do with Evan. One conversation was more than enough to last me another decade."

"Noted. If she's ballsy enough to bother you again, give me a call. I'll take care of her. If you know what I mean."

A laugh slips out, my anxiety already starting to fade. After all, why should I be the one to leave when she was the one who marched up to *me* and got in *my* face?

It looks like she's closing her tab anyway. She deposits her empty glasses on the counter and heads for the exit, her fingers laced with the brunette woman. I'm pretty sure she was the hostess when I treated my parents to lunch for their anniversary a few weeks back. We chatted while waiting for an available table, but it was mostly small talk. Nothing memorable.

She traipses outside now, her face split into a dreamy smile. She better be careful. I'm sure, eventually, Evan is going to hurt her, too.

CHAPTER 7

EVAN

My phone pings, a sharp beep against my ear. I blink awake, my stomach heavy as a brick. I'd say I'm never drinking again, but that would be a lie.

I'm barely functional without my glasses, but even through the blur, I can tell the room is all wrong. I scramble upright, cracking my skull against the headboard. It takes a second to remember I've been crashing with my parents. Another second to realize it's not their house, either.

Brooke is crunched on the other side of the bed, a foot with heart tattoos poking out from the comforter. Her face is covered by blankets, but judging by the gentle rise and fall of her shoulders, she's sound asleep. Thank Christ. I need a minute to jog my memory.

Fiona is the first thing that snaps to mind. Her and her damn bracelet. I wasn't going to strike up a conversation with her, but then I noticed the material, the inscription, the font. It looked suspiciously similar to the necklace ordered under her sister's name. Almost a matching set. Sure, it could have been a coincidence considering rose gold has been in style the last few years and the font was my most popular choice. But still. I needed to see what she had to say for herself.

Or maybe I needed an excuse to talk to her.

Either way, I'm not sure whether her and her little friend were telling the whole truth. The guy sounded genuine, but my gut warned me not to trust him. He was a smooth talker, a salesman type who said exactly what I wanted to hear. If he'd ordered from my shop before, *he* could have bought the necklace. I wasn't going to watch him and Fiona make googly eyes at each other all night, so I stormed back to Brooke and insisted on leaving. I was set to head home and chalk the date up to a failure, but she sheepishly admitted to shipping her kid to the sitter's house for the night. Her apartment would be empty until morning.

We shared an Uber back to her place, swapping tipsy kisses in the backseat, her hands streaking through my hair and pulling, her short nails digging crescents into my skin.

"We should probably slow down," she panted midway through the ride. "Don't want to drop you to a one-star rating."

"Worth it," I said, squeezing her thigh.

When we rolled up to her apartment, she led me through a cramped kitchen with plants soaking up sunlight on the windowsill, past a door decorated with neon butterfly stickers, and into a black-and-white bedroom. We spent the rest of the night alternating between sex and shots, getting way more wasted off her liquor cabinet than the oversized, overpriced drinks at the bar. It felt like a better idea when my head wasn't pounding.

I paw the nightstand for my glasses, then check the phone resting on my pillowcase. I'm guessing the text that woke me is from my parents. I'm not a teenager anymore, but it's only right to fill them in on when they should expect me home. I'm already enough of a burden without making them wonder whether I drank myself to death overnight.

When my eyes adjust to the bright light of my phone, it turns out the message isn't from my mother or my father. It's a group text from an unlisted number. It says: ARE YOU READY FOR THE MEMORIAL DINNER?

At first, I think it's some spammy reminder sent out to everyone in town, an automatic alert. But the bubbles at the top of the screen state there are only three other people in the chat. I click on the number to reveal the names. Two are saved in my contact list. Raven and Cameron.

I assume the third is Seth. He must have changed phones since our last conversation.

I scoot up even straighter, suddenly wide awake. On its own, the text would be harmless since the whole town has been treating the memorial like a celebration. But the fact that an outsider grouped us together is a problem.

So is the time stamp. Three thirty-three was listed on Faith's birth certificate. She used to bring it up whenever she fought with Fiona, her killing blow. She would insist on having the final say in which snacks to buy or games to play because she was born five minutes earlier, which made her *older and wiser*. Spoiler alert: She wasn't even close.

My phone buzzes in my hand. Another message pings into the group chat. From Cameron this time. "That's not funny, man. I don't know how you got this number but screw you. I'm blocking this chain."

I massage my temples, calculating my best move. I'm not sure what to add to the conversation. Or whether I should even bother replying. I type and backspace, type and backspace, until another notification pops onto the top of the screen.

"I think we should talk," Raven says in a new, private group chat. The four of us, minus the blocked number. "Are you all free later today? We could meet at the diner?"

Another ping. "I don't know if we should be seen in a room together," Seth says. "We better do this privately. It's the twenty-first century. A video call would be easiest."

Brooke stirs beside me, her bed-head poking out from the covers. I should've turned down the volume. Then I could've slunk out of the apartment without an awkward goodbye.

"I need to get out of here," I whisper. I consider brushing back the bangs that have tumbled in front of her eyes, then think better of it. I'm not sure whether this is a one-time thing yet. I'm not sure whether I want it to be. "I didn't mean to fall asleep on you. Or wake you up."

"No apology necessary," she says through a yawn. "I'm used to early mornings. My little terror is getting dropped off first thing, so it won't be long until I'm running around after her."

"Sounds exhausting."

"It's the worst. But still the best thing to ever happen to me."

My lips twitch. "I better pick up the pace, then. I don't want her to walk in on a half-naked stranger."

"Good thinking, we don't want to confuse her before we make things official."

I stiffen. "Are you *planning* on making things official?"

"Oh, I mean, I don't want to come across too forward but… Hold on." She scoots herself into a sitting position, rummages around in her nightstand drawer, then hands me an old, cracked iPhone.

"What is this?" I ask. "Payment?"

She flips it over in my palm, tapping the logo on the back. An apple. A laugh tumbles out of me. "You are ridiculous."

"I think you mean *the most romantic ever*," she grins. "We don't have to commit to anything serious right this second, but I definitely don't want this to be the last time we see each other."

I swing my legs off the mattress, concealing a goofy grin. "I guess we'll have to plan another date, then."

"Good. How does popcorn and a movie sound? *It's Always Bloody* is playing. Did you see the trailer? There's this corny line: *Gutting monsters is brave—but having the guts to love, that's real bravery.* We can make a drinking game out of it. Take a sip whenever there's a cringy kiss or bad CGI."

I tense up. Visiting the theater is asking for a reunion with Fiona. Of course, Brooke has no idea about our run-in last night. The bar was packed, so she didn't pick up on the fact we were having a conversation. I didn't explain why I had the sudden itch to leave, either. I blurted out an excuse about needing air and that was good enough for her.

"Or we could see a rom-com," she shrugs. "I just figured we could walk to the cinema from here, so if the movie got boring, we could bail and retreat to bed instead of making out in the back row like animals."

"It's tempting, for sure," I say, but there's something unsettling about being so close to the theater.

I slither into yesterday's clothes while gazing out the window. A short stretch of woods separates the apartment complex from a strip of industrial buildings. Her apartment must have been built on the section of woods they bulldozed. I could've been standing in this exact spot ten years ago, my sneakers crusted in dirt, weaving through the forest in a game of manhunt or capture the flag.

I kiss her goodbye before any more pesky memories resurface, request an Uber, and check the group chat. There are about a dozen missed messages. Cameron was against the idea of a video call at first, raving about the NSA listening in on his conversations, but the others convinced him there isn't any difference between video chatting and texting or talking on the phone.

I fire off a quick message, agreeing to seven, the suggested time. I can squeeze in a few more hours of sleep if I make it home quick enough. Luckily, our places are only blocks apart. Not too shabby for a walk of shame.

A few minutes before seven, I balance my laptop on one of my crafting boxes, then clean off the area behind me, ripping down posters and balling up dirty laundry, so the room looks presentable. If the screen tilted an inch in any direction, they would see piles upon piles of crap.

When the call boots up, four boxes dissect the screen. Seth is sitting in a home office with framed paintings perfectly centered behind him, already wearing a suit. Raven is lounging in her living room, rocking an oversized t-shirt and silk scarf she probably slept in. Cameron is the only one without an image. He must have tape covering the camera, but I picture him on a half-inflated air mattress.

"Hey. It's so good to see your faces," Raven says as if we're getting together for virtual happy hour drinks. The rest chime in with equally polite greetings—*how are you? You look great. It's been so long*—but it all sounds stale. Everyone wants to cut to the chase, to cross the meeting off their checklist so they can move on with their lives.

It's weird seeing them in a new context, with less pimples and more wrinkles. I still imagine them as kids at the theater, goofing off when they should've been working. I picture Raven braiding my hair with rainbow rubber bands, twisting the strands into elaborate patterns. Cameron sharing earbuds with me, blasting obscure bands on his iPod. Seth drawing penises on the backside of tickets and pretending to be confused when customers complained.

"Okay, let's start with the obvious question," Raven says in between sips of a mug stained with lipstick marks. "Did any of you send that text this morning? Come clean now and we won't be angry."

"Speak for yourself," Seth mutters.

"Well, it wasn't me," I say. "You saw my number included in the chat."

"I'm telling you, it's someone playing a prank," Cameron slurs. It sounds like he started his morning with an Irish coffee. "The anniversary is coming up. The dinner is this weekend. Someone wanted to rattle us and it worked. We're giving them what they want by losing our minds about it."

Seth shakes his head. "My bets are on Fiona. She played a similar prank on my wife recently."

"What sort of prank?" I ask.

He tells us about a therapist appointment booked under Faith's name.

"Did she admit to making the appointment?" Raven asks.

"Of course not. But she didn't deny it either. She looked like a deer in headlights when I confronted her."

"Maybe she was upset. It can't be easy hearing rumors about her dead sister."

"I don't know. Seth could be right," I say. "I had a weird thing happen with her, too."

I tell them about the necklace order directing me to Cameron's address. And the fact that she was wearing a matching bracelet when we bumped into each other at the bar.

It never sat right with her that we were at the theater when her sister went missing. Or that we leaked rumors about her. Or that we cut contact with her without warning. She has a million reasons to mess with us. If anything, I'm surprised she didn't get revenge earlier. Lord knows we deserved it.

Besides, if it's not her, someone in our group is most likely guilty. And I can't consider that possibility. Not yet.

"That settles it," Seth says. "It's definitely Fiona. I could contact my lawyers to see about issuing a restraining order, but I don't think she's done enough to warrant it. However, if she keeps this up, then there are going to be serious consequences. I thought I got through to her when we spoke, but apparently not if she's sending anonymous texts now."

Raven clucks her tongue. "I'm sorry. I'm still not convinced. It doesn't seem like something she would do."

"Are you suggesting it was one of us?" Seth asks. "Because, if I had to guess, the person who was spared from pranks is probably the one pulling them."

"I wasn't *spared*," she says, then puffs out a sigh. "My salon has a website. The other day, someone hacked into the program. They changed my log-in information too, so I haven't been able to fix it."

"What did they do, exactly?" I ask.

"They erased all the information—my biography and my prices—and replaced it with insults. Then they swapped my customer photos with photos of Faith. Most of them were from the newspapers or her old social media pages. I reverse image searched them all to double-check. But there were a few that weren't anywhere online. I had never seen them before. I don't know where they came from."

Seth tosses up his hands. "That settles it. Who would have pictures like that? Fiona. All signs point to her. She's not hiding it well. She's unhinged."

"Hold up," Raven says. "Does that mean you don't think it's me anymore?"

"I never said it was you."

"You implied it."

"This is ridiculous," Cameron cuts in. "Whether it's Fiona or us or a space alien, what does it matter? If we freak out over their mind games, we're giving them what they want. Just ignore it and they'll go away. Like little girls getting their hair pulled at the playground."

I wince. "That's crappy advice for little girls. You realize that, right? It's basically telling the bully what they did is cool. That they can act out and won't face any consequences."

"What are you, our mom now?"

I flash my middle finger at the screen. It's clearly a joke, but my thoughts wander to my ex-husband, who was trying to get me pregnant, then to Brooke, who has a child of her own. I wonder whether I would get along well with the kid, then blink hard, discarding the thought. I haven't known the woman for more than a week. I need to pump the brakes.

"Hopefully this is the last we hear from whoever this is," Seth says. "If not, we need to keep each other updated. Report back with anything odd that occurs. We might not have spoken to each other in a while, but we're still on the same team, right?"

"Yeah, yeah, together until we're corpses," I say, mimicking our old catchphrase. The one we would scream through laughter whenever we came close to dying. When we snuck weed into the raceway and got chased out by a guard with a handgun. When we set off fireworks at the pier and aimed a wick in the wrong direction. One winter, Seth got his stomach pumped after too many rounds of beer pong. One summer, Raven got a concussion while crowd-surfing at a concert. We were always tempting fate. And it finally bit us in the ass.

"All right," Raven says, clapping her hands. "I guess we'll see each other at the memorial dinner."

I flick my wrist. "Count me out. I wouldn't be caught dead there."

"Why?"

"Because I'm not a masochist."

"But you're back in town. You have to go. Everyone goes."

I roll my eyes. "What's that motto about jumping off a bridge?"

"I'm just saying, it would be weird if you skipped it. Especially since you and Fiona were so close. Don't you think they would want you there?"

"Trust me. The family doesn't want anything to do with me. Not after the way I left things."

I was a coward, texting her father that I wasn't going to return to work instead of breaking the news in person. He assured me he understood and explained they were closing for a few weeks anyway, focused on finding their daughter.

As for Fiona, I ignored her long strings of texts, her late-night ramblings asking where I went. *Evan, is your phone glitching? I've been texting you all day. Evan, is everything okay? I was hoping you would come over. Evan, I miss you. Evan, what is wrong with you?*

I stared at her words—some desperate, some angry, mostly confused—and typed out a million flavors of responses. I tried pouring my heart out, explaining the story from start to finish. *Delete.* I tried confessing my feelings for her, asking her to trust me. *Delete.* I tried telling her to fuck off, so she would hate me and be glad I was gone. *Delete.* Every time a new text came through, I drained another six-pack, cracked open another bottle. I had a collection of cans rolling beneath my bed, growing bigger by the day.

I missed as many classes as possible without sacrificing my diploma, skipped prom, refused to walk at graduation. Whenever I was forced to attend class, I carried a flask in my backpack and snuck sips in the bathroom. I couldn't wait to get out of town and leave for college upstate.

I promised myself I would never come back. But I've never been great with promises.

"If anything goes down, you guys have it covered," I say to the video chat. "I believe in you."

It's not entirely true, but I need them to think I'm with them, one million percent. If they sense any tension between us, they could turn on me. It's better to have them on my side. They need to know I've got their back. Then they won't stab me in mine.

CHAPTER 8

FIONA

My mother isn't pleased to see me. "You can't knock on our door at six-thirty in the morning without warning," she says, but she's already dressed. Black slacks. Long-sleeved shirt. Full face of makeup.

"Sorry," I mumble. "I know your alarm goes off at five. I didn't think it would bother you."

"You scared me half to death. It could've been the police at the door, telling me—" She catches herself, shaking her head. "Come on. Get out of the cold. You should've worn your gloves."

She steps aside, allowing me into the cozy, one-story home. A sage green couch faces a flickering fireplace. Bookshelves line the adjacent walls, tall as the ceiling itself. My father is puttering around the room, watering a hanging plant with long, thick tendrils. He's about to move onto the next one when he spots me.

"Hey, pumpkin," he says with a one-armed hug. "What are you doing here? Aren't you opening this morning?"

"Yeah. I was early and had to pass the street anyway, so I figured I'd stop in and say hello."

In reality, I had a nagging feeling they were in trouble. I had flashes of them bruised, bleeding, and broken, so I wanted to make sure they were okay. But I'm not admitting that—and they're staring like my first excuse isn't good enough—so I scramble for more.

"My car heater is busted. I wasn't sure if it was something you could fix or whether I should have a professional handle it."

"That might be in my wheelhouse. I'll take a look-see," my father says. He deposits the watering can on the coffee table, catches my keys, and heads out.

My mother bangs around the kitchen, grabbing a cast-iron skillet and egg carton. "While you're here, you might as well have a healthy breakfast," she says, waving me over. "Not those processed toaster pastries and hot pockets you eat straight from the sleeve."

"I'm not an animal. I warm them up first."

"Either way. Meals should be cooked in ovens, not microwaves."

I don't have the energy to argue. I seat myself at the wooden table, sinking into my old cross-back chair. Faith's seat is stacked with newspapers and magazines, so no one takes her place.

My parents have done their best to preserve everything she's touched. My side of our bedroom has been stripped and replaced with a mini-office area, but they kept her side intact—the antique globe, the vintage postcards, the makeup made by European designers. Her big dream was to travel the world, actually visit the places we projected onto movie screens. Especially Britain. Trench coats hung from her closet in every color. Her blankets and pillowcases were printed with Union Jacks. And she kept resetting our desktop picture to the London Eye, no matter how many times our parents tried to change it back to our family portrait at the Cinderella castle.

My mother trashed that bulky computer a few years ago, but she transferred its data to a clean laptop, which is unfolded in front of me. She must have been reliving the past again. The laptop is a glorified time capsule, filled with ancient photos, emails, and AIM transcripts from accounts our parents forced us to share. Faith had more internet friends than real friends, people she never met in person but would talk to on forums about her favorite shows, mostly British dramas no one in school watched.

We combed through every conversation when she first went missing, but she must've deleted threads, because all the chats were G-rated. I know for a fact she spent hours on that keyboard, flirting with boys.

Plus, there were only a few messages from Perry Pierce, and they talked every single day. They met on Tumblr freshman year, ignoring *stranger danger* warnings and exchanging numbers.

They didn't see each other in person much since Perry went to a private school in the Hamptons, but sometimes Faith slept over Perry's place. Or Perry drove to the theater to watch free movies. But she never set foot in our house. When our parents asked why Faith refused to invite her over for dinner, she snapped, "I don't need Fiona to steal my best friend." As if that would ever happen.

The only time I talked to the girl was when we got stuck on the theater bathroom line together. "Wow, you two really *are* twins," she said, readjusting her pocketbook strap as she stared me down. It looked expensive, black leather with red trim. "It must be bizarre having a doppelganger."

I shrugged. "It's just normal life for me. You get used to it."

"I don't know. I wouldn't be able to resist playing the comparison game. I would either be staring at my twin nonstop, jealous of any little detail that made her look better than me. Or I'd be focused on the pieces I hated and would wonder whether people see me like that, too. It would be like a mirror following me everywhere, taunting me. Must be exhausting."

Before I could correct her, Faith cut me in line, shutting down the conversation.

We didn't speak again until the incident. Perry never showed at the search parties or vigils—she was hospitalized with pneumonia at the time—but I tracked down her email address and shot her a message. I asked whether she knew anyone who had reason to hurt my sister, if Faith had said anything strange lately or mentioned anyone having an issue with her, but Perry was clueless. She promised to get in touch if she remembered anything important, but I never heard from her again.

There's nothing more to gain from searching through my sister's emails, so I click open an old AIM conversation between me and Evan. My icon was a dachshund wagging its tail. Hers was a painted nail flashing the middle finger.

"Would you rather marry a werewolf or give birth to a werewolf?" I asked her on a random Wednesday afternoon.

"Give birth," she answered. "Next question."

"Hold on. What's the explanation? Because it would look like a puppy?"

"Because marrying a werewolf would suck. You'd be paranoid half the time, wondering if they're out late howling at the moon or cheating on you. Plus, there'd be all that hair in your teeth."

I hate the laugh that slips out. I hate missing her.

"Moving on," I said with a straight-faced emoji. "Would you rather spend a night in a haunted house or the middle of the woods?"

"Alone or are you with me?"

"Does it make a difference?"

She replied, "If I was on my own, I'd pick *woods* because there's plenty of places to run and hide. If you were with me, we'd explore the haunted house. Set up some sleeping bags and ghost-gaze."

"Aww, Evan, are you saying you're braver when we're together?"

"Shut up."

My heart squeezes. I can't read anymore. I can't think about the countless nights in bed, half-conscious, stirring whenever my phone buzzed to text her again. She would message me rambling thoughts at one in the morning when she was just getting to bed. And I would message her when I sprung awake from nightmares, shaking and sweaty.

But those days are long gone.

I switch off the computer and flip through the mail piled on the table. Sometimes my parents accidentally bring home bills from the cinema that I should be working into our budget. Other times letters get sent to the wrong address. I'm only halfway through the heap, but it looks like it's happened again. One envelope says FLYNN FAMILY FILMS in capitalized letters. There isn't a stamp in the corner or a return address scribbled on top. Someone must have slipped it directly into their mailbox.

I poke a finger through the side and tear open the seal. I wriggle out a greeting card from the ninety-nine-cent store with two wine glasses clinking. Above the sketch, it says HAPPY ANNIVERSARY in golden bubble letters. It must be a belated gift for my parents. It was their thirtieth anniversary last month. I bought them a custom painting of the night sky, as seen from the theater. It cost a fortune to have framed, and it took me a while to figure out the right coordinates for the engraving on the bottom, but the looks on their faces were worth all the trouble.

"Did you know you got a card?" I ask my mother as she salts and peppers the eggs. "You never opened it. There could be money inside."

"Who's it from?"

I unfold it. On the right-hand side, more letters are stamped. *"Happy anniversary!"* it says. *"Can you believe it's been ten years already? I bet you're still wondering what happened to your precious Faith. It's a shame you've had to wait so long for answers. Lucky for you, I can make all your questions go away. But I'm going to need something in exchange. Fifty thousand dollars should do the trick."*

Below, there are instructions on how to wire over the money. I skim them, but my eyes are drawn to the left-hand side of the card. Hair is taped to the paper. A few strands of long, black hair.

"What's wrong, Fiona?"

I shiver from top to bottom, picturing the black hair outside the theater, whipping in the wind. The black hair at the grocery store, weaving between aisles. The black hair, there and then gone, disappearing into thin air, like it never existed in the first place.

"Fiona?" my mother repeats again and again. At least, I think that's what she's saying. The heartbeat in my ears is drowning everything else out. I can't respond, not with a nod or a tear. My body has gone numb.

I don't feel a thing until my mother rips the card from my hands, slicing a cut across my palm. I stare at the little white scrape, harmless at first. Then the blood bubbles, spilling across my hand.

My mother's beady eyes flick across the page. When she's done reading, she clutches the countertop and calls for my father—screeching like the world is ending, like she's about to die herself. She crumples onto the tile, wheezing and sobbing and gasping for air.

My father rushes inside, his head whipping for signs of trouble. "What's wrong? What happened?" he asks, dropping near my mother. He tilts up her chin to examine her, thinking she's physically hurt.

"Faith is alive," she sobs, thrusting the card toward him. "Our baby is okay. She's out there. They're going to give her back to us."

He reads while her head is cradled in his lap, snot dripping down her nose. When he finishes, his cheeks are snow-white and slick with sweat. I haven't seen him like this since the day she disappeared.

"It might not be her hair," I say. My voice sounds far away, like it belongs to someone else. "If someone had her, why would they wait to ransom her? It doesn't make any sense. If they took her for money, they would've asked for it right away."

"Fiona is right. Let's not get ahead of ourselves," my father says, rubbing circles on my mother's back. "We can hope for the best, but this letter never suggests she's alive. It only says they'll give us answers about what happened. The person who... who hurt her could be giving us a confession, that's all."

"That doesn't make sense, either," I say. "Why would they come forward now? Are they starting to feel guilty out of nowhere? If they hurt her and got away with it, they would've moved on by now."

"We haven't moved on." He coughs, clearing the emotion from his voice. "Who knows? Maybe it was an accident. Maybe they want to set the truth straight now that the statute of limitations is up. Or maybe they just need quick money. There's no telling what this person is thinking."

He kisses my mother on the forehead, then shimmies away so he can rustle in his pockets. He removes his pay-as-you-go phone and flips it open.

"What are you doing?" I ask.

"Calling Officer Patel. We need a DNA test on the hair. And we need to figure out who slipped the card in the mailbox."

"She's alive," my mother mumbles. "I know she's alive."

That can't be possible. She can't make a comeback after ten years of mourning. She was gone. Everyone knew, deep down, that she was dead.

Someone else had to be behind the letter. It could be Evan. I doubt it's a coincidence the note arrived right after she returned to town. Or maybe it's Seth. He could've accused me of impersonating my sister to throw me off his scent. Unless it's a stranger who would never cross my mind, a guest invited to the restaurant this weekend.

"He's not picking up," my father says, lowering his phone. "He must be asleep still. He usually works nights."

My mother sniffs. "Good. We should pay this person first. They might flee town if they hear we contacted the authorities."

"No way. We don't have that kind of money," I squeak. "Not unless you take it out of the business. And you can't risk losing the theater to pay this person. The police are going to warn us not to negotiate with them, anyway."

My father raises a hand. "Don't get yourself worked up, sweetie. We'll cooperate with the police. We'll head down to the station today and talk to them in person, so they do their job right. Patel won't be able to look us in the eyes and screw us."

"I'll come with you," I say, pushing up from the table. My legs wobble, but I'm able to stand. I need to put on a brave face for them. Seeing me crumble will only make it harder for them to hold themselves together.

"That's all right, pumpkin," my father says. "You have responsibilities at the theater. We don't need all three of us crowding up the station, anyway. We'll talk to them alone."

"Are you sure?"

"Yes. Keep yourself busy. That's all you need to do today."

I don't want to cause more pain by putting up a fight. Besides, a part of me is relieved to be saved from the station, the scrutiny, the stress. The police insisted they were on our side after Faith disappeared, then interrogated us like we were their main suspects. They questioned my mother's parenting, my father's temper, my relationship with Faith.

Like it was our fault we lost her.

CHAPTER 9

EVAN

I pull up to the police station, a squat brick building that hasn't been updated since the eighties. In middle school, I went to a few dances with a scrawny guy who grew into a pudgy, card-carrying cop. Back then, he was at the top of the popularity ladder, so I couldn't turn him down without admitting I had the hots for someone else. I remember his wiry hands on my waist, ogling my cleavage while I stared across the gym at Fiona. I felt more chemistry during the fast songs, when she got excited over some overplayed pop music and we danced across from each other in a circle.

I came close to unfriending him after one too many selfies with guns and deer carcasses, but I thought he might come in handy in the future. He leaves fire emojis under every photo I post, so hopefully he'll bend some rules for me.

Here goes nothing...

I step into his cramped, cluttered office with American flags tacked to the walls. He's the only one behind a desk, but there are muffled voices coming from one of the back rooms. Men chatting. A woman crying.

"Evan O'Connor?" the officer says, eyebrows shooting toward his nonexistent hairline. "Is that really you?"

"In the flesh. I hope you didn't miss me too much."

"Only every shower."

I blink hard, wiping the disgust off my face. "You haven't changed one bit."

"That makes one of us. What are you doing here, anyway? Turning yourself in?"

"There are better ways to get into handcuffs."

He raises a smarmy smile. "What brings you here, then?"

"I have a friend who needs some help."

"A friend, huh? Why aren't they with you?"

"She isn't a fan of cops. And, full disclosure, I *might've* volunteered to handle the situation in the hopes of running into you."

In reality, handing over information about Raven is my safest way forward. I *could* ask him to trace the necklace order back to a credit card, but it's not like ordering jewelry under the wrong name is illegal. It makes more sense to use her story.

"What's wrong with your friend?" he asks, leaning back in his chair, trying hard to look cool. I give him two minutes until he topples over.

"She owns a hair salon in town. Her website was hacked. We were hoping you could figure out who's responsible."

I pull up the page on my phone. Instead of listing her beauty school qualifications, her biography section repeatedly calls her a whore and bitch and a homewrecker.

"Can you try to trace the IP address?" I ask. "Find out who's behind the prank?"

"If they have half a brain, they used a VPN to make themselves untraceable."

I tilt my head. "Are those hard to come by?"

"It's cake. Type those three letters into Google and you're halfway there. It doesn't take a mastermind to download one. It could be any dude with internet access."

"Do you think you could check it out for me, just in case they got sloppy?"

"Not my job. She should report the issue to the website service provider. If she's still not happy, the FBI handles computer intrusion."

"*Come on.* I bet you're smarter than those FBI guys," I coo, and he puffs his chest, sitting up straighter. I run a hand through my hair, making sure he catches my bare ring finger. The hidden perks of divorce. "If you help me out, I'll return the favor."

He bounces his head, like he's considering the offer. "It *is* a pretty slow day on my end. I could squeeze you in. If you're serious about your favor."

"Of course. I'm free next weekend. You pick the place."

It shouldn't take longer than seven days to get the results back to me. Plenty of time to cancel on him.

Unfortunately, he leans forward, clutching the back of my hand with his warm, sweaty palm. "Why wait? Shouldn't take more than ten minutes. I could do my thing with the hacker while you do yours. Two birds with one stone."

My stomach churns, but calling him out for being a sexist pig would get me kicked out at best, shot at worst.

"Are locals allowed to use the bathroom?" I ask. "I want to freshen up first. I don't charge extra for kissing."

He snickers. "Help yourself. It's the first door on the right."

I follow his instructions, then circle back and swing left. I need to move quickly, but I'm not exactly sure what I'm hoping to find. There are file cabinets along one wall, but they're sealed with locks. There's a bulletin board with strings connecting mugshot photos, but it's for an unrelated case. I could take my chances with the cop, but there's no guarantee he would discover new information. I'm not going to sacrifice my self-respect over a *maybe*.

I'm about to search an empty cubicle when a woman chokes out a sob. It's hard to make out what she's saying from afar, but I swear I hear the word *Faith*. It could be my imagination, but I might as well check while I have the chance. I follow the sounds to a dented metal door labeled INTERVIEW ROOM. I peek through the window embedded in the door and listen in.

An officer with buzzcut hair and neat goatee is seated behind a desk, talking to a couple. Even by the backs of their heads, I can tell it's the Flynns.

Goosebumps prick my arms. I haven't seen them in person since the incident. The police investigation overwrote my warm, fuzzy memories of them as my bosses—setting out homemade snacks in the break room and inviting us to private movie screenings. When I pictured their family, I pictured the photograph every news outlet blew up and analyzed. Mrs. Flynn was doubled over, sobbing, while Mr. Flynn shooed away the cameras. Fiona stood in the background, staring straight into the lens, her face blank as a mannequin. The cameras clearly caught her in an unfortunate moment, but it added fuel to the conspiracies. Everyone started wondering whether the rumor was true, whether she had what it took to murder her sister. News channels ate up the good versus evil twin angle. Viewers wanted the juiciest story and hers would sell the most papers.

I don't know how their family navigated this town for a decade, Matrix-dodging so many dirty looks. I needed an escape and my name never even made it to print.

"We'll have the results back to you in two to five days," the officer says, jotting notes onto a form.

"Can't you finish it sooner?" Mrs. Flynn asks, her voice raspy and raw.

"I can't make any promises, but I'll see what I can do."

"And what if the hairs are a match?" Mr. Flynn asks. "What's the next step?"

"Forensics will test for fingerprints to figure out who sent the letter, then bring them in for questioning. See how much they know about your daughter."

"They have Faith," Mrs. Flynn says. "It's her hair. It's her. I can tell."

I take a sharp breath. Looks like we're not the only ones receiving messages from a dead girl. I'm not sure whether her parents being roped into this mess is a positive sign—or the worst possible one.

"I promise," the cop says. "I'm going to do everything possible to speed the process along. This is the biggest lead we've had in years and I don't intend on botching it. But I'm going to need you to keep it between us for now."

Mrs. Flynn nods, hiccuping out more tears.

The cop leans forward. "Would you like a drink? We have a water cooler near the entrance."

"I'll grab it for her," Mr. Flynn says, rising. "I'll scrounge up some tissues, too."

Shit. I scramble away from the door, retracing my steps so we don't bump into each other. I squeeze around the front desk and slither out the exit before anyone can stop me. Officer Horndog must have noticed my escape, but he doesn't chase me outside. At least he can take a hint.

I lean against the building, tugging out my phone. It might be smartest to keep the information to myself, but I want to show the others I'm a team player, that they have my complete trust. I text the group chat, updating them on the breadcrumbs I discovered. *A little birdie told me the Flynns got a letter with hair stuffed inside. They think it's from Faith.*

The replies are lightning fast. *What do you mean, hair? How do you know? Did Fiona tell you that?*

I'm typing out answers when someone calls my name. For a second, I think it's the cop, wondering what happened to his *favor*, but it's Mr. Flynn. A pack of cigarettes is gripped in his shaking hand. I guess the water was an excuse to sneak outside.

"Evan?" he says, inspecting me with red-rimmed eyes. "My God, it's good to see you. It's been years."

"Don't do that. You don't have to pretend you missed me. I wasn't exactly employee of the month."

"Are you kidding? Why do you think we *gave* you the job? Pure nepotism. You were practically family."

I swallow hard, heat rising to my cheeks.

"You were a great friend to Fiona. I'll never forget your sock puppet shows. Or the choreographed dances. Or the synchronized—"

"Please don't remind me of how awkward we were."

He chuckles. "Come on. You two were top-notch entertainment. You know, you should get in touch with her now that you're home. She doesn't go out much these days. She could use a friend. Another woman."

"Maybe. I'm still getting settled here. Trying to adjust."

"Is everything okay with you? And your parents?"

"Of course. Why wouldn't it be?"

He gestures to the police station.

Oh. Right.

I could tell him about the texts, the necklace, the hacking. The information might help the police track down their target faster. But I want to talk to this mystery person first, learn how much they know.

"I'm friends with one of the officers," I lie. "I was just dropping by for a chat. What about you?"

"My wife is inside, filling out some paperwork. Standard stuff."

"It's too bad I missed her. Tell her I said hey."

"You can tell her yourself. At dinner. You'll be at the memorial tomorrow, right?"

I hesitate, wishing he would stop staring at me like a sad, wounded puppy. When we were kids, he was always so calm and in control. Him and his wife were stricter than my parents, with a no-phones-at-the-table policy and a magnetized board on the fridge distributing chores. My parents let me curse and call them by their first names, but at the Flynn house, I helped Fiona fold the laundry and wash the dishes without daring to complain.

Only one of her parents were around at a time, since someone had to run the theater, but they overcompensated when they were home. Mrs. Flynn baked us shortbread cookies and warm, gooey brownies with peanut butter drizzled on top. Mr. Flynn helped us roast s'mores at sleepovers, assembled doll houses, and set up tents in the backyard.

This one time, we were splashing around a kiddie pool when a wasp stung my shoulder. I started bawling my eyes out, so he rushed into the kitchen to grab honey, then slathered the wound with it. He gave this big, emotional speech about how the bee's stinger might've hurt me, but its honey would heal me. It blew my ten-year-old mind.

Goddamn it.

"Obviously I'm coming to the memorial," I tell Mr. Flynn. "Wouldn't miss it for the world."

CHAPTER 10

FIONA

My anxiety is sky-high, but the sooner the memorial dinner starts, the sooner it ends. Tomorrow, I can return to my regularly scheduled life. At least for eleven months, until the cycle repeats itself. Sometimes, I feel like a ghost, trapped in a loop and searching for closure.

I used to dream of my sister surprising us, arriving on our stoop alive and unharmed, but it's gotten to the point where I would be just as happy if we found her body. At least the waiting would be over. We could hold a proper funeral and put her memory to rest. She deserves peace.

I think I do, too.

But I'm not getting it today. Simply climbing out of the car is a ten-minute task. I slide my key in and out of the ignition. Buckle and unbuckle my seatbelt. Swing open and slam my door. The only reason I'm able to stop myself is because a waitress on a cigarette break is staring.

I don't want to draw extra attention, so I ignore the alarm bells in my head—Mom is going to get into a freak accident, Dad is going to drop dead—and enter the restaurant. The gold-painted doors slide apart automatically. They deposit me in a lobby strung with black-and-white photographs of the original owners.

I proceed to the main dining area. The lights are dimmed low with ivy strands dangling down the walls, acoustic music humming in the background. The restaurant has never seemed like the right spot for such a somber occasion. The atmosphere is too charming, almost romantic, but my parents reserve its main hall every year.

For a decade, the owners have offered us a discount on pasta dishes and an open bar. Our guests never pace themselves with the drinks, so they must lose money by hosting us, but they make it back during the rest of the season. They earn major brownie points by helping *people in need.* That's what tragedy has turned our family into. A charity case. It sounds awful, but I've been waiting for another disaster to strike our town, so the spotlight can shift onto someone new. Anyone other than us.

I keep my chin down while clacking across the waxed hardwood floors, picking up speed when passing a photo collage pinned with Faith's face. No reason to stop and stare. I know the order by heart.

The first shot shows us as toddlers in color-coordinated bathing suits, splashing in a public pool. In the corner, there's one of us playing badminton in our backyard with matching rackets. And dead center, there's a candid shot of us prepping for a middle school dance. I'm standing in front of our water-spotted mirror. Faith is hovering behind me, piling my hair into a bun. It's a cute photo—if you don't know the backstory.

Before it was snapped, Faith threw a hissy fit about my lipstick because she intended on wearing a similar shade. I didn't see the issue. It wasn't the same exact color. I wasn't stealing her makeup. I was using my own.

"You're already wearing your hair down like me," she said, pouting. "You can't wear red lipstick like me too. We're going to look—"

"Like twins?"

"Like losers."

I stole a glance in the mirror, admiring my hair. The thick curls tumbled down my shoulder blades. Shorter tendrils framed my face, drawing attention to my bee-stung lips. I looked pretty, which was never a word I used to describe myself. But Faith spent the next hour whining about how she had the idea first, how I was ruining her night, how she would never forgive me. With only twenty minutes until our carpool arrived, I ended up folding. I let her swap out my lipstick and style my hair however she wanted. It was better than watching her mope around the entire night.

Once every bobby pin was in place, she was happy, but I still thought we looked similar. So did the rest of the town. For a good year after she went missing, people would call me by the wrong name and then apologize profusely, like they murdered her themselves. My parents were the worst culprits. They would holler her name when dinner was ready or while scolding me about chores. Sometimes their slipups would have me fuming. Other times, it was oddly comforting. If only for a moment, it made me feel like she was still alive, still around in an abstract way. The idea of her watching over me used to be reassuring.

Now, it gives me the chills.

"Fiona," a smoky voice says. I spin toward a woman draped in scarves, the first of a hundred guests. Before I can recall her name, she envelopes me in a hug. "You're so brave. I don't know how you do it, dear."

"Thank you," I say with a tight smile. "It's nice to see you."

"You, too. Look at you. You look good. You look healthy."

"That's kind of you to say."

"And your parents? How are they holding up?"

"I haven't seen them yet. I should probably track them down, actually."

"Of course. Go. Go. You should be together on a day like today. Poor thing."

She gives me one last hug, her mouth bunched to the side, before chasing after a server carrying bacon-wrapped scallops. This is only a taste of how the whole night will go. Half the guest list treating me like a fragile, lost lamb. The other half, like a murderer.

With wobbly steps, I cross the restaurant, finding my parents huddled in the coat check room.

"Hey," I say, keeping my voice neutral until I can gauge their mood. Some years they collapse into sobs in the middle of eating. Other years, they socialize without a drop of water beading their eyes. I'm not sure what to expect today, but it's not the stunned, deer-in-headlights stare they exchange.

I'm about to ask what's wrong when I notice Pranav Patel hovering beside them. He was one of the original cops assigned to my sister's missing person case. He was younger than I am now when he started, starry-eyed and optimistic about tracking her down. I think that's why he's entertained my parents for so many years, listening to their late-night concerns, nodding along as they blurted out a hundred different conspiracy theories.

She ran away with a boyfriend. There were so many boys with crushes on her. She was bound to get attached to one.

She was kidnapped by a stranger she met on the internet. She was always typing away at that computer, chatting with Lord knows who.

She took a wrong turn on her way home and got lost. For someone who had their heart set on traveling, she sure was hopeless with directions.

Over the years, the theories grew more and more eccentric. But Patel never stopped looking into her case, even when it was officially, legally closed.

"I'll talk to you folks later," he says now, tipping his head. "If anything else comes up, you have my number. Use it."

My parents mutter agreements. I wait until Patel is officially gone, the door swinging shut behind him, to say, "What's going on? Did he get the results back from the DNA test?"

My father nods. "Apparently, there was a match between the hair provided by your mother and the hair in the letter. Which means the person is a blood relative. It really could be Faith."

My lips peel apart, but I've lost the ability to speak. To think. To breathe.

"What does this mean?" I ask. "They think she's alive?"

"We're not sure yet," my father tells me, but my mother is grinning like my sister has already come home.

"It's hard not to have faith when something like this happens," she says. "We named her that for a reason."

I wet my lips, unsure how to respond. I don't want to break their hearts, but I don't want false hope to shatter them, either. "Mom," I start. "I don't think you should get too—"

"Please, Fiona. I'm a grown woman. I'm entitled to my feelings. Tonight doesn't have to be sad. It can be a celebration. At least try to enjoy it."

With that, she disappears into the dining hall. My father squeezes my shoulder, then shadows her out the door.

I stay behind, my feet fixed to the floor. How do they expect me to play hostess after the bomb they just detonated? How can they possibly—

A woman bumps my shoulder, deliberately shoving me aside to check her coat. She must be one of the guests convinced I'm a murderer. Lovely.

It takes a minute to remember how my legs work and carry myself outside. I collapse onto a metal bench by the sidewalk, shielding my face as our guests flood into the building. They all took the start time seriously, arriving as one mass, a parade of cars and wafting conversations.

I drown them out, pulling in deep breaths of frigid air. The DNA test must have been wrong. If Faith was roaming around the world, she wouldn't have gone ten years without a text. She would've worked out a way to contact us. Wouldn't she?

Sometimes, I wonder whether the version of her in my mind is anything like the girl who once existed. I wrote over her memory a million times, like putting a filter over a filter, smoothing out her features, blunting her sharpest edges. Even our fights have a nostalgic, sepia-toned tint to them. Remember when Faith packed her luggage and threatened to move out at thirteen? *How funny*. Remember how she would pout and stomp around the den whenever we told her *no*? *She was so passionate, so strong.*

"Fiona?" a voice calls, startling me. I snap my head up as a woman with choppy brown hair and a suit prances over. Evan's date from the bar. "Hey. I'm Brooke. We met at the diner, but we were never officially introduced. I'm still pretty new in town, so I felt weird coming tonight, but I also felt weird missing it."

I cross my arms, tucking my fingers into my armpits to keep warm. "Did Evan send you to talk to me?"

Her long forehead wrinkles.

"I know you're dating," I say. "I saw you at the Cider Shack."

"Oh. Yeah, we were there the other night. I didn't know you guys were friends. You should've come over and said hello."

I purse my lips. It's no surprise Evan is keeping secrets. What else is new? I would warn the woman to be careful, but it's not my business. Let them wreck each other.

"Sorry if this is a bad time. I'm not trying to bother you. I just wanted to give you this." She sticks a card under my nose, scribbled with my name. "I couldn't afford much, but it might be enough to—well. You'll see."

She waits, like she expects me to open it. I muster a smile and undo the flap, tugging out a card with THINKING OF YOU in gold bubble letters. My vision blurs, imagining the card in my parent's mailbox, written with the same color, same font. But they were cheap, generic cards from the dollar store. The hub where everyone in town shops.

Still, my breath catches as I slowly unfold the card, envisioning strands of long, dark hair.

Of course, there's only a short SORRY FOR YOUR LOSS message, paired with a gift card for *Anarchy Ink*.

"It probably won't cover an entire session," Brooke says. "Unless you get something small. You don't have to go for prayer beads or a giant cross with their name on it. Those can be nice, but you can try something personal. Like…" She rolls up her sleeve, exposing a minimalist plane tattoo. One curvy, unbroken line with a hollow center. "This is the most recent one. My dad passed away last year. Heart attack." She rolls her jacket higher, twisting her arm to point out different designs. An hourglass. A hummingbird. A paw print. "This one was for my mother. My grandmother. My cat."

I lean closer. "Doesn't it make you sad to look at them?"

"I'm going to think of them anyway. Might as well do it on my terms."

"Right."

She winces. "You hate it, don't you?"

"No. No, it's sweet." I'm not the tattoo type, but it's nicer than the misty smiles or empty prayers people usually offer. "I appreciate it. It's definitely... thoughtful."

"What can I say? I'm used to losing people."

A pang hits my chest. Maybe I *should* warn her about Evan—that she'll pretend to be your friend then desert you, that she'll alternate between making you feel loved and lower than dirt. Brooke won't believe me at first, but at least my voice will be in the back of her head, urging her to run.

I crack open my mouth as a blocky brown car swerves into the parking lot. And miraculously, the night gets a little bit worse.

CHAPTER 11

EVAN

I unroll the window, letting crisp air whip my cheeks until they turn numb. My father mans the wheel and my mother rides shotgun, retouching her plum lipstick in the dropdown mirror. I feel like a little kid, crammed in the backseat where it's hard to hear the adults talking. But that's fine by me. There's no sense in putting extra miles on my car. And I'm not making it through the night without hard liquor.

"Why so gloomy?" my mother asks as she folds her mirror back into place. She twists sideways, craning her neck to get a good look at me. "You should be excited."

Excited? About being surrounded by my ex-best friend's family after moving one-hundred miles to escape them? Or getting a front row seat to watch them mourn when I couldn't stomach it the first time around?

She must read my expression because she clutches her chest. "Oh, I know it's a morbid thing to say, considering the occasion, but this will be like a family reunion for you. You moved back here a month ago and have hardly seen anyone. You need to get out there again. Who knows, there might even be someone there who can offer you a job."

"That's not the way businesses run in the twenty-first century, Mom. And these people aren't my family. They're overinvested neighbors who are going to take joy in the fact I got sucked back here after making such a big deal about leaving."

She waves a hand, bangles tinkling. "I didn't raise you to be such a pessimist. Everyone is divorced these days. I bet some people will even congratulate you on it. No one is going to hold it against you."

"And if they have anything rude to say about the rest of it, you can point them in my direction," my father says, tapping the pin on his lapel. A pride flag. It sticks out like a sore thumb on his dark navy suit.

"Oh. Speaking of which, is your friend coming?" my mother asks, meaning Brooke.

I texted her earlier to ask the same question. "She has to work," I say. "She doesn't know the Flynns, so no one is going to miss her."

"Except us. I was looking forward to meeting her. And thanking her for getting you out of our hair."

"Slow down. We're not U-hauling yet. I'm still your problem for the foreseeable future."

The conversation sputters to a stop as we pull up to the restaurant, a red brick building draped in white fairy lights. The trees peppered around the parking lot are illuminated, too, their bare branches strung with bulbs. I'm not sure whether they decorated for the holidays early or whether they're going for a cottagecore aesthetic year-round.

We clamber out of the car and cross the parking lot, my parents clutching mittened hands as they walk. Judging by the packed parking lot, we're fashionably late, which is good news for me. I can sit back and observe.

We're halfway to the entrance when I spot my crushes—past and present—and trip forward, catching myself on an outdoor ashtray. It wobbles, coating my fingers in ash.

"What's wrong?" my father says without slowing. "Did you just get your sea legs?"

I wipe the grime on my jumpsuit. "My heel came loose. Give me a minute. I'll meet you inside."

It's too cold for them to stick around and argue. They pass through the automatic doors while I stroll over to the bench, casually, like my heart isn't about to vomit out of my chest.

Brooke is wearing a tight-fitting, teal suit with the top two buttons undone. Her hair is loose around her face, the choppy layers coming to a stop at her chin dimple. Fiona is bundled in a ski jacket, a loose black dress, and leggings with her signature ponytail. She flinches when she sees me, but Brooke breaks into a smile, her teeth nipping her plump, red lips.

"What's going on?" I ask her, grazing the small of her back. "What are you doing here?"

"It was a slow day—probably because everyone is grabbing dinner here—so the boss let me leave early. I have a sitter for another hour, so I thought it would be nice to stop over and pay my respects."

It's not a funeral, but I don't correct her. Neither does Fiona. We lapse into an awkward silence, looking everywhere except at each other.

"Why are you being so weird?" Brooke asks, poking me in the side. "You guys aren't exes or something, are you?"

Fiona scrunches her nose.

I scratch my ear.

"*Oh,*" Brooke says. "In that case, I'll give you guys a second alone. I want to introduce myself to your parents, anyway. We can gossip about you behind your back. Maybe they'll have embarrassing baby pictures to show me."

She pecks my cheek and bounces toward the door, leaving us alone.

But Fiona doesn't stick around to chat. She springs from the bench, a card fluttering from her lap. She abandons it on the ground and brushes past me.

"Hold on. Fiona. I'm sorry about the other night. I was rude. I was drunk."

She grinds to a halt, whipping toward me. "Were you drunk the *whole* decade you were ignoring me or…?"

"It's not just you. I haven't been in touch with anybody."

"But I'm the only one you blocked on every single form of social media."

"I thought you'd be happier without my face on your feed."

"Why are you still lying?" she pants, like the conversation has already exhausted her. "I don't understand why you can't be honest with me, even now. We were fine the last time we hung out. We had fun. What happened? I don't even care at this point. I just hate the *not knowing*."

"I guess… Seeing you made me too sad."

She sucks her teeth. "Wow. Okay. I'm sorry I was upset after my sister went missing. I didn't mean to bring the mood down."

"No. That's not what I said. I was a punk kid. I wasn't able to handle—"

"Me. I was too much to handle. Understood."

"Fiona. Would you listen to me?" I seize her arms, tightening until I feel the bones under her jacket. A thousand fragments whoosh through my head, about how sorry I am and how hurting her was the last thing I wanted to do. But my mind snaps to a blank when I realize how close our bodies have shifted. My eyes dart to her lips, resisting the urge to tuck a stray curl behind her ear.

"I had feelings for you, okay?" I blurt out, the words flying from my mouth before my brain can catch up.

She steps back, breaking my grip. "Excuse me?"

"That's why I stopped talking to you out of nowhere. I didn't want to ruin our friendship by telling you, so ironically, I ruined it by running away."

She squints, trying to read me, but it's true enough. As a kid, I poured out my feelings in a little red diary, but I never spoke a word of them out loud. I even gushed about fake crushes to throw her off. Unless she was faking, too. Pretending not to see it to avoid the embarrassment of shutting me down.

"You really didn't know?" I ask.

"No. Not at all. But I…" Her whole face softens, her voice barely above a whisper. "I would have been fine with it. I would have wanted… We could have… Is that really why you disappeared?"

"Yes," I breathe out, relieved she's finally looking at me the way she used to, the anger dimming. Then her gaze drops. She watches me crack my knuckles with my thumb, a motion I hadn't realized I was doing until that exact moment. *My tell.* She used it against me during every game of rummy and Uno for years. It only ever happened around her, the one person I didn't have to put on an act around, who gave me permission to relax and not think so hard about every move I made.

"Oh my God," she spits, her head rattling. "You're still lying. Why would you do that? What is wrong with you?"

"No. Listen. It's not a lie. That's not what this was."

Her nose wrinkles in disgust as she races to her car, fists buried in her pockets.

"Where are you going?" I call out, slapping my hands against my thighs. "You can't leave."

"I don't want to be anywhere where you are," she says, slamming her door. She speeds away without snapping on a seatbelt.

God damn it. I need to be more careful. No more letting my guard down, not even for a second. Not in this town.

A headache forms at the base of my skull, small but razor-sharp. I'm going to need that drink.

Forcing my chin up, I stride through the front entrance and swing into the main hall. Dozens of familiar faces stare back at me. The drama teacher who cut me from the school musical when I dropped an F-bomb on stage. The driving instructor who made the sign of the cross whenever I slid behind the wheel. The math tutor who claimed my brain wasn't the problem, my attitude was.

Coming here is starting to feel like more and more of a mistake.

I start toward Brooke, but she's in the middle of an animated conversation with my father. She flashes me a subtle thumbs up while he flails around his arms, lost in a rant. He only gets that worked up over vintage cars and ghost-hunting shows, so they must be bonding over one or the other. She drives a Toyota, so my bets are on the latter.

I don't want to interrupt, so I mosey toward my mother. She's hovering near the snack table, trying to grab a shrimp while balancing two drinks in her hands.

"You could try bobbing for them," I suggest.

She snorts, passing me a cup. "It took you long enough. Brooke introduced herself while you were outside. She seems sweet. Good looking, too."

"Are you saying she's out of my league?"

"I'm saying you must've lied through your teeth on your dating profile."

"You like her that much, huh?"

She smirks.

"What? What is it?"

"You didn't tell me she had a *daughter*," she says, wagging her brows.

"Nuh-uh. Stop. I don't want you getting attached to the idea of some magical granddaughter. We've only been on a few dates. I can't make any promises we're going to work out."

"But you *might*. I swear, Evan, I don't know when you became such a downer."

She turns her back to me, sampling more appetizers. I busy myself with my glass—a vodka cranberry, light on the vodka—and scan the room, taking stock of the guests. Raven is plucking olives from a tray, looking cute as hell in a pineapple updo. Seth is hovering in the corner with his arm wrapped around his wife, massaging her shoulder. Cameron is hunched over the furthest bar, knocking back one beer after another. Fiona's friend is standing beside him, ordering his own concoction.

"Hey, do you know that guy?" I ask my mother, nodding in his direction. "I ran into him the other night and he recognized me. He said you and his mom are friends."

She shuffles sideways, peering around heads blocking her view. "Oh, that's Jonah, Shannon's boy."

"He told me he ordered a few things from my website."

"He did. Thanks to yours truly. I bragged about you so much that Shannon parroted the information to him. She's a single parent, so he does his best to take care of her. He spoils her with vacations and spa days and these big, gaudy earrings. He's smart with the stock market, which is why he can afford to work at the theater while making short films on the side. Anywho, I think he spent a few hundred dollars on his shopping spree, so you're welcome."

I guess he was telling the truth about the bracelet he bought for Fiona. But that doesn't rule him out as a suspect. If he knew about my history with her, and knew about my shop, he could've ordered the necklace as revenge for ghosting her.

"What else do you know about him?" I ask between sips. "I'm not caught up on all the gossip. Enlighten me."

"See? A little alcohol, a little trip out of the house, and you're interested in our boring little town again." She chuckles. "Do you want me to formally introduce you? I can wave him over."

"No, no. You don't need to—"

She shouts his name. He does a double-take, scouring the crowd. When his eyes land on her, he raises a shit-eating smile and shoulders through bodies to reach us. He wraps my mother in a bear hug, lifting her toes off the ground. She plants a lipstick mark on his cheek.

"Jonah," she sing-songs. "This is the darling daughter I never shut up about. She says you met the other night, but I doubt either of you remembers it with the way you drink. You're probably the only two in town who could outpace the other."

"I don't know, O'Connor. You're sucking that sangria down pretty quickly," he teases.

She swats him. "It takes more than one to get this old bag tipsy."

"Oh, stop. Your skin's not a day over twenty-one." He goes in for a hug with me next. I stiffen but let it happen. "It's nice to meet you in the daylight, Evan. I wasn't sure if you would show. Since you and Fiona aren't close."

"Oh, no, no," my mother says. "These two were thick as thieves when they were younger. They would spend whole weekends building blanket forts and putting on magic shows and drawing comic books. They were so creative. They might not keep in touch anymore but love like that never goes away. Right, sweetie?"

I nod, even though my mother is already strolling away, chasing another tray of snacks.

"Listen," Jonah says, moving a step too close. "It's nice that you showed up for the free food tonight, but you really upset Fiona at the Shack. I don't want you causing any more trouble for her."

"Is that a threat?"

"A friendly suggestion."

I plant a hand on my hip. "You know, I'm happy she has someone like you, looking out for her. But it must be hard, stuck in the friendzone. How long have you had a crush on her?"

"Not as long as you." He winks. "That's why you keep asking whether we're dating, right? You're hoping she's single? That she'll forgive you for all the crap you put her through. You think you actually deserve someone as good as her?"

I swallow, my whole chest tightening. "I have a girlfriend. So, no. I'm not—"

A set of clinking glasses cuts our conversation short. The owner of the restaurant, a plump man with a bald patch, informs us the food will be out shortly. He urges everyone to find a seat and thanks us for choosing his restaurant. As if it were our decision.

Groups break apart as guests settle into their cushioned chairs. I nab a corner spot, jammed between Brooke and the wall so no one else can squeeze beside me. A vase bursting with petunias blocks the couple across from me, making small talk impossible. The best seat in the house.

Especially with Brooke caressing my thigh under the table.

"Your parents are the cutest," she whispers as we dig into the first course—skinless chicken breasts, fettuccine noodles drenched in alfredo sauce, and speckled brown baguettes. "They're literally holding hands right now. And he was carrying her pocketbook earlier. I can't get enough of them."

"Are your parents not together?" I ask between bites.

"My mom died when I was pretty young. My dad got remarried a few times, but it never stuck. He wasn't around much anyway, because of work, so I never bothered to get close with them. I was mostly on my own—until my little girl came along."

"That must've been tough."

She shrugs. "I've made my own family. At the end of the day, DNA means nothing. Total strangers can save you, and relatives can be the death of you."

I cup her hand with mine. She squeezes, and heat rushes through my lower half.

"Enough about me," she says, spinning pasta onto her fork. "We're supposed to be celebrating Faith, right? Tell me your favorite memory of her. It's okay if it includes Fiona. I promise not to get jealous."

"I don't know." Only one night comes to mind. I play with my earring, twisting the stud. "It's a little morbid."

"All the best stories are."

"All right. Fine." I shift toward her, sitting sideways on my chair. "There was a blackout once, when I was sleeping over at their place. Faith had nothing better to do with the internet down, so she came up with a game for the three of us to play. It was basically a blindfolded makeup challenge. We covered our faces with neon eye shadows and lipsticks, and it looked like we flunked out of clown school. Faith was in a surprisingly chill mood, laughing and joking around like we were actual friends. But when the lights flipped on and she saw herself in the mirror, she started crying. Like, mascara running down her face, convulsive sobbing. Her parents thought she was being ridiculous and snapped at her to stop, but I felt bad for her. It was when I realized how much she hated herself. She was one of those people with ten-thousand Facebook friends, but no real friends. Guys would jump to hook up with her, but not date her. She acted stuck-up, but she was secretly super insecure."

Brooke cocks her head, worrying at her lip, and I regret being so honest. We're at Faith's memorial, for crying out loud. I should've made up a feel-good story, or told her about our fashion show, the catwalk in the living room.

"I wasn't *happy* to see her upset," I explain. "It was just… a human moment, you know?"

"No. I get it. One of my favorite memories of my dad is watching him break down at my mom's funeral. He was always so stiff and proper. I wasn't sure if he ever loved her, but watching him fall apart in front of everyone… I finally knew."

"Talk about morbid."

She shoves my shoulder, snickering. Maybe my mother's optimism is trickling down to me, or maybe the vodka is stronger than it tasted, but I'm starting to imagine a future where we work.

The next hour is filled with flirting and food, and guilt about enjoying the flirting and food. I should be interrogating guests, searching for leads, taking advantage of the fact the whole town is crammed into one room.

But it's impossible to concentrate when waiters, dressed in matching black slacks, trickle out of the kitchen with baked goods. They serve cake to each guest on square, gold-rimmed plates while cookie platters are placed around the room—assortments with snickerdoodles and gingersnaps and lemon drops.

Brooke covers her head with her hands, fake sobbing. "My sweet tooth is screaming at me, but I should've been out of here twenty minutes ago. I don't want the sitter to teach my kid how to call me a bitch."

"I'm sure she'll figure that out on her own."

She laughs, planting a kiss on my crown since my parents are within snooping-distance. Then she hugs my mother goodbye and shakes hands with my father.

"She's got a good grip," he says once she's gone, sliding over a seat. He and my mother take turns passing along useless tidbits they've learned about neighbors throughout the night. I nod and *mhm* while chewing, my mouth filled with heavy cream.

Halfway through my second serving of chocolate chip cannoli cake, the Flynns stand to say a few words. Around the room, conversations sputter and die.

"I wanted to thank all of you for coming," Mrs. Flynn says, the glass in her hand trembling. I wonder whether she gives a speech during every memorial dinner, and why anyone in their right mind would want to witness this. "Even though we've been holding this dinner annually, this year is far different than the rest. Not only because it marks a decade, ten whole years since our little girl was ripped away from us, but because we're closer than ever at finding closure."

Her voice breaks at the end. She brings a napkin to her eyes, dabbing her makeup. Mr. Flynn squeezes her hand and takes over the speech. "Anyone who has lost a loved one knows some days are worse than others, and boy have we had our bad days. During the first anniversary, it felt like our little family was falling apart. We almost foreclosed on our home. The theater was failing. Fiona was in and out of the hospital. We weren't sure whether any of us would recover from the pain of having a daughter ripped away from us. But with support from all of you, we were able to pull through and..."

Raven shoves her chair away from the table, like the speech is too much for her. She flies across the room, slipping a pack of cigarettes from her high-waisted jeans. She makes eye contact with me along the way and jerks her head, inviting me to follow.

I lean toward my father. "This is pretty heavy stuff," I whisper. "I need to take five."

He nods without tipping his head at me. His full focus is on the Flynns.

I march through the dining room and out the automatic doors, arms tucked across my chest. The wind lashes me, but the chill is refreshing after being crammed in a hall with the body heat of a hundred other people.

I follow Raven into a slender alley shrouded by shrubs with dead leaves. Every wall is solid brick, without a single window, so no one can spy on us.

"Do you still smoke?" she asks.

"Nope. But after that speech, I decided to pick it up again."

She smirks, slipping out an extra cigarette for me. I pinch it between my matte black nails while she lights the tip. We take a beat to inhale, sagging against the building.

"Could Fiona have sent her parents that letter?" Raven asks, severing the silence. "I didn't want to believe it was her the other day, but twins have the same DNA. She could've pulled out her own hair and threw it in the mailbox to make it look like her sister was still alive."

I blow out a cloud of smoke. Honestly, I *wish* Fiona was responsible. It would ease my guilt about being such an ass to her. But she would never put her parents through that. There's no point. Which means the odds aren't looking good for my friends. I don't want to point fingers, but Raven owns a salon. She could have trimmed Fiona's hair, saved a chunk, and framed her with it.

"I don't think it's Fiona anymore," I say. "But I know it's not you. And can't imagine it being Cameron or Seth."

Her eyes roll at Seth's name. I guess the split is still fresh, ten years later. The messiest heartbreaks are always the hardest to get over.

Before their breakup, they were obnoxiously adorable. Raven would attend Seth's football games with clip-on colors in her hair, holding up signs that said #13 ON THE FIELD BUT #1 IN MY HEART. He would leave surprises in her locker, a love poem ripped from a textbook or fresh cupcakes from the cafeteria. If they made it until prom, they would've been in the running for king and queen.

But everything fell apart before then.

"Come on," I say. "Are you telling me you guys haven't kissed and made up after all these years?"

"The four-way call we had the other day was the most interaction we've had since we were teenagers. He has a whole life now. Kids. A house. A wife. Have you met her? She's a *therapist*. That's basically my job, except my paycheck is smaller. At the salon, I hear all the gossip. I know about everyone's cheating husbands and missing pets and work problems. None of it helps me here, unfortunately, but I'll keep my ears open. Or, who knows, the police might do their job for once and figure it out for us."

"Now you're talking nonsense." I stub my cigarette out with a heel. "I don't know about you, but my ass is freezing. I'm in a thong, not thermals."

"I'm with you."

She drops her cigarette next to mine. We take a step, maybe two, before beeping stops us.

I check my cell. A group message appears on the screen, from a blocked caller. I flit my eyes across the random clump of numbers they've sent. Gibberish. But it could help us crack the case.

I sprint out of the alley, swinging around the side of the building and cupping my hands over the closest window, but the panes are made from frosted glass. It's impossible to see inside. "Goddamn it." I slap the bricks, stinging my palm. "If we were still in there, we could've checked to see who was on their phone. We could have narrowed down our options."

"I'm not so sure," Raven says. "If they're smart, they would have hidden in the bathroom or sent the text with a timer, don't you think?"

It's possible, but even serial killers slip up every once in a while. If we're lucky, the boys caught a detail we missed. Seth, at least. Cameron is too wasted to recite his ABCs. I start toward the entrance again, but her swearing stops me.

"What?" I ask Raven, pausing mid-stride. "Do you know what those weird-ass numbers mean?"

"No... That's not the number I'm worried about right now."

She flips her phone toward me, pointing to the top of the screen. In the little bubbles stating how many people are involved in the group chat, it says six.

"The last message included five of us. Our group, plus the blocked number. They added someone else to the chain this time."

"What? Who?"

Raven clicks on the bubble to view the names, but the newest one isn't saved onto her contact list. "I could call and see who answers?" she says.

"Hold that thought."

She has more connections in this hellhole than me, but I check my cell for kicks. I tap the bubbles, skim the names.

My stomach lurches. It turns out, I do have the final number programmed into my phone. I never had the heart to delete it.

"What's that face?" Raven asks. "Who is it?"

"I'll give you one guess."

CHAPTER 12

FIONA

After my conversation with Evan, I hobble through the parking lot and collapse into my ice cube of a car. I can't believe I used to beg to hang out with her. I'm embarrassed for my younger self. It's humiliating to think we share the same memories. I wish I could rip them from her skull. Especially our last argument, before my sister went missing, before she cut me out of her life for good.

"I want to come with you guys," I whined as she tucked an accessorized coffee container into her backpack, zipping it tight. "We can get all the theater kids together, if you want. We can all go."

"Then your sister would be involved. No one wants her there."

"She's seeing a movie with Perry. She won't be around, either way."

Evan groaned. Normally, she would toss out another excuse. *There's only room in the car for four. We're going while you're working.* But that night, she said, "You wouldn't have any fun. I'm not the same person with them. You wouldn't even recognize me. It's like how you talk to your grandparents differently than you talk to your cousins."

"But we all get along. Raven is super nice to me. So is Cameron. Seth's not my favorite person, but that's three out of four."

"You're the bosses' daughter. Of course they're nice to you during work hours."

I frowned. "What about employee movie nights? All of us have played manhunt, and cards, and a million other games."

"But other people are there. And we're still technically at work. I'm telling you, it's different when it's the four of us. We're kind of assholes."

"If I'm not cool enough for your other friends, just say it."

"Jesus. Stop overthinking it." Evan put a hand on my shoulder and squeezed. "I don't want to corrupt you, okay? You're not the type of person who sneaks out in the middle of the night, or smokes weed in the woods, or buys shots at bars with fake IDs. You're not like us. And I like that about you."

"I'm not a saint. Or a baby," I grumbled. "We're the same age. You don't have to protect me."

"I'm never going to stop taking care of you, Fiona. You might as well get used to it."

With that, she stormed out of the theater, her backpack bouncing.

She apologized the same night Faith went missing—but she must not have meant it because stopped speaking to me days later. "I'm sorry about your sister. But you're strong. You're going to be okay," was the longest text she sent. Then she reduced our correspondence to one-word answers and lies about being busy. When she fled town after graduation, she ripped the bandage the rest of the way and blocked me.

I don't want to waste any more energy on her, so I twist my key. Switch the gear. Blast the radio to drown out my spiraling thoughts.

I roll by a gas station with a two-dollar newspaper stand and posters of bikini-clad couples advertising beer. The turn to my apartment is coming up, but my mind is so scrambled I miss it. I continue straight, past a bakery illuminated with a neon sign of a dancing donut, then a farmer's market with stands of plump pumpkins and tall husks of corn.

Soon, the scenery disappears, the buildings replaced by forests. The street ahead is empty, a long stretch of straight road without any curves or hills in sight. It feels like those nightmares where you keep running and running down the same hall without making any progress. Even the trees lining the pavement look like they've been copied and pasted. Doubles of doubles. Twins.

I sigh, one hand gripping the wheel and the other fiddling with the sound settings. Every song on the radio feels *wrong*. I skip from station to station, but if I listen to this bouncy, upbeat love song, a truck is going to ram into me at the next intersection. If I listen to that slow, drawling country song, lightning is going to strike my mother on her way home. Or cancer is going to chew apart my father. Or my cat is going to get run over by a car. Or Jonah is going to get gunned down in the street.

I smack the stereo to cut the music and swerve to the roadside, my tires bouncing onto the dirt. My bumper edges alarmingly close to a tree, but I don't care. All I can think about is how I can't lose someone else. I can't go through the pain again.

I can't.

I can't.

I won't.

I spend at least an hour sobbing, ignoring the phone buzzing away in my cup holder. But I can't avoid my parents forever. I peel my forehead from the steering wheel, mop away the tears with a sleeve, and scroll through my missed messages.

Surprisingly, only one of the texts is from my father. It says: *I understand if you need some space, pumpkin. We'll make an excuse to explain your absence. Talk soon. Love you.*

I tap out a short text about loving them too, then return to my inbox. I have several messages from Jonah—*Where are you? Did you bail? Should I be worried?*—and one message from a restricted number.

I click to unfurl it, but it's nonsense. A series of numbers without any words attached. At first, I assume it's the tracking information for kitty litter I'd ordered, but I count up the digits squished together. Sixteen of them. Tracking numbers are usually twenty. It's probably a glitch, a message from a gas or electric company attempting to send me a payment reminder.

I extend my arm to drop the phone, then stop myself. Someone contacted my parents, promising to reveal details about my sister. They could be contacting me, too.

It seems unlikely, but so does everything else that occurred this week. Seth raging about the therapy appointment. Evan interrogating me about the bracelet. Hair being dropped into the mailbox.

I plug the numbers into the search engine on my phone. I have enough bars to connect to the internet, but an error message appears. YOUR SEARCH DID NOT MATCH ANY DOCUMENTS.

The longer I stare at the numbers, the harder they tug at my memory, but it could be wishful thinking. My brain forcing patterns where none exist.

I unlatch the center console and extract the pocket-sized notebook where I track my OCD symptoms. On a crisp, clean page, I jot down the numbers and assign them letters—A is one, B is two, C is three—but it doesn't make out a real word. I rearrange the numbers next, testing whether another order holds more meaning. Then I add some numbers together. Subtract some. Multiply. Divide. Nothing makes sense.

Back to square one. I stare at the original spread, before I jumbled it all up. The sixteen digits could be a credit card number. Or an account number. Unless…

I fumble for my phone and click open my camera roll. In between candid pictures of my cat kneading and swatting string toys, there's a screenshot of the constellation painting I'd bought for my parents. The seller sent me a mock-up to confirm the details before physically creating it.

I pinch to zoom in on the bottom of the frame, where the coordinates are printed. The first half of the numbers match the ones in the message. The last few digits are different, but that only means the text is referencing a specific spot at the theater. Maybe the person who sent the letter to my parents is going to meet me there with additional information on my sister.

Or maybe I'm reading too far into things.

Either way, the theater is closer than the restaurant after so much driving. I have no desire to return to an empty apartment, either. All this crying would upset the cat.

I smear away snot with a sleeve, then flick my turn signal on and off, on and off. My gaze snags on my rearview mirror, my eye makeup dribbling down my cheeks in ragged lines. Even with my hair pulled into a tight ponytail, it's a frizzy mess with my bangs pointing in every direction. Somehow, I still look better than I feel.

It takes five minutes to reach the cinema, but it feels closer to five seconds. I can't remember merging onto streets or making turns or slowing at stop signs. It's scary how well the brain can run on autopilot, how much you can filter out without even realizing.

A few cars are peppered around the parking lot we share with salons and clothing stores, but the pavement on our side is empty. Normally, Saturday nights are swamped for us, but we shut down the cinema in a *moment of silence* for my sister.

I park near the curb, dart across the sidewalk, and unlock the doors. Moonlight streams through the windows, bathing the room in a blue glow.

I bolt the entrance behind me and switch on the lobby lights. They flicker, illuminating the room in strips—along with a man standing near the ticket booth, blood splattered on his cheeks.

I stumble backward, crashing into the velvet ropes by the registers, before realizing it's only a cardboard cutout. A disheveled actor with a rifle propped on his shoulder.

I release a shaky breath and circle around the abandoned ticket booth. The television above the counter activated with the lights, displaying movie times. Every two minutes, the screen flashes a silent, thirty-second ad. The man from the cutout, blasting a zombie into ribbons.

I continue toward the concession stand, an oval counter at the heart of the building. There are theaters to the left and theaters to the right, making snacks easy for customers to access, no matter where they're seated. But the walls separating the inner kitchen make it impossible to see straight across. Someone could be standing on the opposite end right now, waiting, watching. I creep around the perimeter to check, shuffling forward an inch at a time.

A crash stops me cold.

I whip my head fast enough to strain my neck, but it's only the ice machine. *Get ahold of yourself, Fiona.* I shake out my wrists while running through a grounding exercise, cataloging the surrounding smells, sounds, and sights. The lingering scent of burnt popcorn. The hum of the soda machine. The butter dispenser drip-drip-dripping onto a grate below.

Once my breathing is steady, I download a navigation app and input the coordinates. Arrows direct me across the lobby, toward the emergency exit. Is the mystery texter waiting outside?

I peek through the window embedded in the door. Growing up, the woods out back sprawled for miles. Whenever we tossed trash in the dumpsters, we were ordered to bring a buddy or a walkie-talkie for protection. Sometimes there were trespassers in the woods swapping needles or homeless men sleeping in thin, flimsy tents. There were even hunters on occasion, scoping for wild turkeys and deer.

On employee movie nights, when our adrenaline was pumping after an R-rated film, we would dare each other to creep into the woods. It was like weaving through a haunted maze, wondering whether a ghost would spring out and snatch us.

Now, twisting between those trees sounds like a nightmare, even though the remaining branches are skinny and stripped of leaves. A real estate company purchased the land a while back, bulldozing most of the forest to build a cheap apartment complex.

I swing open the door and squint into the distance, but I don't see a silhouette in the shape of a woman, waiting for my approach. I don't hear anyone shuffling around in the woods either, crunching on leaves or squelching through mud.

I have a growing fear that whatever the coordinates are leading me to, it isn't alive.

My cell buzzes in my pocket, making me jump. Another text from Jonah. *There's no way you went out without your phone, so do me a favor and answer it. For real. You're scaring me. Where are you? Tell me what's going on.*

I want to accept his help, but dragging him into a potentially dangerous situation wouldn't be right. I can't lose him, too.

I have to do this alone. She was my sister. My responsibility.

Jonah will hunt me down if I don't reassure him, so I activate my voice-to-text software. "Calm down," I say while walking toward the utility closet. "You don't have to worry about me. Today was stressful, that's all. I needed a break from socializing. I'll see you tomorrow." I tap *send* without checking the grammar. No time to waste.

I rummage through the closet for a shovel, holding it across my chest like a spear while circling the guest service area. Then it's into the back office. The room is tight, crammed with three desks, a series of computer monitors displaying security footage, and a safe my parents issued me for personal use, more secure than the employee lockers upstairs.

I twist the dial, spinning past the correct number twice. *Focus, Fiona.* I give myself a second, rubbing my sweaty palms against my coat, my nails whining against the fabric. When I try the safe again, the mechanism clicks, unlocking.

Hidden behind a mound of paperwork is a little black pistol, loaded with bullets.

After my sister went missing, I found a stranger online who was willing to exchange a single-action revolver for a thousand dollars, no questions asked. That money was supposed to be put toward a used car to drive around campus on the other side of the country, but moving was suddenly out of the question. I couldn't leave my parents alone. They wanted the theater to be a family-run business. And I was the only family left.

But I couldn't shake the fear that my sister's kidnapper—some sick pervert with a fetish for twins—would target me next. Another part of me worried some neighborhood vigilante, who believed the lies about me killing my sister, would try to punish me in her honor. The gun was a better investment.

I keep it tucked under my jacket while wading into the woods, hyper-aware of every cicada and cricket chirp. The darkness is thick, murky, so I activate my phone flashlight to avoid tripping over a stump and snapping my neck. I keep my movements slow too, swiveling the light to both sides before risking another step forward.

When a bat bullets past, its leathery wings beating by my ear, I flail, nearly dropping my phone into a brown patch of snow. *Jesus.* What is wrong with me? Why would I think I could handle this? I whirl back toward the building, tempted to retreat to the office and lock myself inside, but the text was sent to me for a reason. I need to know what's waiting at those coordinates.

With a few cleansing breaths, I creep further into the trees, covered in goosebumps. As the woods start to thin out, I glance between my toes and the app. The triangle marking my location and the X marking the coordinates pinch closer and closer together.

When I reach my destination, I'm not technically on the theater property, but I'm not technically in the apartment complex, either. However, I am on the edge of an unfenced yard. If the owner opened their back door to smoke a cigarette or let their dog pee, they would have a perfect view of me in between the final rows of trees. There could be cameras around the property, too, capturing my every move.

I should return to the restaurant, explain the situation to the police, and ask them to acquire the necessary permits. But the cops move like molasses, even in this small town. Especially in this small town. If I leave the work up to them, I'm not going to get answers tonight. They would fail our family again.

Someone promised my parents closure. This could be what they meant. Her body wouldn't answer all our questions, but it would answer the most important one. I can't risk that chance being stripped from me.

I need to reach the finish line before Evan and her friends. Half of the names in the group message were missing from my contact list, but she popped right up. So did Cameron, which meant Raven and Seth were most likely the remaining numbers. And I don't trust a single one of them.

I get to work, digging the spade into the ground and using my foot for leverage. The ground is rock hard, making it tough to break through the crust. My ballet flats aren't helping, but at least I skipped the heels.

I lean all of my weight onto the shovel, jumping on the spade until the ground splits apart. The first few scoops strain my arms, but I gradually pick up speed. The dirt beneath is looser. Still back-breaking work, but manageable.

I burrow about a foot deep before wondering whether I'm in the wrong position. It's not like I'm following a professional compass or an expensive, state-of-the-art GPS. This app has a three-star rating. It could be off by a few inches. Or yards. I could be digging in the completely wrong place.

I shake my head. I already committed. No stopping now.

With a grunt, I plunge the shovel down again, forming haphazard piles on either side of me. The ditch expands to the size of a football, a basketball, a manhole. Wiping my brow, I step into the uneven, narrow hole. Dirt from the edges of the pit crumbles onto my shoes, coating them brown. My cheeks are probably streaked with dirt too, unless I've sweated it off.

I'm panting by the time the shovel strikes something other than a tree root. The tinny, high-pitched clang echoes through the forest.

My heart races, the blood pounding in my ears. A part of me expected to come up empty, but now that the endpoint is within reach, all I can imagine are bone shards. Bruised skin. Chicklet teeth scattered beside dark, matted hair.

I freeze with the shovel poised over the patch. I've spent a decade wishing on shooting stars and birthday candles for answers, but I'm not sure whether I'm ready to reunite with her. She isn't going to appear peaceful, like the bodies tucked into caskets. She's going to be decomposing—caked in grime, coated with worms or thick, writhing maggots.

I retch at the thought, but curiosity keeps me moving. If she's been in the woods, less than a mile away from the theater where I spend almost every single day, I need to know.

But the shovel could skewer her if it hits the wrong spot, so I drop to my knees and scrape the rest of the grime away. My heart throbs in my throat, braced to find a sliver of an arm, the shard of her hip, but there aren't any bones after all.

CHAPTER 13

EVAN

This town isn't used to much action. Half the guests at the memorial dinner are gone by eight. All that booze tuckered them right out.

The stragglers putter around the dining hall, giving slurred goodbyes. I do more schmoozing than usual on my way out the door, smooching cheeks and setting dinner plans I have every intention of canceling. I want to see who has trouble looking me in the eye, who fidgets or swerves to avoid me. Unfortunately, no one triggers any warning bells.

I wish I had the chance to discuss suspects with the boys. Seth excused himself early in the night, eager to hurry home to the kids. I can't blame him. Honestly, I'm surprised he even showed up after his spat with Fiona. His wife probably roped him into attending. Meanwhile, Cameron hasn't budged from the bar, but it's pointless to pick his brain when he's so far gone. I doubt he even read the message.

I stop at the collage on my way out the door, gravitating toward the most familiar shots. The twins in side-by-side beds after an allergic reaction sent them straight to the hospital—with my GET WELL SOON balloon bobbing in the background. The twins blowing out birthday candles on a mint chocolate chip ice cream cake—with my poorly wrapped present perched on the table. The twins feeding goats bottles at a petting zoo—with my knobby elbow sticking into the frame.

There are hardly any shots of Faith without Fiona, like her parents considered them a packaged deal.

I almost feel bad for her.

Then I remember all the days Fiona turned to me, teary-eyed, wondering whether she'd done something wrong because her sister exploded at her. I was tempted to throw punches more than once, but I had to walk a fine line. Fiona appreciated it when I stood up to her sister, but not when I badmouthed her. Once, I made the mistake of cursing her out behind her back, and Fiona's whole face turned red. *"Take that back. She's my sister, Evan."* As if being family made the abuse okay.

I pry myself away from the photo board as my phone vibrates in my pocket. I steel myself for another cryptic text, but it's a phone call. SETH ADAMS spans the screen. He doesn't have a contact photo attached, so a generic silhouette appears.

I'm not surprised he's reaching out to one of us, but I'm surprised he picked me. It's been ten years since we've spoken one-on-one, and our final few conversations got heated. Then again, tensions are high between him and Raven, and Cameron is a trainwreck. I'm the best of three crappy options.

"We have a problem," Seth says, skipping the hellos. An owl hoots in the background.

"Another one? What is it now?"

"I'm not sure how much I should say over the phone, but you guys should get down here. ASAP."

"Where are you?"

"At the theater," he spits. Like I should already know.

"Why are you at the theater?"

"Didn't you get the message? You were included on the text chain."

"Yeah. Me and Raven didn't know what those numbers meant."

"Jesus Christ. I didn't think I needed to hold your hand. I would've approached you at the dinner to explain the obvious, but my wife was with me. I had to bring her home and sneak out of the house like I was meeting a mistress. I don't want her getting dragged into this ordeal. It's bad enough she was harassed at work."

"So," I draw out. "What were the numbers?"

I can practically hear his eyes roll. "Coordinates to the capsule."

"Capsule?"

"The time capsule. I'm looking for it now, but the damn thing could be buried in the apartment complex for all I know."

"Hold on," I stumble. "Wait. I'm confused."

"Do you need me to speak slower? If we don't find the capsule before Fiona, she's going to take it to the police. She was added to our group chat if you two couldn't parse that part out, either. Which means we were wrong about her being the prankster. Or, maybe blackmailer is more like it. This is about money, guaranteed."

My vision swims. I grip the nearest chair to steady myself. This is bad. Apocalyptic bad.

I used to have sweat-drenched anxiety dreams about the police knocking at my door with the container covered in dirt. Those fears slowly faded, but they made a comeback when the apartment complex was being built. For months, I felt nauseous whenever a deliveryman pounded on the door or a police cruiser pulled behind my Mustang. It got to the point where I considered packing my bags and fleeing the country, starting from scratch with the clothes on my back. Just to be safe.

Of course, nothing came of it. The construction was completed without a hitch. I assumed workers had dug up the capsule with an excavator and dumped it in a landfill. I thought it was out of our lives. Permanently.

"Even if Fiona locates it first, hopefully she won't realize we were the ones who buried it," Seth says. "But I would rather hedge our bets. I don't need the extra gray hairs."

"She'll definitely know it was us. We talked about it in front of her."

He heaves a sigh. "You mean, *you* did."

"No. You're not blaming this on me. All of our names are in that chat. It wouldn't take a rocket scientist to put together who was involved, either way. We can't start turning on each other. I'm sure this person *wants* us to split apart."

"Just round up the others," he hisses.

"Got it. We'll be there in a few."

I pocket my phone and make my way across the room, threading around a handful of families who haven't called it a night yet.

"Rise and shine," I say, slapping Cameron on the shoulder. He's folded over the counter with his head hanging low, bangs drooping into his beer.

"What do you want?" he slurs, shrugging away from me.

"We need to leave. You need to come with me."

"I told you I don't want anything to do with anything."

"I don't have a choice, so neither do you. Get up. You can't drive yourself anyway."

"I took the bus."

"I don't care if you flew in strapped to a jetpack. You're—"

A hand cups my arm.

I snap my head sideways, ready to swing, but it's only Raven. I would be happy to see her, but if she overheard our back-and-forth, others could too. We need to stay under the radar.

"What's wrong?" she asks, her forehead bunching.

"We need a ride," I say. "My parents drove me. I don't have a car."

"I was about to leave anyway. You want me to bring you both home?"

"I want you to bring us to the theater."

Her eyes grow to saucers, but she doesn't utter a word. She's too smart to ask questions in a room with so many ears.

"Come on, Cam," she whispers instead, speaking soft as a lullaby. "Let me help you. I've got you."

And he actually lets her.

I was always jealous of how well she could read a room, pinpoint what a person wanted and provide it. She could stand on her tiptoes, whisper in Seth's ear, and stop him from getting into a fistfight at a club. She could tie my hair back while puking and make the world stop spinning. The movements were so small, so subtle, you almost didn't notice them at all.

I leave her to work her magic on Cameron while I beeline toward my parents. They're hovering by the exit in marshmallow thick coats, waiting for me.

"Hey," I say, combing a hand through my curls. "Change of plans. I hope you don't mind me ditching you, but I'm heading out with some friends. We can handle our booze better than you boomers, so we figured we'd extend the night."

"That's wonderful," my mother says. "I knew going out would be good for you."

My father pats me on the back. "Make sure they have you home by midnight, kiddo."

They latch hands and totter toward the car without me. I linger near the exit, waiting for the others to catch up.

Raven has her arm looped around Cameron's bony waist. He tilts against her, like a crutch, as she leads him across the restaurant, then the half-empty parking lot. Her car is a two-door with folding seats, so I volunteer to climb into the back. Cameron would never be able to fumble his way out again.

Raven leans across him to click on his seatbelt. I grab a warm water bottle rolling around the floor and toss it to him. "You better sober up," I say.

"Why?" Raven asks while he chugs. "What is going on? I'm a little freaked out. Am I right to be freaked out?"

I run them through my conversation with Seth, filling them in on what the numbers mean.

"Only we knew about what was inside of that thing, right?" Cameron mumbles. I'm impressed he's managing to follow the conversation. "We're the only ones who know it's important. That means it's one of us. One of us is sending the messages. One of us is trying to tell Fiona the truth about her sister. One of us is trying to get the rest of us locked up."

"Why the hell would one of us do that?" I ask.

Out of guilt? Resentment? A death wish? Cameron would be the first to break in my book, but he can barely hold himself upright. I doubt he has the stamina to screw with us. Unless he's faking it.

"If it's one of us, they must have a second cell phone," Raven says. "Because all our numbers were in the group chat. The anonymous text came from another device."

Cameron groans. "I don't even like carrying *one*. I mostly keep mine turned off. So no one can track me."

I keep my mouth shut, but Seth probably has a separate cell phone for work calls. There's no point in planting that seed in their heads right now. If they turn on him, they could turn on me next.

"We don't know for sure it's one of us," I say, drumming my armrest. "Either way, we need to get the capsule, and Seth has a pretty big lead on us. How fast does this baby go?"

"The speed limit," Raven says, merging onto the main road at a reasonable sixty. "What are we going to do when we get ahold of the capsule?"

"Dig it up. Burn it. Toss it in a river. Whatever works. We just have to get there before Fiona. Otherwise, we're screwed."

"Maybe not," she says. "Maybe we don't have to do anything. What's inside doesn't matter. We didn't do anything to Faith, right? It's not like we hurt her."

"Obviously. But that doesn't matter. We thought it would look suspicious back then and it's not going to look any less suspicious now. Especially since we hid evidence for years."

"Is it *really* evidence?"

"The cops will think so."

Optics were always our big worry. Whether we were responsible or not, we all had reason to hate the girl. We had motive *and* opportunity. The police could have pinned the crime on any one of us and convinced a jury to convict.

And honestly, even though the other three never admitted it out loud, I think there was another, hidden layer to the coverup. We were worried one of us was responsible, that we were lying about our whereabouts when she was murdered. There was a period of unaccounted time for each of us. We all disappeared during some point in the movie. Cameron claimed he was smoking a joint by the dumpsters. Raven and Seth swore they were arguing in the break room. And I told them I was sneaking extra candy from the concession stand.

Turning against each other would do more harm than good, so we agreed not to ask questions. We took each alibi as the truth. Then we shook the suspicions off us by tossing them onto Fiona.

Or technically, Seth did.

He leaked the rumor to the tabloids about her killing her sister. I blew a fit when I read his quote, shouting about how he should've discussed it with us, about how we were supposed to make decisions as a team, but he convinced me it was harmless. They would never arrest her. She had no real motive. She loved her sister too much to see what a witch she could be. Besides, his statement was already in print. It wasn't like he could walk it back.

I should've defended her in an interview of my own, but I didn't want the attention to shift toward me. None of us wanted to get dragged into a missing person investigation. Even if we weren't officially charged with murder, it wouldn't be a great look. Seth would get his acceptance revoked from the fancy-pants college he was supposed to attend. Raven's Black, so we didn't trust cops within a hundred feet of her. And Cameron would never make it as a Christian rocker if he had a record.

The evidence in the capsule might not have damned us to life in a prison cell, but it would have been a shit-stain on our names. We didn't want to take the risk ten years ago, and we're not taking it tonight.

CHAPTER 14

FIONA

A dog howls as I heave a wide, cylindrical container out of the hole in the ground. A time capsule, converted from an old coffee grounds container. The label has been ripped off and replaced with a laminated, hand-drawn picture of a skull and crossbones. TOGETHER UNTIL WE'RE CORPSES, it says in a cartoony speech bubble.

I recognize the container. It was the one Evan crammed into her backpack during one of our arguments. She didn't even bother to hide it from me. Her and her friends spent months planning what they would seal inside to commemorate their senior year together. They discussed it constantly, regardless of who was around to overhear. It was cruel, like discussing a party in front of guests cut from the invite list.

I turn the container over in my hands, considering tossing it in the hole and dumping dirt back on top, but I came all this way. No. Someone specifically *sent me* all this way.

I flex my sore, calloused fingers and attempt to unscrew the lid, but it's rusted in place. I jam my thumbnail around the seal, dislodging dirt that has snuck into the crevices.

It takes a few tries, but I finally wrench open the top. I expect to find photographs of the group playing around at the theater, letters to their future selves, or the matching skull pins they wore on their backpacks. Useless trinkets only they would be excited to see again.

I reel out the largest item, a sandwich baggie. The plastic is discolored from age, so I unzip the top to peer inside. At the bottom, there's a chunky, capped pregnancy test. I wrinkle my nose, wondering which one of them added it to the capsule. Seth is the only one with children, and he hadn't even met Angel at that time.

I dig into the container for the next items. Another, smaller baggie with white smears of powder. Then a series of crumpled papers, ripped from the NOTES section of our high school agenda. I shine my phone light over them, trying to make out the bleeding red marker. Half the letters have faded, but it seems to say: YOU WHORE, KILL YOURSELF, and ROT IN HELL HOMEWRECKER.

A gust of wind slams into me, scattering the dirt piles and nearly pulling the papers from my hand. I stuff everything back into the capsule, my heart in my throat. Why would the four of them want to preserve such awful things?

I almost fasten the cap, then spot another item clinging to the side of the container. I tug loose a bow-tie-shaped ribbon. It's smeared in dirt and the color has faded, but the pattern is still visible. Small, pinprick-sized polka dots.

"Oh my God," I whisper, bunching the ribbon in my fist. "No. No, no, no."

I press the fabric against my heaving chest, tears beading in my eyes. It feels like a vice has clamped down on my lungs, sapping all the oxygen from me.

This ribbon was attached to the center of a collared, ruffled top. We described that shirt to every police officer who rang our doorbell. We found old photographs of us wearing it. We sent digital copies to news outlets so they could ask whether anyone had spotted it around town. It was the outfit Faith was wearing on the day she went missing.

I knew it better than anyone because she swiped it from my side of the closet.

My eyes flick back to the pregnancy test, streaked with two pink lines. I always wondered why she borrowed my clothes that night. Even though we were twins, we never traded outfits. Faith wore tight, form-fitting clothing in dark shades. I wore baggier sweaters and stretchy jeans, even back when there wasn't much weight on me. Did she need looser clothes because she had trouble fitting into hers?

No, I tell myself, struggling to breathe through the panic. It couldn't be her pregnancy test. Sure, she made-out with pretty much any guy my parents hired, but we took birth control every night with dinner. Mom had encouraged us to get prescriptions sophomore year to prevent acne and period cramps. Those pills are never one-hundred percent effective, but I would have known if she had a pregnancy scare. If she was going to become a mother. I don't care how distant she was acting those last few years. We were still sisters. She would've told me.

Wouldn't she?

I think back to all the nights when I caught her sneaking to the family computer, clacking away at the keyboard, checking over her shoulder every few seconds to see if anyone was watching. I thought she was messaging random boys, but she could've been researching abortion clinics. Or adoption centers. Or tips on how to raise a baby when she was practically a baby herself.

I ram each item back into the time capsule, reseal it, and stagger to my feet. I assumed my sister drank the night she went missing. The whole crew was mixing liquor with soft drinks and taking vodka shots, but maybe she turned down the alcohol. Maybe she poured water into a cup and pretended to join us. I can't remember. I wasn't paying attention. Not to her.

There's a chance the test belonged to her and she never mentioned it. Of course, if that's the truth, if she died while pregnant…

A twig crunches, ejecting me from my thoughts.

I jump, clutching the capsule against my chest. I tell myself it's only an animal, a squirrel scampering through the leaves, but then there are more crunches. The sound of two feet, not four.

I'm not alone anymore.

It must be someone else who received coordinates. They must be combing the woods for the capsule. I don't want to be cornered with it on me. I need to hide it, to maintain the upper hand.

I switch off my phone light, shrouding myself in darkness. With the shovel clutched in one hand and the capsule tucked beneath my armpit, I tiptoe toward the building, making as little noise as possible. Trees work as my guides, my fingers grazing their trunks for balance. Sap sticks to my skin and my knees buckle with nerves, but I march forward. I need to make it to the gate. I'll be safe inside the theater.

"We have a problem," the trespasser whispers, freezing me.

He sounds even more agitated than Thursday, when he threatened me.

I scramble behind a thick tree trunk, making myself as small as possible so he doesn't spot me. I wet my cracked lips, scanning the forest for signs of him. I was distracted earlier, running on adrenaline, so I didn't register how chilly it had gotten. Now that I'm trying to hold still, I start to shiver and can't stop. My hands are numb. My ears are ice. It slowly dawns on me how isolated I am in the forest, how easily he could kill me.

How easily he could've killed Faith.

A woodpecker hammers a nearby tree, and my heart races. I fumble for the gun in case he charges me, but I'm carrying too much. With trembling hands, I prop the shovel against a neighboring oak, leaving my hands free to pull the trigger. I switch the safety on and off, on and off, as the steps grow closer, the voice grows louder.

When Seth enters my line of sight, he's lugging a shovel over his shoulder. It looks out of place against his light gray, tailored suit. He must've been at the memorial, pretending to care about my family before driving here to betray my family.

"Do you need me to speak slower?" he hisses into the phone pressed against his ear. "If we don't find the capsule before Fiona, she's going to take it to the police. She was added to our group chat if you two couldn't parse that part out, either."

That settles it. If there was any doubt their group knows something about my sister, it's gone.

My stomach lurches as Seth slithers closer, passing directly in front of my tree. I hold my breath, praying he doesn't turn toward me, doesn't give me a reason to shoot. He pauses every few footsteps to scan the ground, but he always takes another step. And another.

He continues deeper into the forest, heading in the wrong direction. I push out an extra-long breath and resume my walk, treading carefully through the trees. As I approach the dumpsters, the howls and hoots are replaced by honks and hushed conversations. The noises could be coming from customers at the neighboring shops.

Or it could be the other three, arriving to back up Seth.

I slink into the theater, bolting the door behind me, and beeline for the office. I never shut the safe, so I slip the capsule into the compartment and seal it away. Then I arrange a row of chairs—a wheeling one and a few metal ones. If Seth is sneaking through the woods, the others must be close.

And I'm going to get answers out of them, no matter what it costs me.

CHAPTER 15

EVAN

I knew the capsule was going to backfire on us eventually. We met at the theater, and grew close at the theater, so we figured the forest was the perfect burial site. Once the capsule was hidden underground, we pinky promised we wouldn't touch it until we were old and wrinkled. But we almost immediately broke that promise. On employee movie night, we dug it back up, dumped out our ticket stubs and photos, and replaced them with evidence. The woods were thicker then, spanning miles. We took a chance no one would notice a small patch of disturbed dirt, and our gamble paid off.

Until today.

Raven swings us into the parking lot, rolling past a beat-up, old Thunderbird parked near the theater. The rest of the cars are clustered by the mall-like strip of stores. Raven points out Seth's minivan mixed in with them, parked out of the way to avoid drawing suspicion. Raven eases into the spot beside it, inching so close she nearly scratches its paint.

We pile out of the car and sneak around the side of the building, toward the snow-speckled woods. Cameron wobbles with each step, his path a zigzag. I start second-guessing my bright idea to bring him along.

"Maybe he should wait in the car," Raven says, echoing the thought.

He mumbles.

"What was that?" I ask. "Use your outdoor voice."

"I said, all I had was a few drinks. I've played shows on way harder drugs. I had to remember lyrics and chords and smile and wink at the audience. I think I can handle a little walk." A pause. "Besides, I need to piss. I can't do it in public without getting another indecent exposure ticket."

Fair enough. We already dragged him down here. No turning back now.

We continue around the theater and into the sparse stretch of woods. The area is eerily quiet, except for the shrill, whistling wind. My heels sink into the ground every few paces, muddying their stems and making me unsteady on my feet.

Once we're deep enough that the road disappears, Cameron leans against a skinny tree trunk and unzips his jeans. I don't want him to fall behind, so I fish out my phone to text Seth. I tell him we're here, explain we're on the lookout for him, but he never responds. There's no trace of him, either, except for footprints in the dirt.

Fantastic. We came straight from the restaurant, so we didn't bring a shovel. I was relying on him to be prepared since he was the genius who deciphered the text. He'd better show soon.

"Do you two remember where this thing was buried?" Cameron asks as we knit through the trees. There aren't any rocks or stumps that stand out from the rest. Just trees and more trees.

"Not a clue," I say, booting up a navigation app. "That's why we wrote down the coordinates back then."

"Too bad we didn't remember them."

"I'm lucky if I remember to put on underwear in the morning."

"See? That's why technology sucks. We never think for ourselves anymore. We have one big robot brain."

"I don't need your techno-crap right now, okay, Cam?"

"What are we going to do if it's too close to the apartments?" Raven cuts in. "We can't dig up someone's backyard."

I shrug. "Why not? We'll blame it on a dog."

"They could have cameras. They would know we were liars."

"Then we'll find a dog. I don't fucking know. We'll figure it out when we get there. This thing says we're close. Like, it should be up-our-butt close."

I don't want to alarm the others, but the footprints have multiplied. At least two sets are stamped in the dirt. Half of them come from a wide pair of sneakers, a grown man. The others are smaller, pressed tighter together, like the owner was shuffling, scared. Arriving this late isn't great for us. Especially since we're inching close to the edge of the forest and haven't hit our mark. There's a chance we—

"Holy shit," Cameron yelps as he trips, sways, and comes crashing onto the ground. He catches himself with splayed fingers, coating his nails in dirt.

"Quiet," I snap. "You couldn't have gone one night without drinking? Haul your ass to an AA meeting every once in a while. I don't need you dead, too."

He shoves himself onto his butt, groaning. "That wasn't on me. I'm fine by the way. No broken bones. Thanks for checking."

I shine my phone light near his sneakers, illuminating the pit that tripped him. I'm praying Seth dug it, but judging by my unanswered messages, the odds aren't in our favor.

"What are we going to do?" Raven asks, chewing her thumbnail.

"We need to come up with a new story," I say. "A reason for why we would bury those things. Fiona's car was parked outside. She must be nearby. We can convince her not to call the cops. And if she already has…"

"Then it's three against one," Cameron says. "We can steal it back."

Raven winces, but she nods. "And then we can team up, tell the cops we have no idea what evidence she's talking about. They'd believe us. Just like last time."

And I would be drowning in guilt for another decade. Still, it's our only option. Fiona might *think* she knows what's best for herself, but she's wrong.

"All right. Sounds like a plan," I say. "Although, it would be nice if Seth was with us so we could all stick to the same story." I kick at a rock, sending it flying. "I can't believe he ditched us."

"Maybe something happened to him," Cameron says.

"Or maybe he took off when he realized the capsule was missing and we were screwed. Sure, he has ties to the evidence, but we're going to look way worse by trying to destroy evidence."

"Nah, no way. His car was outside, wasn't it? He's always the first one saying we're supposed to stick together."

"Sure, when we were teenagers, but he has a family now. They're going to come before us. If he thought he would be taken away from them, who knows—"

A branch snaps to our right. A shadow appears, long and skinny in the moonlight.

A heartbeat later, Fiona steps out from the tight cluster of trees. A pistol is gripped in her trembling hands. She waves it wildly, pointing it at each of us. "What did you do to my sister?" she asks, her voice ringing out through the forest.

Raven throws up her arms, palms facing forward. Cameron does the same from his spot on the ground.

I leave my arms at my side, balling my fists, but my pulse beats hard in my stomach. I fight the urge to turn away, to look at anything other than my ex-best friend dripping snot and tears. It's why I skipped the search parties, the candlelight vigils, the news conferences. I couldn't look her in the eyes and pretend everything was going to be okay.

"What did you do to my sister?" she asks again, jerking her arm. "Why did you bury a container filled with those things? They were hers, weren't they? Everything in there was hers?"

"What container are you talking about?" I ask, keeping my voice neutral while scanning for the capsule. It isn't cradled in her arms or propped against a tree. She must have hidden it already.

"Don't lie to me, Evan. I know it was you. I saw you with the capsule when we were kids. And you came looking for it now. There's obviously something important inside that you don't want me to see. There's no point in pretending anymore. It'll only make me madder."

I swallow. I need to play this right.

"Say something," Fiona shouts, her voice cracking. A squirrel takes off from a branch, shaking the limb. I wouldn't be surprised if a light or two turned on from the apartments, but the area remains cloaked in darkness.

"Listen. I know today sucks for your whole family," I say, slow and steady. "But we're not the enemy here. So why don't you do us all a favor and put the gun down?"

"You're lying."

"You're overreacting."

"Let's not yell," Raven says in the same calm, soothing tone she used on Cameron earlier. I only saw her raise her voice once, and it was for a damn good reason.

"I'm sure you have a million questions, which is understandable," Raven says. "You have a right to be upset, but we can clear everything up for you, okay? We'll answer any question you ask. But it's freezing out here. Why don't we go into the theater to talk?"

Fiona's mouth twitches. Her gun lowers for a brief moment, but then she steadies her aim. "Fine. Throw down your phones first. Drop them into the hole. I don't want you calling the cops on me. I should be calling them on you."

"No way," I say. "Not happening."

Cameron glares at me.

Raven shakes her head at me.

Fiona cocks the gun.

"You're not a killer," I say, risking a step toward the barrel. "You're too good of a person to pull that trigger. You would never hurt me. Remember when we made those crummy origami cranes and you gave me a paper cut? You cried for an hour."

"We were kids. That *me* died with my sister."

"Okay, well, if you gunned down one of us, the others would rat you out. You would go to prison for the rest of your life. You wouldn't want to be stuck in a crowded cell. All those people. No privacy. You can't live like that."

She readjusts her aim, so the gun is parallel with my chest, hovering over my heart. "I'm not going to prison," she seethes. "I have enough bullets for all of you. Plus, one for me."

Fuck.

A lump forms in my throat. I hope to God she's bluffing, but I launch my cell into the hole just in case. The others follow my lead. Their phones clatter on top of mine, cracking the screen. Fiona nudges dirt onto the pile with the heel of her shoe, letting chunks rain down.

"Come on," she says, gesturing toward the theater.

She ushers us toward the back door, warning us to walk slowly and keep our hands to ourselves. It would be the perfect time to make a run for it. The trees would grant us cover and the parking lot would provide witnesses. Not many, but enough to prevent her from taking a shot.

Still, none of us veer off the path. Cameron shoves his hands in his pockets, hunching over so far he almost takes another tumble. Raven is the opposite, ramrod stiff. She shoots me a wide-eyed look as we march, like she's trying to send a telepathic message. I hope she's thinking what I'm thinking. *We're lucky we're getting a private escort inside. It will give us a chance to hunt down the capsule. It must be stashed somewhere nearby.*

We hauled ass here to destroy evidence—and we aren't going to leave before that happens.

We file into the theater, one after the other, with Fiona bringing up the rear. She trains the gun on the person in front of her, which happens to be me. She doesn't jab me in the back with it like a wannabe movie villain, but I can feel her body behind me, her breath on my neck.

She leads us through a deserted lobby, which is almost unrecognizable. The walls have been repainted, the loud yellow tones swapped out for a sleek black. The floor tiles have been replaced with a different palette too, a tasteful monochrome instead of a checkered bowling alley design. And, of course, the crystal ball is gone, replaced with a self-serve soda machine.

But some things are exactly like I remember, their colors and textures swapped but their aura the same. Movie-themed cups and buckets stacked on the concession counters. Freezers carrying miniature water bottles and pre-wrapped ice cream cones. Signs advertising their loyalty card program—*free popcorn upgrades with every ticket!*

I take in the eating area where Raven and Seth would split pizzas on break. The employee-only elevator where Cameron would sneak naps. The lobby couches where an after-hours spin the bottle game led to me kissing Fiona. My mind sticks on that last memory. It was the same night Faith kissed Cameron, straddling his lap and making out with him so long that his current girlfriend, whoever she was at the time, broke up with him over it.

But I couldn't be that obvious. A crowd was watching, and girls who landed on girls weren't supposed to enjoy themselves unless they were pretending for the boys. So we rushed it. There was no hand on her waist, fingers through her hair nonsense. The briefest touch, skin against skin, and it was done.

I squeeze my eyes closed, blinking away the memory to keep inspecting the theater. There are approximately zero signs of Seth. Nothing suggests he's breached the building and is hiding in the shadows to save us. If I could peek into the parking lot, I bet his car would be long gone. He sent us on a mission, then ditched us to do the dirty work ourselves. Unbelievable.

He might not be with us in person, but he'll be here in spirit. If anyone is going down for what we've done, he's the first one getting thrown under the bus.

CHAPTER 16

FIONA

The days after my sister went missing had a surreal, dreamlike hue to them. My vision felt hazy, cloaked in fog, like nothing was real. Nothing mattered.

I feel that same dreamlike sensation now, guiding the group through the theater, struggling to hold the pistol steady. Evan called me out for being weak in the woods. I don't want to prove her right. If her group senses any vulnerability, if they think for even a second I don't have the heart to hurt them, then they're going to gang up on me. I need to use all my tools to my advantage, and right now, the gun is all I have going for me.

I train the barrel at Evan's back, switching the safety on and off, on and off again. I've never fired a weapon, not even at the range down the street from my apartment. The field is so close I can hear faint pop-pop-pops while warming up microwavable dinners or changing the kitty litter in the morning. The explosions used to make me jump, but it's become background noise, as normal as the birds chirping or the crickets singing.

I march the group around the guest service desk, guiding them into the managerial office. Once they're clustered inside, I plant myself in front of the door, blocking their only exit. Two high, skinny windows face the woods, but they're too tight to fit a toddler through, let alone a full-grown adult.

Cameron sags onto the rolling computer chair. He jiggles his knees and itches his chest, unable to sit still. Raven seats herself on a hardback chair beside him, folding her hands across her lap, like an executive at a conference meeting. Evan ignores the remaining seats and perches on the edge of a desk, her long legs crossed. If any of them are going to cause trouble, it's her.

"Ten years," I say. My finger hovers over the trigger as a warning— but pulling it would be a last resort. "I've spent *ten years* wondering what happened to my sister and you knew the entire time. You all kept the truth from me. From my family. You could've told us. You could've done the right thing."

"We don't know anything," Evan says. "I have no idea what you found in that capsule that has you convinced we were involved in her murder or kidnapping or whatever happened to her. We buried that thing before Faith went missing so I'm not sure how there could be anything incriminating inside."

"You must have dug it back up. It was a good hiding spot."

Her eye twitches. She probably thought it would be easier to fool me. "Can you at least show it to us, so we know what you're accusing us of hiding?" she asks. "You keep yelling about what you saw in that capsule and we don't even know what you allegedly found."

"Nice try, but it's staying hidden until the cops come. I heard you in the woods, talking about how you need to come up with a good explanation about what's inside, but here's a refresher. A positive pregnancy test. A note calling my sister names. A bunch of drugs. And the most interesting piece, in my opinion... A ribbon from the outfit she was wearing the day she went missing."

Silence. Pin-drop silence.

Evan screws her lips to the side, but her gaze never wavers from mine. The others are easier to read. Raven drops her eyes, staring at the floor like she's too ashamed to face me. Cameron swivels back and forth in his chair, restless.

"Where do we want to start?" I ask, but of course, no one sputters out an answer. Not even Evan. "Okay. That's fine. I have a feeling the killer isn't going to come right out and admit to what they've done, so we can start with an easy question. A simple yes-or-no." I twist toward Cameron, waiting for him to meet my eyes. "Did you get my sister pregnant?"

He blinks hard, like he's trying to focus his vision. "Me? No. No way. I never touched her. Why would you think it was me?"

"You had a crush on her. You broke up with your girlfriend for her."

"My girlfriend broke up with me because of her. Not the same."

"So you *did* sleep with her?"

"No way. We never even came close to having sex. She was a tease. She flirted with me. Led me on. We made out a few times during lunch breaks, but she wouldn't even let me put my hand up her shirt."

"Did you force her?"

"Whoa. No." He throws up his hands, nearly tumbling off the chair. "I've never done anything like that to a girl. Never. My band was killing it back then. I had plenty of other chicks who were interested. They threw themselves at me. I didn't have to put in any work to get their clothes off. If your sister wanted me, I wouldn't have turned her down. But she wasn't swayed by the band thing, so I dropped it."

I take in his bloodshot eyes, his sweat-beaded forehead. "I don't believe you."

"Why? What else do you want me to say?"

"I want you to say what you did to her. You must have done something wrong or you wouldn't have been creeping through the woods in the middle of the night to keep this capsule from me. You're all involved somehow. Tell me how."

"I swear. It wasn't me. I didn't do anything to Faith."

"You're not here on accident. You know what happened to her. You must. I need you to tell me about the part you played in her death, right now, or I'm going to assume you slept with her. You got her pregnant. And then you killed her because you didn't want to raise her—"

"No. No. No," he slurs. "The drugs were mine, okay?"

"The powder in that baggie? That was yours?"

"Yeah. That's the only thing that was mine. I swiped it from my parents. They were dealing. Dealt ever since I was a kid. It's what killed them."

"I thought heart attacks killed them."

"We lied. They got screwed by their supplier. The dude spied on my parents through their computer camera and caught them testing their own supply, then cutting the rest with sugar. So he sent some guys to teach them a lesson. They took it too far and... and it killed them. I was at a gig that night or they might've got me, too, but I never saw their faces and I kept my mouth shut, so they left me out of it."

He pinches his bloodshot eyes shut, warding off tears, and my heart clenches. Despite the situation, what he may or may not have done, I know how much it hurts to repeat The Story, to relive a death over and over whenever anyone asks, to wonder what would have changed if you made one decision differently.

He sniffs, scrubbing his nose with a sleeve. "Growing up, they had a stash of anything you can think of at the house. I usually handled weed, but I would hook people up with whatever they needed if they came to me directly. Your sister must've heard the rumors because she came up to me, *she* approached *me*, and said she wanted drugs. So I sold her drugs."

"What kind of drugs? What did she want them for?"

He digs his nails into his knees. "I didn't ask any questions. When people flash money at me, I give them whatever they want. I can't get all ethical about it or I would be broke."

"So, what, are you saying she died from overdosing?"

"I have no idea. I don't know how to do an autopsy. All I know is, I didn't want the cops to find a bag on her and trace it back to me or my parents, so I took it off her. That's it. I wasn't sleeping with her. I have nothing to do with knocking her up."

I tilt my head, stuck on the first chunk of his confession.

"You didn't want the cops to find drugs on her?" I repeat, the words coming out strained and slow. "You saw her body?"

He winces.

Raven drops her head into her hands.

Evan whips toward him, her gray eyes bulging.

I'm about to raise the gun, to threaten him to say more, but the alcohol keeps his tongue flapping.

"We did. We saw her," he says, his leather seat squeaking as he swivels faster. "I found her in the woods. I snuck out of the movie toward the end to smoke a joint—you warned me not to do it inside—so I was trying to be sneaky about it. I was roaming through the trees, looking at the snow and squirrels and shit. After a couple of minutes, I noticed her curled up in the grass. I didn't see any blood, but I called her name and she didn't answer, so I freaked. I should've called the cops, but I was high and didn't want to get thrown in cuffs, so I brought the others outside. By then, the movie was over and everyone was leaving, so no one saw us walk into the woods. I don't think."

"Why didn't you come to me? She was my sister."

"I don't know. Me and you weren't *friend* friends, so running to them was my gut instinct. I trusted them." He rubs his neck, a blush creeping onto his cheeks. "We voted on whether we should involve you, but we knew you would go haywire and make us call the police."

"So you moved her instead? You got rid of her body?"

"No. We didn't want our fingerprints on her, so we didn't go near her. We only took some stuff that fell out of her pocketbook. It was dropped in the grass, like she tore it apart looking for something. Her cell phone maybe. The ribbon was there, too. We were sloppy and touched it, so we tossed it in the capsule with the notes and pregnancy stick and pills."

I swallow. My mouth is desert dry, my tongue coarse as sandpaper, but I manage to rasp out, "You kept what you saw a secret, even after it was all over the news that no body was found? No pocketbook, either. There was no sign of her."

"I mean, we're not monsters. We called the police after we got home. We sent in an anonymous tip about a dead girl in the woods. But I guess she was already gone by the time the cops pulled up. When we found out they were calling it a kidnapping a few days later, we were confused. But we didn't want to get involved again. We felt like we did all we could do. It's not like our info would help much anyway.

We didn't know anything important, like whether she was stabbed or shot or whatever. We didn't see a wound. So we shut our mouths and moved on."

My chest heaves. "Guess who wasn't able to move on? For a decade? Me. My mother. My father. My whole family."

"It's not like we know who killed her. All we knew was that she was dead—and we *told* the cops. It's not our fault they didn't believe us. We thought the body would turn up eventually. Or that you guys would assume she was dead since kidnap victims usually don't make it past a few days. That's what Seth said, at least."

I sip in short, rapid breaths, dangerously close to hyperventilating. I don't understand how they can live with themselves—or lie to themselves—so easily.

"You're right," I say, my wrist trembling, the gun smacking against my thigh. "No matter how bad we hoped she was still out there, we've known for a while that she was dead. But what we didn't know is whether she spent days or weeks or months getting raped and tortured before someone finally put her out of her misery. What we didn't know was how long she suffered before she was given peace. It would've been nice to know it was quick, to know her pain only lasted a little while instead of literal years."

The floodgates burst. Hot tears streak down my cheeks, wrecking what's left of my patchy makeup. I swipe away a clump of mascara and collapse against the door. My insides burn white-hot, like a match has been scratched against the walls of my throat. My breathing comes in heavy, heaving gasps.

I'm not sure how long I spend hunched on the floor, my chin buried in my poofy collar—but I know there's more to the story than what Cameron has revealed. I need to wring more answers out of them, so I sniff snot up my nose and lurch onto my feet. Then I flinch, sinking onto the floor again. *Not now. Not now. Not now.* I can't repeat rituals in front of them. I can't keep leaping up and down until it feels *right*. I need to stay in control of the situation. Which means controlling myself.

Luckily, none of them budge while I force myself to stand—and stay standing. They remain as stiff and silent as statues. I'm surprised they aren't scrambling to apologize. Or to attack me. They could have wrangled the gun from my grip while my guard was down. I'm not sure whether they controlled their tempers to come across as harmless. Because they genuinely feel sorry for me. Or because they were scared they would get shot in the scuffle. Maybe all three things are true at once.

"Okay. That's one item explained," I say, counting on my fingers. "We have a few more to go. What do we want to discuss next? The pregnancy test? The notes?"

Evan sighs. "You can keep us here all night, but you're not going to learn anything new. Like Cameron said, we didn't hurt your sister. I'm sorry you lost her, but we weren't involved."

"Evan, honestly, you're the last person I want to deal with right now."

"I thought you wanted us to talk. Which is it?"

"You know what I mean. You were my best friend. If anyone should've come clean about this sooner, it's you."

Evan blinks, emotionless. "We were all friends."

"No. Cameron and Raven were coworkers who were friendly with me. You were an actual friend. We hung out every weekend. We texted every night. You know there's a difference."

"And you know how much drama there was between us."

"Fine. We had a rocky relationship. You didn't care about my feelings, but what about my parents? They let you sleep over. They stocked the fridge with your favorite sodas and ice cream. Not to mention, they gave you a job. And you repaid them by lying to them? By keeping this enormous secret from them? And then you had the nerve to tell the papers it was me?"

She swallows. "I never said it was you."

"You implied it. People still look at me like I'm a murderer. I can't take a walk in the park or grab a drink from the coffee shop without worrying about someone cursing me out or crossing the street to avoid me."

"That's not my fault. No one forced you to stay in town. You were supposed to go to college, leave all this behind."

"I wasn't going to abandon everyone who loved me. I'm not like you. I haven't...I never..."

I trail off, distracted by movement on the computer monitors. There's a blur. A human-shaped smudge.

I race to the opposite side of the room, fumbling for the keyboard. Nine boxes display security footage in three-by-three rows. The camera connected to the upper right-hand corner, where the person appeared, is mounted inside theater three.

"What's wrong?" Cameron asks, doing a double-take over his shoulder. "Is someone else in this place? Is it Seth?"

"I'm not sure," I mumble, clicking for more camera angles. None of them capture the intruder. "It looked like someone was running through one of our theaters. Which is impossible. I know I locked the doors behind me. I always double-check. I couldn't have forgotten."

"Holy shit," Evan says. "I bet someone snuck in through the back while you were stalking us in the forest. You should go check it out. Make sure it's safe."

Liar. She couldn't have seen anything with the monitors directly behind her. She's trying to get rid of me.

I don't want to leave them alone, but they can't call the cops without their phones and they can't steal the capsule when it's stashed in the safe. There's a chance they could flee, but it's a risk worth taking. Someone texted me coordinates to the crime scene. Someone sent a letter to my parents claiming they knew what happened to my sister. Whoever is sneaking around the building could be the person who gathered us all together. I want to meet them, to thank them.

Or interrogate them.

CHAPTER 17

EVAN

Fiona bursts out the door like a firecracker, leaving us unsupervised in the office. It's still for a moment, the three of us swapping unsure looks like it could be a trap. Then Cameron clambers out of his chair, lunging for the door handle. Raven follows close behind, eager to escape, but I swing the opposite way. I wander over to the computer monitor and play with the controls, hoping to see whatever spooked Fiona. Unfortunately, there are no signs of life. When they renovated the theater, they must have skimped on the security updates. It's impossible to rewind the tapes. The cameras only relay live footage.

Fiona isn't even on screen. The cameras are only aimed at select areas. There's one installed in each theater, which makes sense. There are major fines for bootlegging movies. There are cameras trained over the ticket booth and concession stand, too. They're slanted toward the registers to make sure no one is swiping cash from drawers or sneaking extra fries to friends. Managers might check the security feed on occasion, but the cameras are more of a visual deterrent than anything else. Which makes them useless to us.

"Let's go," Cameron says, waving me over. "It was probably Seth on camera. He probably created a distraction so we could sneak out."

"You're giving him way more credit than he deserves," I say. "Seth doesn't even know we're stuck. Because he *bailed* on us. He's probably at home, screwing his wife by now."

"Nah, he would never do that to us."

"I hate to burst your bubble, but I don't see him as our big hero, saving the day. I'm not convinced anyone was even on camera. Fiona could've been seeing things. She's not thinking straight. She threatened murder-suicide."

"I'm surprised she hasn't fired with your mouth," Raven says. "Would it kill you to be nice to her?"

"Weirdly, when someone aims a gun at my head, my gut instinct isn't to shower them with hugs and kisses."

"It should be if it keeps you alive."

"Hold on, why am I getting all the heat? I'm not the one who ratted."

"Whoa, don't turn this around on me," Cameron says, brushing back his stringy hair. "Who cares what Fiona knows? She doesn't matter anymore. All that matters is that she bolted. Let's go. There's no lock on the door. We're home free."

"Sorry," I say. "I'm not leaving without the capsule. We marched through the forest because we needed to get our hands on it. That hasn't changed. If anything, it's even more important now because she has a piece of our story. I don't want her to have evidence to back it up. The damn thing has to be around here somewhere. It shouldn't be too tricky to find."

I drift past the safe embedded in the back wall—reserved for stacks of cash—and move to the smaller safe propped on a filing cabinet. I twist the lock left and right, pressing my ear against the metal.

"We're not hot, hardened criminals in a Bond movie," Cameron says. "You can't break in without the combo."

Raven nods. "I hate to say it, but he's right. Besides, it might not be in there. We might be wasting our time trying to crack it."

"Only one of us has to play around with it," I say. "I know their family the best, so I can take some guesses at the combination. One of you can check the concession area and pantry. There are a million drawers where she could've stashed it. And the other person can check upstairs.

This place has changed a lot, but the layout is the same. The projection room used to be packed with crap. It would make a good hiding spot. Remember, it's not like we were sent the coordinates *that* long ago. She didn't have hours to spare. She would've thrown it somewhere easy and called it a day."

Raven nibbles on a nail. "Are you sure it's smart to separate?"

"This isn't a Scooby-Doo cartoon. Spending a few minutes apart isn't going to make a difference. But if you're paranoid…"

I curve toward a desk cluttered in paperwork. In between thick stacks of receipts and work schedules, walkie-talkies are perched on charging ports. Two are empty, but I pluck the rest one by one, to see which have full power. I distribute three with steady green lights and say, "We don't have our phones, so these are better than nothing. If we find the capsule, we can give each other the OK and meet in the car. Otherwise, we'll regroup in ten minutes and leave without it."

Raven and Cameron murmur their agreement. They clip the walkies onto their waistbands and tiptoe out the door while I fiddle with the safe. Luckily, it's the old-fashioned kind with a twistable lock, not an electronic keypad that could lock me out after a few wrong attempts or trigger a security alarm.

I try the obvious combinations first. Her birthday. The date her sister went missing. The year the theater first opened its doors. But the lock refuses to budge. I move onto more niche dates, our graduation and junior prom and senior banquet. Still no dice.

Sweat prickles my brow. My gaze keeps sliding back to the clock on the computer monitor, warning me our ten minutes are almost up. I want to check in on the others, but they would say something if they found something. Their silence means we're shit out of luck.

I slap the safe, once, twice, three times, stinging my palm. I was lying when I said we could get out of here if our treasure hunt failed. I have no intention of resorting to plan B. We can't let Fiona hang onto the capsule. The fact we hid evidence is going to look sketchier than the evidence itself. And if she learns the truth…

It's my own fault. I should've snuck onto the property earlier. I should've decoded the coordinates without step-by-step instructions from Seth.

I pace in tight circles, trying to think outside of the box. Solving the combination isn't the only way inside. Any lock can be broken. I scour the room, rummaging through every drawer and cabinet. I need a wrench, a hammer, a screwdriver, anything hard and heavy. If the safe is as old and outdated as the security system, I can bash my way inside.

I tear the office apart, but there's nothing useful. The best I can find is a bright orange box cutter. There are dozens scattered around the building like roaches. Employees used them for everything—to slit open packages to stock the shelves or to break down cardboard boxes to fit in the trash.

I slip the blade into my romper, thankful it came with actual pockets. If Fiona pulls anything sketchy with the gun, I can use the knife to knock it away from her. I could've lunged at her when she broke down earlier, but my emotions got the best of me. If I want to get through tonight, I need to return to thinking with my head, not my heart. I learned that ten years ago.

Static fizzles from the walkie. I unhook it from my belt and hover it near my ear. I can't make out what's being said, but I can tell it's Raven.

"What's wrong?" I ask, cranking the knobs, raising the volume. "I can't hear you. Repeat it for me."

"I need you," she says. "I need you to get over here."

"Oh, thank Christ. You found the capsule?"

"No. He's not moving, Evan. He's dead. I think he's dead."

CHAPTER 18

FIONA

I sprint down the hall, snapping my head every which way. According to the security cameras, the intruder was in the east end of the building. I check every theater on our right-hand side, stumbling through aisles and ducking behind seats, but it's impossible to pin them down. They vanished—or never existed in the first place.

No, I correct myself, *I'm not hallucinating.* But I *am* panicking. My OCD forces me to touch every single armrest as I weave from side to side, checking each row. If I miss one, I backtrack and start the line over. I'm wasting precious seconds, minutes even, but I can't stop myself.

I remember doing the same thing freshman year, after an argument with Faith, which ended with a panic attack between seats. Except that time, Evan stumbled across me.

"Fiona," she called while I was rocking back and forth on the sticky floor. "You in here? Your parents are looking for you." She froze when she found me, her knuckles turning white around her broom. "What did she do to you?"

"Nothing," I said, sniffling. She already hated my sister enough. Besides, her comments were always so small, so pointless. Calling my shoes ugly. Pointing out my pimples. Teasing me about the hair under my arms. But teenagers are mean. Sisters, especially. It was my fault for getting upset.

"I can't fix it when you're playing *mime*," Evan said.

"I don't need fixing."

"Not even close to what I meant."

She propped her broom against a seat and slumped onto the carpet with me, shoulder to shoulder. She counted slow and steady while I breathed, the way I taught her the first time she found me hunched in a corner, hyperventilating. Five seconds in. Pause. Five seconds out. Repeat.

After a few rounds of inhales and exhales, she said, "How are we doing?"

"Better. Not perfect. But decent."

"Okay. Good. Most people would kill for decent."

She bumped my shoulder with hers, smirking, then vaulted up from the ground. I joined her, rising slowly, dusting off my work pants.

"Thanks for that," I mumbled as we headed for the exit. "Sorry I'm so annoying."

She looked me dead in the eyes. "Fiona. Do I waste time with people who annoy me?"

I didn't answer.

"I'm serious. When someone annoys me, do I waste a single second on them?"

"Not unless you're yelling."

"Exactly. So don't talk about yourself like you're some burden. I don't want to hear it again."

I don't know what happened from that moment to this one, but there are more important questions to answer tonight. And they start by finding our mystery guest.

They have to be *somewhere*. I continue my search, running into each theater and checking each row in case they're crouching behind seats. Then I move onto the next one and repeat the process. But I'm coming up empty.

I'm almost done inspecting the final row of the final theater—for the third time—when the screen bursts to life. A spray of light. An explosion of sound. I stumble backward, my legs heavy beneath me.

"Stop it. Come on. What are you doing?"

Faith. That's Faith. Her voice booms from every speaker, shaking the floor, stopping my heart cold.

I haven't heard her voice since her number was reassigned. I used to call her every single night while brushing my teeth, just to hear her voice message: *"If I'm not picking up, I must have a good reason, so don't bother trying again."* I can't count the amount of times Mom and Dad yelled at her about changing it, so she didn't look unprofessional when *future employers* called her. She argued it didn't make a difference when she was being forced to work at the theater. They never came up with a counterargument.

"I'm filming the first episode of our travel vlog," the girl behind the camera says, and I trip toward the screen with my arm outstretched. My fingers skim the fabric, tracing my sister's chin. Her face stretches across the theater, larger than life.

"Nuh-uh. Turn that thing off," Faith replies, but instead of raising her palm to shield the camera, she poses, Vogue-style. "I don't want you filming unless you're capturing my good side."

"If I found a bad one," her friend says, "I'd get a refund on this camera because it *must* be defective."

Faith laughs, flashing the uneven teeth she usually hid behind close-lipped smiles. "Why do I have to be cursed with liking the douchiest guys? You're clearly my soulmate."

"Friends can be soulmates, too. Besides, you're not my type."

"You wound me." Faith clutches her heart, faux hurt. "By the way, how is this a travel blog? We're still on shitty, soul-sucking Long Island."

"Not for long. I have a surprise."

Faith taps her empty wrist. "I'm waiting, Perry."

Perry? I squint, picturing her glossy red hair and plaid, pleated skirts. Since she never stepped foot in our house, the closest I came to seeing the two of them interact were their one-sided phone conversations. My sister would sprawl across the bed on her stomach or paint her nails while propping the phone against her shoulder, gossiping about hookups and period cramps and hot actors. She never laughed with anyone the way she laughed with Perry.

"Ta-da," the girl says now, her freckled arm appearing on screen. Two tickets wave in front of the camera, blurry until the lens refocuses. PARIS, FRANCE is stamped across the top. One-way. Booked for the end of June, days after graduation.

The room spins, my vision gone fuzzy. Why wouldn't Faith mention a vacation to us? Was she going to spring it on our parents at the last second, so they weren't able to stop her? Was she going to call from the plane once they've already landed? Or was she going to keep it a complete secret, disappear on us in the middle of the night without explaining why?

On screen, Perry flips the tickets to show Faith, and she squeals. "Are we seriously doing this?"

"We're doing this! I have joint hotel rooms booked, close enough to see the Eiffel Tower from our balconies. I figure, we'll stay until we're bored, then head to Britain. Italy. Greece. Throw a dart at a map and I'll take you there."

"I fucking love you," Faith says, charging toward her friend with her arms outstretched.

Then the camera cuts. The screen snaps to black.

And I snap to my senses, bolting up the carpeted theater steps to the top aisle. The intruder must be hiding out in the projection booth. It's the only way they could've played the footage. And the only way they could've *gotten ahold of* the footage was if they recorded it themself.

I race to the window where the projector is installed and cup my hands over the glass, but the machine blocks my view. There's no back door connecting the room to any of the individual theaters, so I need to take the long way—out the door, up the stairs, down the hall.

I fly down the steps, tripping and catching myself on an armrest. I limp down the rest of the steps, then pick up the pace once I'm on level ground, zipping out of the theater with my heartbeat pounding in my ears.

With each thump, it feels like I'm coming closer and closer to solving this mystery.

I just hope Perry is on my side.

CHAPTER 19

EVAN

"He's dead. I think he's dead," Raven repeats into the walkie. I haven't answered her, haven't been able to pry my feet from the ground.

She could be wrong. Cameron could be fine. He *had* to be fine. He couldn't drop dead before getting clean and hearing his band on the radio and moving into a new place without the ghosts of his parents to haunt him. It wouldn't be right.

I can't wrap my head around him dying so young, so sudden—not even in a practical sense. Did Fiona trap him in the hallway and gun him down? I didn't hear a shot. She didn't have a silencer attached to the barrel.

I scramble to check the security cameras, hoping to catch the killer fleeing the scene. Instead, I find Fiona pacing back and forth in a theater, her OCD dialed up to one hundred. When her symptoms spiked the night before big tests and presentations, I would calm her down with bad Dad jokes and cat videos. I wish fixing tonight was that simple—but she's not my concern right now. Cameron is.

Since the security cameras aren't any help, I tear out of the office and across the lobby, following the map from my memories. The only elevator is located on the west side of the concession stand. It's reserved for crates, not bodies, but we used to ride it anyway.

I stumble to a stop when I reach Raven. She's kneeling on the ground, tears streaking her cheeks.

I circle around her to peer into the elevator. A shovel is propped against the wall, its blade spotless. Beneath it, a man is crunched up with a slash in his shirt, a gash in his chest. Blood snakes down his torso, forming a crimson pool around him.

My gut twists, bile rising in my throat. I gulp it down and force a straight face, holding myself together for Raven's sake.

"I took a look upstairs," she chokes out. "The projection room was locked, but there wasn't anything in the lockers or the break room. I figured I would ride the elevator down, but the button wouldn't work. That meant the gate was open at the bottom." She pauses, gulping down air as tears streak her cheeks. "I ran downstairs to check inside. We used to store a bunch of junk in there to keep it out of the way of the customers, remember? I thought she might've dropped the capsule there. But I found *him*."

"I guess he didn't desert us after all," I say, staring at his clean-shaven jaw, his crisp suit. Even in death, Seth Adams looks completely put together. "Fiona couldn't have done this. Who else is in the building?"

"I don't know," Raven says, shivering like a chihuahua as she shoves herself onto her feet. "But we need to leave before whoever it is comes back and finishes off the rest of us."

I can't argue with her. She isn't going to listen to reason with her ex-boyfriend sprawled out on the floor. Besides, now that there's a body, walking away is probably our best option. We need to get to the phone.

When the police show, they're going to be more concerned with this murder than the one from ten years ago. Luckily, out of everyone in the building, I have the least incentive to kill Seth. We haven't hung out in years. He didn't even introduce me to his wife at the memorial dinner.

Then again…

I'm the last person on his call log. I spammed him with texts when we arrived on the property. The police are going to have plenty of questions about why we were meeting in a forest in the middle of the night. We could show them the group text, confess someone lured us to the spot, but we would need to explain why the coordinates were important. Which meant explaining the capsule.

I rake my fingers through my hair, tugging at the roots. The police-paranoia that hit after we found Faith comes whooshing back. I was terrified of getting pulled over for rolling through a stop sign or having an expired inspection sticker slapped on my windshield. Every interaction with the cops was an accident waiting to happen. It was safest to dodge them, even if it meant making my life more inconvenient by taking back roads and avoiding detoured streets.

Or trapping myself in a theater with a bloodthirsty killer.

"We can't leave without Cameron," I say, stalling. "Where the hell is he?"

She raises her walkie to her lips. "Cameron. Do you hear me? We need to leave. Come on."

She swaps the radio with her keys. They dangle from her small, shuddering fist, jangling with each stride she takes.

"Where are you going?" I ask.

"To the car. He can meet us outside. I wouldn't be surprised if he's out there already."

"No way. We came together, we leave together. What if he got hurt?"

"Sticking around is too dangerous, Evan. It's not our job to—"

An extra pair of footsteps echo across the tile, stopping us short. Raven gasps. I smush a finger against my lips, shushing her.

The footsteps continue, a heavy clomp-clomp-clomping. It can't be Fiona in her flimsy ballet flats. It must be someone else, someone new. A millisecond later, my suspicions are confirmed. A man with shoulder-length hair strides into the lobby.

It has to be the intruder Fiona saw on screen. The person who lured us here.

Bolting toward the front *or* back exit would put us directly in his eyeline, so I slink through the closest door. The elevator. I climb over Seth, squeezing myself against the side wall, then wave Raven over. We're forced to straddle his corpse to fit.

The stench of blood gags me, sharp and sickly sweet. It soaks into my shoes, staining the stems. I study the control panel to avoid looking at him, pretending there's nothing more than rotting meat below me. Then again, that's not far off. This morning, he was a father, a husband, a respected businessman. Now, he's nothing but flesh.

Raven cups her mouth as she crouches over him. She reaches beneath his suit jacket, blinking back tears as blood snakes onto her hands. She rummages in his inner pocket, removing his cell. A wedding photo smiles up from his lock screen, the happy couple kissing on a rocky, white sand beach.

She winces, and I imagine what must be flicking through her mind. The evenings spent snuggling against his chest while we were out smoking joints, his jacket unzipped and wrapped around her to keep warm. The mornings spent passing notes in class, then making out against lockers in between periods, putting on a show that made everyone in school jealous. The forehead kisses. The cuddles. The late-night pillow talks. Intimacy in every form.

I think of what my mother said earlier. *Love like that never goes away.*

Raven taps the emergency button, replacing the wedding photo with a red screen. "I'm calling the police," she rasps.

We're pressed so close together that I can hear the officer on the other end of the line. The guy at the station yesterday, who requested a blowjob.

"We need help," Raven whispers after he asks for her emergency. "You need to get down here. Please. We're trapped at the movie theater, Flynn Family Films, with a dead body. Seth Adams. He was stabbed. The murderer might still be in the building. We're not safe."

"A dead body?" he repeats, excitement laced in his voice. "What's your name, ma'am?"

"Raven Clark. You know me. We went to high school together. Fiona and Evan and Cameron are with me. And another man just broke into the building. I'm not sure who."

"Did you say O'Connor is with you?"

"Evan? Yes, she's right here."

He sucks on his teeth, drawing out a pause. "Unfortunately, no one else is at the station with me. We'll get down there as soon as possible, but our other officers are busy setting up speed traps and rescuing kittens from trees."

You've got to be kidding me. I rub my eyes beneath my glasses, seeing spots.

Raven rattles her head. "You don't understand. There's a dead body under my feet. There might be more bodies soon. You need to get down here."

"We will. We'll be there as soon as possible. Could be ten minutes. Could be thirty."

"But you—"

The line goes dead.

Raven flinches. "What was that?" she asks, breathless. "What did you do to him?"

"Nothing. He's an asshole. He never liked me."

"Like Fiona doesn't like you? And Faith didn't like you? Why does it always come back to you pissing people off?"

"It's not my fault they're sensitive."

She juts out her chin. "Evan. We're not teenagers anymore. We're pushing thirty. Don't you think you should grow up a little? Look what you're doing to Fiona. You two were best friends, even better than me and you were, and you've been nothing but horrible to her."

"I'm just trying to protect her."

"From *what?*"

"Forget it," I grumble, flicking my wrist.

We need a distraction. Something to occupy the stranger long enough for us to sneak to safety. I try the walkie, but Cameron doesn't answer. I can't call him when his phone is in the pit, either. But someone else might be able to help.

"Give me the phone," I say. "I can get us out of here."

"How?" Raven asks.

"Not *everybody* hates me."

She squints, reading my mind. "How is your *girlfriend* going to help us?"

"She's close. She lives right behind the woods."

Raven massages her temples, up to *here* with me, but she passes me the phone. I dial, thankful Brooke made a joke about her number's weird alternating pattern during our bar date. *Every other number is a four because I'm un-four-getable,* she said, and I kissed her to make the puns stop.

I wait for one ring. Two. Three. Then my nerves kick in. I would never answer a number I don't recognize. I would let it go to voicemail, check it later.

Luckily, she's not like me. She picks up at *five.*

"Hey. Brooke. It's Evan."

"Oh. Hey," she whispers. "Perfect timing. My little devil just fell asleep, so we don't have to keep it PG. Why are you calling from—"

"Good. You're home. I need some help." It comes out in a rush, but we're short on time. "There's a fuse box at the back of the movie theater, near their dumpsters. I need you to cut through the woods and shut down the main breaker to kill the electricity. Then run back to your apartment. Don't hang around the building. Get out."

Any advantage will put us in a better position. If the theater is pitch black, it'll be easier to escape. We'll be ready for the outage, and he'll be frantic, wondering who cut the lights, whether there's more people in the building than he realizes.

"I don't understand," Brooke says.

"Just trust me. Please. You need to hurry."

"Evan. You're freaking me out. Tell me what's going on."

"I don't have time. I'll explain later if you just do this one thing for me."

I hear her mouth opening and closing.

"Are you there?" I ask. "Are you coming?"

Finally, she says, "I'm not going to trespass and destroy property, Evan. It's illegal. And expecting me to do that *today,* on the day of the memorial? Their family is going through enough. It's kind of a gross thing to ask."

My stomach drops to the floor. "Sorry. You're right. Forget it," I say, hanging up.

I should've realized how this would look from the outside. Not that it looks any better from the *inside*. Calling her was a mistake. A waving red flag. She's never going to want to see me again.

Of course, I might not be alive for her to make that choice.

"She wouldn't be able to make it for a while, so there's no point in her coming," I lie to Raven while craning my head, peeking out the door. The stranger is still out there, pacing back and forth, swinging closer and closer. It won't be long until he passes the elevator. "We can't stay cooped up in here. Eventually, we'll be along his route. He'll have a clear view of us."

"What are we supposed to do, then?"

"We obviously can't wait for anyone to come save us," I say, feeling for the box cutter in my pocket. "So, I guess we'll need to handle this ourselves."

CHAPTER 20

FIONA

I sprint into the hallway, beelining toward the stairwell at full speed. I'm halfway down the eastern wing when a crash sounds from the storage room. My heart stops. So do my steps. Perry couldn't have relocated from the projection room to the storage room that quickly. Unless she pressed *play* on the video, then took off while I was frozen, gawking at the screen.

I can't let her get away again.

Trembling legs lead me toward the swinging metal door. With both hands on the pistol, I nudge it open with my hip, then creep inside. Rows of tall, skinny pantry racks are half-empty, stripped of their napkins and tray holders. Spare ketchup and mustard packets are scattered across the floor. Cardboard boxes, sloshing with syrup bags, are knocked from their stacks.

I scan the room, searching for Perry's long red hair, but find a mop of brown.

Cameron balances on the pantry rack with one foot on the shelf. His other leg is bent, his sneaker sticking out at an angle. He glances over his shoulder as he unlatches the window, grunting when we make eye contact.

"No. Get down," I say with the same tone reserved for the cat. I storm toward him, but it only makes him scramble faster. He hitches the window and hikes his knee, trying to launch himself outside.

I sweep the gun across him. I could shoot, lodge a bullet in his leg and send him crashing to the floor. But it's hard to aim with him squirming. I might miss and hit his stomach or chest or the back of his head.

I groan, holstering the gun. He's smaller than me, lanky but no more than one hundred pounds, so I lunge toward him. I wrap my arms around his dangling leg and wrench him backward. Hard. The rack wobbles as he clutches the railing, trying to hold himself in place. I tug once more, dragging him to the ground.

I fall with him, landing hard on my shoulder. We're crumpled on the ground next to one another, me on my back and him on his stomach, panting hard. The rack teeters above us. I'm worried the shelves are going to topple and crack open our skulls, but the structure remains standing, spilling a few more napkins and condiment packets.

Cameron's palm crushes one as he scrambles away from me, squishing ketchup between his fingers. I lean forward and lurch for him again, but he shoots out his sneaker and strikes me in the teeth. My jaw aches, my vision spotty with stars. Once the room comes back into focus, I grope for the gun.

With my teeth gritted, I fire toward the ceiling, hoping the bullet doesn't bounce back and hit me. My shoulders jerk. My ears ring. Dark liquid sprays across the floor. I gag, mistaking it for blood, but it's only soda. The bullet pierced one of the syrup bags.

Cameron plugs his fingers in his ears, crab-crawling toward the wall like a cornered animal. It's hard to hear him over the high-pitched ringing, so I have to read his lips: "Please don't kill me, man. If there was anything more to tell you, I would. I don't know anything else about Faith. I swear."

I inspect him from top to bottom, searching for signs of lying, but I always trusted him the most out of the three. I liked Raven, but she was so polite it could sometimes feel fake. Of course, that hollowness was worlds better than Seth, who wouldn't say more than two words to me. But Cameron would yammer on about concerts and celebrities and video games, anything that popped into his head. Despite everything, I believe him.

But that doesn't mean I'll free him. I inspect the room—the pantry shelves and the utility carts and the walk-in freezer. I unclip my keys and finger through them, finding the correct one.

I push myself onto my feet and stagger toward the freezer to unlock the thick, insulated door. Inside, frost hangs from the ceiling. Boxes of ice cream bites and burgers are stacked from corner to corner.

"Go on," I say, motioning with the gun. Even from a few steps beside it, my breath frosts.

Cameron hesitates, his mouth dropped wide.

"That last one was a practice shot. Do you really want me to try again?"

I'm not sure whether he can hear me, but he can guess what I want. He lumbers inside, goosebumps sprouting on the back of his neck. He's going to get frostbite if I leave him in there too long. I shut the door halfway, then pause. I strip off my top coat, the puffy one with heating pads in the pockets, and toss it to him. I have other layers.

He flounders to shove his arms through the sleeves, which are twice his size. He looks like a little kid playing dress-up. "How long until you let me out?" he asks, crossing his arms and rubbing warmth into them. His voice is muffled, like he's talking underwater, but at least I can make it out.

"Until your friends tell me the rest of their story. Where are they? Did they leave the building?"

"They shouldn't have. We were looking for the capsule. Raven checked upstairs. I checked the concession stand and this place. Then I heard them say something about a dead body. I switched off the walkie so the killer wouldn't overhear it and grab me next, then bolted for the closest exit. I didn't want to risk walking back out in the open. We should've been gone already, but they don't listen."

"Wait. Slow down. They found a body? Whose body?"

"I'm guessing Seth." His voice catches on the name. He sniffles and swipes his nose with his knuckles, his eyes rimmed with water. "We shouldn't have come here. I didn't want anything to do with the capsule or necklace or whatever. I told them fifty times. They don't listen."

"What necklace?"

"That's how it started. Somebody ordered a necklace from Evan's store under your sister's name and had it sent to my place. And Raven's hairstyle website got hacked. And someone made a prank appointment with Seth's wife."

That explains why he confronted me in his driveway. And why Evan was weird about my jewelry at the bar. But it's the first I'm hearing about a website.

"I'm sorry about this," I say to him, wishing one of the less cooperative ones could take his place. "I'll try to be quick. But I need you to turn your walkie back on, okay? I might need you later."

He nods, and I seal the door, locking him inside. On my way to the exit, I tap open a browser on my phone. I pull up the bright purple site for *Raven's Beauty Shop And Salon.* Her makeup and hairstyling photos have been replaced with shots of my sister. The first one is the photo from the newspapers, her beaming in her graduation cap and gown. She never made it to the stage, but a photographer snapped our senior portraits at the beginning of the year, so she got to play the part.

The rest of the photos aren't from her social media. In one, she's wearing a silky robe emblazoned with the initials PLP. In another, she's posing in a sweater and tennis skirt. The court behind her looks fancy, the type that would be found at a luxury spa or three-story house in the Hamptons. None of our relatives owned a home anywhere near that size. And our only vacations were to amusement parks where we stayed in cheap, generic hotel rooms.

It must be where Perry lived. If I had any doubts about her luring us here, the photos confirm it.

I wish I knew more about her, but she was a mystery to me. Faith never went into detail about their hangout sessions. She would simply disappear for hours, returning with wet hair or henna tattoos or a new ear piercing.

"Where are you going?" I asked one morning, clipping a magnetic name tag onto my collar. Our shift started in twenty minutes, but Faith was dressed in a low-cut sundress and gladiator sandals.

"I'm getting pedicures with Perry," she said, rolling up a beach towel. "Then we're going to lounge around her pool. It's private. Nothing like the piss-filled hole where Mom and Dad used to take us."

"Aren't you on schedule with me today? You're going to get in trouble."

"What are they going to do, fire me? They'd be doing me a favor."

I sighed, not wanting an eight-hour lecture from my parents about how I should've talked sense into her. "Don't you want to save, so you have spending money for college? Those paychecks add up."

"I'm lucky if I can afford a pack of gum with one. Besides, who says I'm sending out applications?"

"Wait." I leaned forward. "Are you serious?"

She shrugged, picking at her cuticles. "Plenty of rich, successful people quit after high school. Most of the stuff I've learned was outside of the classroom, anyway. I taught myself French on the computer. Some Italian, too."

"I thought you'd be jumping up and down to leave. All you talk about is moving out."

"I am. Just. Forget it." She shouldered her bag. "You can tell Mom and Dad I'm sick. If they ask. I doubt they'll notice I'm missing."

"Of course they will. What are you talking about?"

"All they care about is you and how great you're doing in school. Or you and how bad you're doing with your anxiety crap. Either way, they'll be fine with you there."

"Faith," I started, but she stormed out the door, too stubborn to hear me out.

If she honestly thought they loved me more, she was wrong. Her death proved it. Our parents insisted on staying in this town, even though neighbors swore I was a murderer. They held memorials every year, even though it destroyed any chance of me healing. For the last decade, all they cared about was Faith.

It's too bad she wasn't around to see it.

CHAPTER 21

EVAN

Five minutes crammed in an elevator with a corpse and his high school sweetheart is five minutes too long. I tiptoe toward the door with my pocket knife clutched in hand, careful not to stomp on Seth.

"Do you *want* to get yourself killed?" Raven whispers, grabbing ahold of my arm. "You can't attack him. We should just go. We can make a run for it."

"We aren't getting around him without being spotted. If he has a gun too, we're screwed the second he sees us."

"Then we can wait until he leaves. Or ride the elevator to the next floor."

I shake my head. "We can't close the gate without making noise. Sending the elevator up would make even more noise. He'd meet us upstairs and we'd be fish in a barrel."

"Then we'll come up with something else. We're not *murderers*, Evan."

"He thinks we are. He knows what we did to Faith. He lured us here, and he's going to pick us off one-by-one. Do you really want him to get away with that?"

"The police will handle it," she groans.

"They'll handle our bodies when we're added to the death tally."

She sucks in a deep breath through her nose but uncurls her fingers, releasing her hold on me. It's hard to argue on top of a corpse.

I slide the box cutter's handle, extending the blade, and peek out the door. The man is making his way toward the opposite end of the concession stand. I can circle around the back and catch him off-guard. He won't see me coming.

I creep out of the elevator, walking on my toes, so my clacking heels won't give me away. It's like when we used to play manhunt, stealthily slipping from one hiding spot to the next, trying not to get caught. Moving slow. Breathing slow. Aware one wrong move could leave us vulnerable.

I follow the curve of the concession stand, trying to make out whether there's a gun on him, whether I can disarm him without either of us shedding blood, when a crash reverberates through the lobby.

It sounds like it came from the storage room, but his head snaps every which way, his dark eyes landing on me.

I clench up, recognizing him, and raise the knife toward his neck.

"Whoa. Whoa," he sputters, throwing up his hands. "Take it easy."

"Whatever you have on you, I need you to drop it," I say, creeping closer. I hold the blade high, ready to slash. "I'm not asking twice."

"I don't have anything on me," he says, nostrils flaring now that he's had a moment to process the scene. Process *me*. Jonah clearly isn't my biggest fan, so I can only imagine the swears he's stuffing down now.

"If you don't have anything," I say, "Then you won't mind if Raven searches you."

She steps forward with tiny, cautious steps. "We need to know you're not dangerous," she says, phrasing it like an apology. Like she's as powerless in the situation as him.

An eye twitches, but he nods. "Go for it."

She slips her slender fingers into his jeans, then his coat, flipping each pocket inside out. She dumps everything she collects into a neat pile on the floor. His keys. His license. His cell phone. A pack of spearmint gum. A condom wrapper. Once his pockets are emptied, she runs her hands up and down his thighs and chest, lingering over his abs.

"You're supposed to be frisking him," I say. "Not feeling him up."

She rolls her eyes. "He's telling the truth. There's nothing on him."

"Now that we've established I'm completely harmless, it's your turn. What are you guys doing here?" he asks. "Or, forget that part, why is there blood on your shoes? Because that looks like blood on your shoes."

I press my lips together. If he's the killer, he's already well-aware of what happened to Seth. If he's innocent, it's in our best interest for him to think *we* murdered Seth. It would scare him, and scared people talk.

"You don't get to ask questions," I say, circling him like a shark, tracking blood across the tile. "How did you break into the building?"

"I think I should be asking you two that question. *I'm* a supervisor. *I* have a spare set of keys. *I'm* allowed to be here."

"And how long have you been sneaking around? For an hour? Two?"

"I was at the memorial dinner until twenty minutes ago."

I don't believe him. "What made you stop here?" I ask.

"Fiona texted me."

"She told you to come?"

"She told me she was fine. In a text with a million typos. She always triple-checks what she writes and uses proper punctuation, periods, all that technical junk. I thought she might be drunk, but she bailed from the memorial dinner, and her parents were acting weird, too, so it set off alarm bells. I drove past here on the way home and saw her car parked out front. I wanted to make sure she was okay." He trails off, doing a double take at the ground. "Hold on. That's not her blood, is it?"

"No. Of course not."

But the idea sticks. His chest heaves as he shoves me aside, following the blood trail to the elevator. "Fiona!" he shouts. "Fiona, are you in there?"

"It's not her."

He skids to a stop in front of the elevator, his shoulders dropping. Then he starts gagging and retching, like he's about to vomit. "Who the hell is that?" he chokes out, clutching his stomach.

I lower the blade, letting it flop near my thigh. A real killer wouldn't be so squeamish. He's not involved.

"His name was Seth Adams," Raven says. "He was our friend. This last week, someone has been harassing us. Some of us thought it was

Fiona at first, but we were clearly wrong. She's innocent, but she might be in trouble. Just like us."

He swears, running a hand through his curls.

"What? What is it?" I ask.

"Yesterday," he says, "Fiona's parents wired someone fifty thousand dollars."

My stomach flips. That explains the hair delivered to the Flynns. The mysterious letter that sent them to the police station, sobbing.

"They took most of it out of the theater," he continues. "But they were short, so they borrowed a few grand from me. They were convinced they'd get answers if they cooperated with whoever is trying to squeeze money out of them. They sounded desperate." He heaves a sigh, staring around the lobby. "Now, would you tell me where Fiona went? We need to find her if there's some monster running around the theater. She could be dead next."

"She ran off earlier," Raven says. "But don't worry. If she runs into trouble, at least she's armed."

"I'm sorry, armed?" he sputters. "She has a gun? She doesn't know how to use a gun."

And then the shot rings out.

CHAPTER 22

FIONA

When I leave the pantry, the others are already headed down the hallway, checking rooms one-by-one in search of me. Raven is twiddling with her car keys. Evan has a knife poking out from her palm.

My stomach flutters with nerves, but my weapon will fire faster than they can charge at me with a blade. They would be fighting a losing battle. Still, I unzip my coat, my skin prickling with sweat. Then I zip the whole thing up again.

Down. Up. Down.

Honestly, I'm surprised they stuck it out when they could have escaped the second I slipped away. They must really want the capsule. Which means there must be more to the story than they've shared.

Up. Down. Up.

Even if they were telling the whole truth about the drugs, the pregnancy test and notes are still a mystery. Whoever impregnated my sister could've killed her. Or whoever scribbled those notes could've killed her. I need more puzzle pieces to form a complete picture.

Down. Up. Down.

I groan, fumbling out of my jacket and getting my arms caught in the sleeves. I chuck it across the floor, panting hard.

The girls overhear. Two heads snap toward me in unison. No. Three. Another person comes around the corner. Jonah.

My breath catches. He's not supposed to be here. He's supposed to be home, safe.

"Fiona." He jogs up to me, wide-eyed. "Thank God. I thought you were dead. Why didn't you call me? You told me you were fine."

"I *am* fine," I snap. "You need to leave. I don't want you involved in this."

"I'm already involved." I open my mouth, but he cuts me off. "I lent your parents money. They made me promise not to tell you."

I wince, even though I should've guessed they would wire over money before visiting the station. After ten years without answers from the police, I didn't trust them to handle the coordinates, so why would my parents trust them with the letter?

"You shouldn't have done that," I tell Jonah, but there's no time to argue. Not with a murderer running loose. I turn toward the other two, who are lingering nearby. "Cameron mentioned a body. Where is it?"

Raven's voice goes squeaky. "You were with Cameron? Was that the shot we heard?"

"He's fine. I didn't hurt him. I locked him in the freezer because he tried to run away." The girls narrow their eyes at me, so I gesture toward the radios they stole. "Go on. Ask him if you don't believe me."

Evan unclips her walkie, squeezing the side button. "Cameron? Are you good?"

The speaker crackles. Then a raspy voice comes through. "There's no bullet holes in me, nah, but do me a solid and cooperate with her so we can get the hell out of this place. I don't want to die tonight."

She returns the radio to her hip, huffing. "This way," she says, turning her back to me. I follow her straight down the hall, toward the service elevator. Spotty footprints are spread around the area, from sneakers and high heels. My breath catches, but I shuffle forward to find the source. Arms flopped. Mouth lolled. Eyes forever closed.

His death might be karma, but the sight of his dead body, any body, makes my head swim. Besides, this isn't good news for my family. My parents might be held responsible since they own the theater. And if his wife thought I was the one who sent that weird email to her office, she might point the cops in my direction. It can't help that my last interaction with Seth involved him threatening me. That could be a motive.

"I don't know how he got into the building," I say. "He must've snuck through the back door earlier."

Checking locks is one of my worst habits. I can't sleep without rising three or four times to double-check them. But I left the door propped while I was in the forest, so it was easy to access when I returned. He must've snuck inside to steal the evidence while I was gathering up the others. Maybe that's when Perry snuck in, too. Maybe she's the reason he's dead.

Unless…

I lean forward, stealing another glance at him. Several lines are shredding his shirt. From a knife plunged in and out. "He was stabbed," I say. "It looks like his wound was from a small knife. How long have you been carrying that blade, Evan?"

"You can't be serious." She twists the knife in the air, letting it glint in the light. "It's not wet or bent or dull. It clearly hasn't been shoved into a body. Besides, when would I have even had a chance to kill him? I was in the office until Raven found him."

"By yourself?" I ask, straightening my shoulders. "The whole time? Did anyone else see you there? It doesn't take long to kill someone. A stab and it's over."

"They were doing their own thing. We all were."

"So then, technically, you did have a chance to kill him?"

"Technically, we all did."

I cluck my tongue. "It's just funny how none of this weird stuff was happening while you were gone. For almost ten years, life has been normal. But the second you come back to town, there are weird messages on our phones and letters in the mailbox and more people dying."

"Fine. Don't believe me. Let the cops figure it out."

"You called them?" I squeak.

"There wasn't much of a choice."

My stomach sinks. Once the police get ahold of them, they'll never talk without lawyers. They'll come up with a convincing story. Sell the world another lie. Plus, I might be thrown in prison for holding women at gunpoint, for locking a grown man in a freezer. This could be my only chance to get answers.

"If you give me the real story, you can have the capsule," I say. It shoots out of my mouth fast. Too fast to regret.

Jonah frowns, but Evan and Raven share an amused glance, like they can't believe their ears.

"Okay," Evan says, reaching out her palm. "You've got yourself a deal."

We clasp hands and shake. Her skin is shockingly warm, sending a current of electricity through me. I wait for her fingers to unwrap, but they linger around mine, like she doesn't want to let go. For a fleeting moment, I get a glimpse of the old her, the girl who memorized my food orders and massacred me at *Smash*, who let me borrow her ChapStick and her burnt CDs. That girl would never hurt Seth. Evan is a lot of things, but she's not a murderer.

I clear my throat, yanking my hand away. "Get back in the office," I order, not wanting to look soft.

It's best to keep them away from the corpse anyway. Seth is too much of a distraction. Raven hasn't stopped sniffling since they found him, her eyes moist with film. Even Jonah is nervous, peeling the flesh from his lip.

Evan seems unphased, but she's good at masking her emotions. I might be more shaken than she is, and I have every reason to hate him. Of course, it's not *him* who's going to suffer. His wife and children are the ones who will cry themselves to sleep for weeks, question what went wrong for years.

"Are you sure you're safe with them?" Jonah asks, grabbing my arm before I can follow them through the door.

"Yes. I don't think they hurt Seth."

I think it was Perry. And I think she had her reasons.

I'm curious what she has to say for herself—and hopeful the murder was in self-defense—but I have to compartmentalize, take care of the problem in front of me before moving onto the next. Besides, I think we have the same end goal. To get justice for my sister.

"If someone else is in the building, we need to find them. I can sweep the place," Jonah says.

I rattle my head. "I can't have you walking around unarmed. We only have one gun. I need it, so they don't attack me." I lock eyes with him, frowning. "I know how it sounds, but this is my one chance to get the truth out of them. I need this, Jonah."

He releases a long stream of breath. "I'll stand guard. If I hear or see anyone, I'll bang on the door, and you'll slip me the gun. Got it?"

"Thank you."

With that, I head inside, sealing the door behind me.

Instead of returning to their seats, the women stay standing. Raven shifts from foot to foot, like she's ready to make a run for it. Evan crosses her arms, fingers clenched in tight fists. I squeeze between them and input the combination into the safe, the date that I'd gotten my OCD diagnosis. A code not even my parents would guess. I couldn't risk them uncovering the pistol.

When I remove the capsule, Evan opens her palms, expectant. I shuffle around her, cradling the container against my chest.

"You didn't earn it yet," I say. "Tell me the story first. And don't leave out a single detail."

CHAPTER 23

EVAN

Fiona is never going to be satisfied with an incomplete story. She wants an exciting, big-screen-worthy saga to answer all her questions and give her closure. Offering up a name is the only way she's going to stop digging. Anything less and she's never going to leave us alone.

I take a beat to clear my mind, to wipe away images of Seth with blood seeping through his starched button-down shirt. As vile as it sounds, his death is a blessing in disguise. He isn't around to defend himself—or to face charges—so it doesn't make a difference if she knows the chunks of the story involving him. He would do the same if our roles were reversed. There's no reason for us to go down with his ghost.

"I never mentioned this when we were younger," I start, but Fiona silences me with her hand.

"Talk into the walkie," she says. "I want Cameron to verify whatever you tell me."

"You don't trust him more than me?"

"I do," she says, without missing a beat.

Whatever. I hover the walkie over my lips and start again. "I never mentioned this when we were younger because I didn't think you should hear it from me. But about a month before Faith went missing, Seth told me he got her pregnant."

Fiona chokes out a strangled noise, somewhere between a choke and a laugh. "That's not possible. They weren't a couple. They barely worked any shifts together. She never even mentioned him."

"She wanted to keep their fling a secret. He made her promise not to tell anyone because he was already in a relationship. I caught them in the woods behind the theater when I was taking a smoke break. I didn't see them... *you know*... thank Christ. But I caught them coming out of the trees together."

It was late autumn, the forest dripping with crisp greens, reds, and oranges. Fiona hated when I smoked, so I rushed to finish my cigarette before she noticed me missing from the ticket booth. I was popping evergreen gum into my mouth to mask the stench, ready to head back inside, when laughter echoed from the woods. Curiosity kept my feet planted as two shadows emerged. Seth was rebuttoning his shirt. Faith was tightening her belt. When he saw me, his face crumbled like he was given a bad diagnosis.

"You're not serious," I said, itching to slap him. Raven never skipped a football game, even though Seth was on the bench half the time. She'd been saving for months to surprise him with Giants tickets as a Christmas gift. Plus, she was drop-dead gorgeous and they screwed like rabbits. He couldn't have dreamed up a better girlfriend. "Is there a reason you're cheating on the best thing that ever happened to you?"

"We didn't have sex," he sputtered, his forehead sweaty. "It was only oral."

"Oh. In that case, congrats. Your girlfriend will be thrilled." I whipped toward Faith and her smeared lipstick, her tousled hair. "What about you? Is there a reason you only go for guys who are taken?"

She shrugged, like the conversation bored her. "Single guys are douches. He's cute with Raven."

"Yeah," I said. "With *Raven*."

She rolled her eyes and stormed into the theater. I started to follow her, but Seth begged me to wait. We sagged against the dumpsters and talked, ignoring the walkies on our hip, the managers ordering us to return to our posts. He refused to admit how long they'd been hooking up, but it definitely wasn't the first time. Of course, he promised it would be the last.

"You can't tell her, Evan. It'll break her heart."

"That's on you. She deserves better than a playboy who sneaks around behind her back. I thought she was out of your league before this, but *now*..."

"I know. I swear, it's not happening again. Faith isn't worth it. She's nothing."

"Then why hook up with her? Because you're insecure? Selfish? A self-destructive time bomb?"

"All of the above. I don't have a good answer."

At least he was honest. I wasn't happy about keeping his secret, but I didn't want to get in the middle of their relationship drama. Besides, he was my friend too. We butted heads more than the others, but he chased away handsy drunks who harassed me at concerts. He lent me his jacket when it was freezing. He even made an emergency trip to buy tampons and a clean pair of shorts once when my period came early. The embarrassment he saved me that night alone was worth the favor.

"I blew up on him that day," I explain to Fiona. "I spent twenty minutes telling him what a screw-up he was. I guess I shamed him into staying loyal because he broke things off with your sister. But then she showed up pregnant."

Fiona frowns, tracing her lips with her fingertips. I wait, letting her lead the conversation, choose where it weaves. "Was he angry?" she asks.

I hitch a shoulder, picturing the fear in his eyes, the tremble in his voice. "He wasn't popping champagne over the news," I say. "But he took it relatively well. He came to talk to me about it because I was the only one who knew about him cheating at that time. He told me he wasn't sure whether she wanted to keep the baby or not, but he said he was going to do right by her either way and help her out with whatever she needed. I can't tell you whether he meant it. Maybe he was trying to look like a good guy in front of me to cover his own ass. Who knows what they said to each other in private? He could've killed her. He could've gotten rid of her body so no one could trace back the pregnancy to him."

"What are you doing?" Raven whispers, nudging me in the ribs. "Cut it out."

I ignore her. My focus is on Fiona. She lowered her gun during my monologue. The barrel is tilted toward the ground, like her face, which is twisted in disgust. I wait for more questions about the logistics of the pregnancy, but she turns her attention toward Raven.

"When did you find out he cheated on you?" she asks.

"It was a little while before your sister went missing," Raven says, fiddling with her hoops. "I couldn't tell you the exact day, but I was at work, gushing to Evan about how much I loved him. I told her I was thinking about taking a gap year instead of going straight to college so we could move in together and maybe get married, and Evan was trying to convince me to put my education before boys. Things got a little heated—I accused her of being jealous that I was in a relationship and she was forever alone—so she caved and told me about the pregnancy. She didn't want me to make some huge mistake and ruin my future."

She pauses, her lips scrunched to the side. "I broke up with him later that day. I raced over to his house and pounded on the door. His mom answered and asked what was wrong, so I told her what he did. I didn't see any reason to protect him. I let her know her son was a cheat and she was pissed at him, too. We got along well. That's part of why leaving him was so hard. I thought we would become an official family one day. I thought we were going to be..." She releases a shaky sigh. "Anyway, he wasn't happy that I told on him to his mom or that I believed what Evan told me without talking to him first. It was pretty messy. There was a lot of crying. And cursing. And screaming."

Tears sparkle in her eyes. Probably because the first boy she loved is sprawled out dead in the other room. I had mixed feelings about our group reuniting, but she might've viewed this as an opportunity to reconcile with him, to make peace with the childish ways they hurt each other as teenagers. And now he's gone. She lost her chance.

"I'm sorry," Fiona says. "You guys seemed happy together."

"I thought we were. It's weird, but the reality you're living is nothing like the reality everyone else is living. It's hard to wrap your mind around the fact that someone you love can see your relationship completely differently than you do, but there's nothing you can do except accept it."

Fiona nods, her forehead crinkled and lips pressed together tight. I'm not sure whether Raven is garnering sympathy on purpose, but it's working.

"If we didn't break up because of your sister, we probably would've broken up because of some other girl. We never would have lasted. It wasn't Faith's fault. I don't blame her anymore."

Fiona blinks a few times, like her sight went fuzzy. Then a full-body change comes over her. Every feature hardens, like she's sculpted from ice.

"Those notes in the capsule…" she says. "Did you write those? Were you the one who threatened Faith? Did you kill my sister because she was pregnant with your boyfriend's baby?"

Raven takes a step back. "No, Fiona, no. Of course not. I mean. I was the one who wrote those letters, yes, and I regret it. I never should have taken out my anger on the other girl when he was the one who hurt me. She didn't owe me anything. I barely even knew her. He was the one who made a mistake. Not her."

"Did she know you wrote them? Did she confront you about it?"

"Umm… Yes, actually. A few days before she went missing. I lost my temper and said some more horrible things, but I never hurt her. I wanted *him* dead." She winces, catching herself. "Back *then,* that's how I felt. I'm over it now. It's been a decade. We haven't even been in touch until this week. We're strangers now."

I raise a brow. She *did* shit-talk his wife when we were smoking outside the restaurant. She didn't sound completely over the breakup then.

"Were you relieved when my sister died?" Fiona asks her. "Were you excited she was out of the picture so your boyfriend couldn't live happily ever after with her?"

"I would never be relieved about something so awful."

"Are you sure? You called her a whore."

"There's a difference between wanting her to feel guilty about what she did and wanting her dead. Finding her body was horrific. And when we heard the body was *missing*... It was the worst experience of my life. You have to believe me."

She's lying again.

When news stations reported there were no signs of Faith in the theater or the woods, our group called an emergency meeting to figure out our next move. The forest was bigger back then, but it wasn't a maze. They should have found her. The rain might've wiped away her footsteps, but what about her pocketbook, her phone, her body? Did she get up and leave? Did one of us move her?

Cameron showed up high, barely able to string two words together. Seth rambled about the pros and cons of cooperating with the cops versus keeping the secret to ourselves. I smoked cigarettes, one after another, until my pack ran out. And Raven folded her hands across our picnic bench, the pinnacle of composure.

"This could actually be a good thing for us," she said, and we wanted it to be true, so we waited.

"You already know I wrote some not-so-nice notes to her," she said. "But I never told you guys what happened the day she confronted me about the messages. Faith ran up to me after class, super pissed. She told me it wasn't her fault that my boyfriend was interested in her, that she couldn't help it if she turned him on more than me. I said some mean things back about how she meant nothing to him and how she could only get someone to sleep with her but not date her because her personality sucked. Then she slapped me." Raven unlaced her fingers, talking with her hands as she picked up speed. "I wasn't going to touch her, but then she raised her hand again. I didn't hurt her or anything. I knew she was pregnant and I'm not a monster. I didn't want anything to happen to the baby. I just grabbed her to stop her from attacking me. The best she could do was scratch me up a bit. But I've been worried about her body getting found and her having an autopsy done. If my DNA is still under her nails, the police might think I killed her. I had motive and I had opportunity. We all did. We were all at the theater with her that night. I'm heartbroken for her and her family, but I think it's good for us that her body is gone. I hope they never find it."

Our group fell silent. No one commented about how heartless she was because we secretly agreed with her. Cameron didn't want an autopsy because there might've been drugs in her system. Seth didn't want an autopsy because it would prove she was pregnant. Raven didn't want an autopsy because of what could be hidden beneath her nails. None of us wanted the police to take that close of a look at her.

We parted ways with an agreement to keep what we saw a secret—and to quit the movie theater. We were worried it would look suspicious if we all marched into the office at once, so we were planning to stagger our two weeks. But then our other coworkers quit. Half the staff, gone in twenty-four hours. They were worried a killer was lurking in the woods, waiting to snatch workers from the parking lot. The area was known for being sketchy. There were drug deals at night, petty arrests and noise complaints about couples having quickies in between the trees. It made sense for us to quit together. No one questioned us about the timing.

"What is your problem?" Cameron asks over the walkie, prying me from the memory.

"Me?" I adjust my glasses. "What did I do?"

"You're making it sound like Raven and Seth are guilty. The dude just died. His body is still warm. It's disrespectful, man. I thought we were supposed to be a family."

"I never said anything about Raven," I say. "And Seth isn't here to tell his side of the story, so I'm doing it for him. You were the first one to blab. I'm finishing what you started."

"I was talking about what *I* did back then. I wasn't selling out you guys."

"Everything I've said was true, even if you aren't happy about hearing it. Seth was a cheater. Seth knocked up her sister. And Seth is dead, so what does it matter if she finally knows the truth about the stunts he pulled?"

"He has kids. A wife. A family. They're going to have a hard enough time dealing with him getting murdered. Dealing with rumors on top of that? It's not right. He made some mistakes, sure, but he didn't kill anyone."

"Says who? Can you tell me, for a fact, that I'm wrong about him? Out of all of us, who was the one most likely to attack her? It's not like he had a conscience. He cheated on you, Raven. You treated him like a goddamn king and he snuck around behind your back for months. You still wouldn't have known what he did without me getting involved. That shows what kind of person he was. He only cared about himself."

"Stop," she rasps. A single tear tumbles down her cheek, but she licks it away. "Stop talking. Please. Cameron is right. He just died. We can't talk like this."

"Why not? I know it sucks to hear it out loud, but Seth had to be the one who killed her. Don't you know that, deep down? Isn't that why we buried all that evidence? If all four of us were innocent, really innocent, then why would we go through all the trouble of stealing her shit and hiding the capsule, let alone hiding the fact we found her body? We protected each other because we loved each other. We didn't want anything bad to happen to him because we knew he was a good guy. But we can't keep protecting him anymore. We have to protect ourselves."

The speech does the trick. Cameron goes quiet on the other end of the line. Raven drops her head into her hands, her shoulders heaving.

Guilt surges through me. I don't want to be the monster who makes my friends cry—but neither of them matters in the moment. Fiona is my priority, and she's eating up every word. It might have actually worked. She might actually give us permission to leave—with the capsule. I uncross my arms, eager to head home, but then the lights flicker.

And the world snaps to black.

CHAPTER 24

FIONA

Raven gasps, whipping her head up as the lights cut. Evan shudders beside her. And Jonah pounds the door, asking if everyone is okay.

"We're fine," I call out in a wobbly voice. Light filters through the windows in the rear of the room, bathing us in moonlight. I'm able to see everyone, but they're more shadow than human.

"Damn, it's dark in here," Cameron says over the walkie. "Does this usually happen during storms? The lights at my place flicker whenever there's some wind, but our electric is trash."

I check the window. The skies have been swirling with thick, muddy clouds for days. The air was crisp when we were in the forest, the scent of snow whirling, and it's finally starting to fall. A light dust sprinkles down, speckling the ground, but it's not nearly enough to disturb power lines.

"We have a backup generator," I say. "It turns on automatically, as soon as there's an electrical issue, so that the movies aren't disrupted. Something else must be wrong. There could be a problem with the fuse box. Unless someone cut the lights on—"

"*Evan!*" a woman screams, muffled by the walls.

The breath squeezes out of me. She must be close to the window for us to hear her so clearly, but I don't spot anyone through the panes. I can't place the voice either, but I run through the possibilities, the short list of people who would come here and call for Evan specifically. Only one option makes sense.

"Is that your girlfriend?" I ask, whirling toward Evan. "What on earth is she doing here?"

Evan hangs her head, rubbing her neck. "I called her earlier. Guess she's a little late."

"Why would you call her? You *wanted* her to know you broke onto private property to steal murder evidence? You think she likes you enough to look past that?"

"I thought she could help us escape. I thought it was call her or die."

"So, she knows everything? You told her that I was holding you at gunpoint?"

"Of course not. I was vague. She doesn't know what I wanted."

She winces when Brooke screams again, although it's lower this time. Good. The surrounding shops should be closed by now, but there could be stragglers sharing a smoke or waiting for the bus.

"Listen," Evan continues. "I don't want her involved. She shouldn't be dragged into the investigation on who killed Seth. She wasn't here. She shouldn't be a suspect when the police show."

She's right. I can't risk more people getting wrapped up in this mess. More people who could team up to implicate me.

"Stay here," I say, passing through the door. "I'll get her to leave."

Jonah is waiting on the other side, looking exhausted. Bags hang beneath his big, brown eyes. His lips are cracked. Even his curls have gone limp. "The scream came from the back door," he says. "She must be by the woods."

"All right. Will you keep an eye on them? I'm going to talk to her."

"Are you sure you should be running around alone? At least let me go with you. If they're telling the truth about that body—"

"Then the killer is inside. I'm going outside." I squeeze his arm. "This is almost done. They answered my questions. I got what I wanted. Now, we only need to keep them here until the police arrive. They'll sweep the place, make sure it's safe. And I'll tell them everything Evan told me. I might get in trouble for the gun, but I never hurt anyone. They don't have a scrape on them."

"Okay. I'll back you up," he says. "They're the bad guys here, not you."

I nod and cross through the lobby, caressing the gun, heavy with a full chamber of bullets. I thought learning more about my sister would bring me a sense of peace, but I somehow feel emptier. Like she's officially gone and has taken all hope with her.

When I leave Jonah's eyeline, I raise my arm and press the barrel against my temple. It would only take a second to press the trigger. It would be easy. Easier than living.

I switch off the safety.

No. That's not an option. You can't do that to your family.

Then switch it on.

It should've happened already. You should've died instead of Faith.

Off.

You need to stay alive to avenge *Faith.*

On.

You can't avenge her. Her killer is already dead. You weren't able to put him behind bars. He lived a nice, cozy life in a fancy house with a wife who loved him. You couldn't stop him from hurting your sister. You couldn't stop him from breaking into the theater tonight. You can't even stop yourself from pulling the—

I grab my wrist with my left hand and wrench it down. Before I lose control again, I force open the door. I step outside and travel toward the fuse box, scanning the trees across from me.

Brooke crunches across the freshly fallen snow, still in her suit, wrinkled and sprinkled with dirt. "Fiona!" she calls. "Thank God. Is Evan with you?"

"Evan?" I say, struggling to sound casual. "No. Nobody is with me. I was just doing some inventory work. What are you doing here?"

"I live in the complex, right behind the theater," she says, panting. She looks between me and the building. "Sorry. I'm confused. Evan asked me to come. To cut the lights."

I flutter my lashes. "You're the reason they went out?"

"She called me from a weird number. She sounded like she was in trouble."

"She was probably drunk. Or lying. All she does is lie."

She tilts her head like a confused puppy.

My heart twists, but I can't afford to go easy on her. I ball my fists and clench my jaw, inviting in the anger I've spent most of my life trying to ignore. After all, the most believable stories have some truth in them.

"Did she mention we had an argument earlier?" I ask. "When you left us outside of the restaurant? That's why I drove away. Drove here. I needed to be alone. She said some horrible things to me. Just like when we were kids. When my sister disappeared, she avoided me at school. Ghosted my texts. She didn't stop by the house with a GET WELL SOON card or give me a hug or ask whether I was okay. She moved away without a word. She's not a good person, Brooke."

She rattles her head. "No. That can't be the reason."

"You don't know her."

"That's not what I mean. I tried calling her a million times. It wouldn't go through. Her Snap location says she's at the theater. Well, it actually says she's in the woods, but that can't be right."

I swallow, thinking of her cell, stuck at the bottom of the pit where the capsule was buried. Where this whole thing began.

"I don't know what to tell you," I say. "If she even tried to buy a ticket at the theater, I would kick her out. I don't want her anywhere near me. You should probably stay away from her, too. She's only going to hurt you."

Her forehead creases. She runs her hand through her choppy hair and says, "Right. I... I'm sorry. I didn't mean to bother you."

"It's fine. Just go. Please."

I think I've convinced her. My acting was a success. She's going to leave it alone.

Then I spot the walkie attached to her belt. The walkie she couldn't have possibly stolen—unless she was already inside the theater.

She notices me noticing and lunges forward. Fast as a rattlesnake, her stubby nails cut into my wrists, drawing blood. I yelp and twist to escape, one arm breaking free, but her hold is too strong. I trip forward, losing hold of the gun and landing hard on my palms. The pistol bumps across the ground, sliding into dirt far beyond my reach. I crawl toward it—but her heel kicks it further away.

"That was easy," she says, wiping imaginary sweat from her brow. "Should've done that an hour ago."

I collapse onto my butt as she swipes the revolver. With a wicked grin, she steps under our fluorescent lights, giving me a clearer look at her suit. The dark splatter isn't dirt. It's blood. Seth's blood.

She must have dropped out the emergency exit and circled around the building, then tampered with the lights to lure me outside. Alone.

Before I can exhale a question—about how she broke into the theater, how she knew about the capsule at all—she says, "Now that you're unarmed, we can talk honestly."

I blink. "About what?"

"Evan. What she told you about your sister isn't true. Seth didn't kill her."

"How would you know? You didn't even meet Faith."

She fake-pouts. "Oh, Fiona… I knew her better than anyone."

I cock my head, raking my eyes across her, and it clicks. Cobwebbed memories come surging back. Her laughing with Faith during lunch breaks, her long legs rustling in her plaid uniform, her red hair flowing down her shoulders. She sounds different than in her home video, her voice deeper, raspier. But if I squint, I can make out the freckles hidden beneath her tattoos.

"Perry?" I whisper.

A laugh bursts out. "Took you long enough. I'd give you the benefit of the doubt, since it's pitch black, but you didn't recognize me earlier, either. I gambled on that happening, though. People are simple. They boil you down to one thing. The redhead with freckles. The rich girl in the uniform."

She steps further into the patch of light. Then she pinches her eye and pops out a contact. The color changes. One brown. One green.

"Colored contacts," she explains, flicking it onto my lap. "Hair dye. Haircut. Tattoos. Contour to change the shape of my nose and cheeks. There are a million little ways to turn yourself into a new person, but I don't want to give myself too much credit. Hiding in plain sight, when you barely paid attention to me in the first place, wasn't much of a challenge."

"I didn't get the chance to pay attention to you," I say. "You were never at the house."

"Faith was embarrassed for me to see your place when mine is three stories with an indoor pool and tennis court. I think she was embarrassed about your family, too. She told me I was more of a sister to her than you ever were."

"Does that mean you know what happened to her? Is that why you're here?"

A nod. "I was the last person who saw her before she died. I sat with her. Held her hand. Told her everything was going to be okay. She was scared, but she was brave. You should be proud of her."

"You're admitting you killed her? It was you?"

She laughs, but there's no humor in it. "No. No one killed her. Although they tried pretty damn hard."

"I don't understand. What are you saying?"

"Let me rewind." She crouches in front of me, spreading her knees and letting the gun dangle between her legs. She looks comfortable with a weapon. Like she's handled one before. "The day your sister was 'kidnapped' wasn't the day she died. She lived for months after she went missing. The baby made it, too."

"I don't..."

"She was torn up over the way Evan and the others treated her, but she begged me not to contact the police. She didn't want to go back home and face you and your parents and neighbors. She decided she would hide out with us until she gave birth, then give up the baby for adoption and return home. That way, no one would ever realize she was pregnant. It would save her the embarrassment. In fact, it would make her a small-town star. Everyone would be thrilled to have her back home after her brush with death. She would be sitting pretty."

No, that can't be true.

"If her plan was to come home, why didn't it happen?" I ask.

"She died during childbirth. It's bittersweet, isn't it? She lost her life, but she created a life in the process. I named her little girl Destiny. It's corny, sure, but it was the least I could do to honor her."

"No…" I tighten my fists, trying to stop my eyes from spilling over with tears—for my sister *and* my niece. I can picture her. A scrunchy-faced newborn with dimples and amber eyes. Of course, the girl wouldn't be so little anymore. She would be grown now, a pre-teen, only a few years younger than Faith when she was ripped away from us.

But her existence is too good to be true. It's only another lie.

"If she was safe and sound for nine months after she went missing, then she would've contacted me," I pant. "She wouldn't have made us wait to figure out what happened to her. She would know how worried we all were. She never would've put my parents through that. Or me."

"I don't think you know your sister as well as you think you do. In any case, I had a feeling you would be suspicious, so I brought some proof. I thought the video I played earlier would be enough to earn your trust, but you're as stubborn as Faith was."

She rummages through the crossbody bag at her hip, extracts a stack of papers, and drops them onto my lap. The sconce hanging overhead illuminates every word, sending my heart crashing to a stop. I would recognize her writing anywhere. The way she dotted her I's with hollow bubbles. The way she curved the bottoms of her letters like she was writing in script instead of print.

"She kept a diary while she was with us," Perry says. "She wrote most nights."

My pupils fly across the page as snow flurries down, smearing the ink. I want to savor her words, stretch them like taffy and make them last, but I'm desperate to devour the last remaining pieces of her.

"I wonder whether my parents have been worried about me," it says. *"I bet they've been doing a lot of crying. Fiona, too. I'm sure Evan is using it as an excuse to cozy up to her, cuddling in our room and kissing away her tears. It's not fair my goodie-goodie sister gets straight As and clear skin and a goddamn girlfriend without even trying. Without even* noticing. *Whatever. Let her cry. Let her blame herself. And our parents? They've screwed me over for years, so I'm not going to feel guilty about doing what's best for myself. Maybe they'll appreciate me more after suffering through a few months without me. Or maybe I'll change my mind by the time the baby is due and refuse to go back. Like Perry always says, you choose your real family."*

My gut twists, like she thrust her hand inside and squeezed. Faith was always throwing snarky comments around—about me passing tests without practice flashcards, or selling a dozen loyalty cards during a single shift—but I didn't think she actually cared. It's not like my accomplishments minimized hers.

I keep reading, the next entry dated later that week: *"Finally, some good news: I'm the most popular girl in NY! My photos are splashed all over the local channels—my senior portrait and the full-body one from junior prom that makes my butt look great. My FB and Insta are blowing up with people worried about me, mostly girls but hot guys too. Plus, there are all the search parties. Perry's been worried that not showing up would make my parents suspicious, but I don't want her to slip up around them and ruin our whole plan, so she's faking an illness to get out of it. I need to start figuring out my own lies, about what I'll tell everyone when I go home—maybe a kidnapper locked me in a basement—but people will wonder why there aren't any scars or bruises on me. It might be easier to fake memory loss. Pretend I have no idea what happened so no one can poke holes in the story. Either way, when I get back, they'll never confuse me with Fiona again."*

I feel sick, so I skip to her later entries. Most of them revolve around the baby. Her pregnancy cravings. Her stomachaches. Her sore breasts. With each passing page, she sounds more and more agitated.

Her final entry is messy, scrawled with a quick hand. It says: *"I'm going to have the baby soon. It could happen any moment now, even while I'm in the middle of writing this. I'm sure it's going to hurt like a motherfucker, but it'll be nice to have my body back again. I hate feeling like someone else is in control, like we're sharing the steering wheel. I don't want to be this baby's mother. Just like I don't want to be Fiona's twin. I don't want to be tethered to some other human for the rest of my life. I just want to be me."*

I clutch my side, sick to my stomach. I want to run the papers through the shredder, pretend I never learned about this side of my sister. But she's not around to focus my rage on. Perry is.

"You're not her friend. You're her murderer," I croak. "You had no right to keep her hidden at your house. She didn't belong with you. You should've let her come home. Sure, our parents might've been mad about the baby at first and some people in town might have talked, but we would have gotten through it. Together. There was no reason for her to stay with you. To die with you. You could've taken her to a hospital, at least. If she had real doctors around, she wouldn't have died while giving birth. She would still be alive. It's your fault she's gone."

My chest is on fire. If I still had the revolver, I would empty it into her gut.

"Deep breaths, Fiona." She smirks. "I understand your emotions are high right now. But your sister was nearly eighteen. In fact, she turned eighteen while she was with me. She was an adult. She could make her own decisions. And she decided to stay with me. She decided to give birth at my big beautiful house, in secret, so she wouldn't have any legal ties to the baby."

"What happened to her? To Destiny?" She could be lying about the baby. Or she could be lying about how my sister died. She could have killed Faith and wrenched the baby from her limp, lifeless arms. "You kept her, all this time?"

"We had more than enough room for her. My father was always on business trips and my mother died when I was young from a tumble down the stairs. No one realized Faith was in the house, except for our maid, who didn't want me to have her deported. So it stayed our secret.

"When the baby came, it was easy enough to pass her off as mine. My father gave me an extra credit card for toys and diapers, but when he passed last year, he left me debt instead of an inheritance. Without anyone around to help with the bills, I've been low on money. Kids are expensive. Between the food and clothes and rent, I barely have enough left over to buy her toys or take her to the movies. I just want her to grow up happy."

There we go. The reason she came back. Not to set things right. Not to reunite us. For money.

"I considered moving back here permanently to get help from your parents. I almost rang their doorbell a million times, but I couldn't gather up the courage to tell them the truth. I knew they wouldn't care about Destiny growing up with me for nearly ten years. They wouldn't care that I'm the only family that little girl has. They would have me arrested for kidnapping since we never signed any formal adoption papers. I couldn't risk them ripping my little girl away from me, so I took a safer approach."

"You sent my parents a ransom note. You used their grief against them."

"I felt horrible about it, obviously, but I knew they would *want* their granddaughter to receive the best care possible. I almost skipped town once their payment went through, but I figured I could squeeze out a little extra cash before going on my way. From the others, not you. You were only invited so they would cooperate."

"What do you mean?"

"I'm going to blackmail them into buying my silence. Call it another way to honor Faith. They don't get to hurt her and walk away clean." She latches onto my arm, dragging me onto my feet. "Up you go. Let's finish this."

CHAPTER 25

EVAN

Once Fiona leaves us alone in the blacked-out office, I snatch the capsule from the ground, hugging it against my chest. It's disgusting, musty-smelling and crusted with dirt, but it's mine. We can get rid of it, get home, and get back to our normal lives.

"Okay, Jonah, we told her the story," I call through the door. "You can let us out now."

"That wasn't part of the deal," he says. "You need to stick around until the police get here."

"What do you mean? We need to get rid of the capsule before they show up or this whole thing was pointless."

I wonder if that was the plan. If Fiona never planned to meet us halfway. The cameras weren't programmed to record, so she'd look guilty as sin if she was alone in the building with the body. She couldn't trust that we'd return, tell the truth about our whereabouts and motives.

"Jonah," I try again, my cheek smushed against the door. "If you let us go, we'll tell the police you cooperated. You won't get in any trouble."

"I'm sorry. You're not leaving."

"Why? Because you want to bang Fiona? This isn't going to get her clothes off."

He snorts. "That's not… She's my friend. She asked for a favor."

"Driving somebody to the airport is a favor. Renting a moving truck is a favor."

"Oh, like you didn't do Seth a favor by lying about a dead girl's body?"

I flash a middle finger he can't see. "Do you want to try to talk sense into this guy?" I ask, swiveling toward Raven, who's busy chewing her nails to the quick. "You clearly have a hard-on for him. Maybe you can get him over Fiona."

She sighs, but she approaches the door and attempts to sweet-talk him.

I pace the office, cracking my knuckles, then my neck. I'm hoping to find something, *anything*, we can use to our advantage. Some sort of beam to use as a battering ram and break through the door, or a tool to smash the window.

Unfortunately, with the electricity killed, the room is pitch black. Or close to it. A green light slices through the darkness.

I roam toward the dot, pushing my glasses further up my nose. The glow is coming from beneath a desk, so I drop to a crouch for a closer look.

What the...?

I snatch the walkie lying on the ground. The green light indicates it's turned on, but it's set to a different channel than we've been using. Frequency Two. I turn the device over in my hands. Tape is sealed over the side, holding down the button used for speaking.

My pulse quickens. There were two radios missing earlier. That's one of them. Whoever has the other knows everything we've said when we were in this room. They heard every confession, every truth and mistruth. If they weren't aware of our roles in the murder earlier, they are now.

I lift the device, presenting it to Raven. "Someone planted this here. They've been listening to our conversations."

"What? Why? What are they getting out of this?" She runs a hand over her face, trembling, and calls through the door. "Did you hear that, Jonah? That's even more reason for you to let us go."

"I told you," he says. "I'm not going to—"

The walkie crackles. "Do it," Fiona says through its speakers. "Let them out."

We pause, swapping unsure glances, wondering what triggered the change of heart. But we aren't going to question our luck. When the door creaks open, we join Jonah in the lobby, which is significantly brighter thanks to the glass block windows out front. I take slow, cautious steps forward, cradling the capsule against my chest, worried it's a trap. Raven isn't as subtle. She makes a break for it, flying across the floor and tugging at the doors.

"I would rethink that," a familiar voice says, freezing her.

Fiona shuffles across the lobby, her hair dusted in snow, her palms raised. A woman follows one step behind her, pressing a pistol between her shoulder blades.

"Brooke?" I choke out as she steps into view. My first fleeting, childish thought is: *She showed up to save me. She's holding Fiona at gunpoint because she thinks I'm in danger. She's trying to protect me.* The follow-up thought is: *You're delusional, Evan.*

My stomach churns as the truth sinks in. Brooke sent the text messages. Brooke purchased the necklace. Brooke swiped right on my dating profile, not because she was interested in me, but because she knew what I'd done. Everything between us was orchestrated. Our conversations. Our dates. Our sex.

"The name's Perry. Although I might have to change it after tonight, so call me what you want." It comes out matter-of-factly, like she's announcing she's going to the bathroom. "By the way, Raven, do me a favor and step away from the exit. Or I'll have to shoot you in the head."

Raven doesn't hesitate, skittering toward Jonah so quickly they almost collide. Between the three of us, I'm the only one with a weapon. The box cutter is weighing down my pocket, but I'm not reckless enough to reach for it. Not yet.

"I'm so glad we're finally getting the chance to talk," Brooke—or, apparently, Perry—says. "I was worried I wouldn't be able to gather your whole group together. You're so stubborn. The coordinates were the best way to get your asses moving. I needed to scare you into cooperating."

"Is that why you killed Seth?" Raven swallows hard. "To scare us?"

"Killing him wasn't part of the plan."

"Why should we believe you?"

"Trust me. I would've rather taken his money than his life. He barely had any cash on him and I'd be arrested on the spot if I used any of his credit cards. His death is only an inconvenience."

"Got it," I say, clenching my fists to stop them from shaking. "You want to steal from us. Fair enough. You could've done that without the weird emails, and letters, and texts."

"Blackmail is risky. I was worried you would refuse to pay me. Then I would be forced to tell the police the truth and we would all be screwed. Nobody would've been happy with that ending. I figured it was smarter to give you a taste of how easily I could mess with your lives so you would take me seriously."

"Right. Because ordering a necklace from my e-shop is *so scary*."

Perry barks out a short, shrill laugh.

I wince. Only this morning, I would've killed to hear that sound.

"Give me some credit, Evan. I did my research. I social media stalked you and collected as much information as possible from everyone around town. Your neighbors sure do love to talk about things that are none of their business." A smirk. "I messed with Seth's marriage by emailing his wife. I told her I wanted to set up a therapy appointment about him being unfaithful. I was talking about him cheating on Raven, but I kept it vague so she might think he was cheating on her as well. Who knows? Maybe he *was* cheating. People don't change as much as they like to think.

"The necklace was about Cameron, not about you. I wanted to show him how easy it was to track him down. He tries so hard to stay off the grid, but he can't even remain hidden from a random woman with Google. As for Raven, I know how important the salon is to her, so I hacked into her business page. I graffitied the site with the same names she called Faith to make her lose customers."

Raven flinches, like she's been slapped. Unlike Fiona, there's no doubt in my mind Perry will put a bullet in any one of us. I'm sure she senses it, too.

"What about Fiona?" I ask, pausing to clear my throat. I don't want my voice to crack. "Or me? How did Frenching me help your grand plan?"

"I went to the memorial because Faith was my friend. I miss her. I wasn't purposefully screwing with Fiona. But Destiny and I *did* run into her a few times—at the grocery store, near the theater—and I had to force her to run and hide. She looks so much like Faith that I had to stop bringing her outside." I don't know who Destiny is, but before I can ask, she blabbers on. "As for you, Evan, I messed with your most vulnerable place. Your heart. I was starting to worry you'd drop the L-bomb."

I roll my eyes, but a blush burns my cheeks. Raven reaches out and squeezes my arm.

"If you wanted money, you could've asked for it earlier," Jonah says, stepping forward to guard us. "What was the point in trapping them here all night?"

"I know, I could use a nap too." Perry yawns. "I didn't intend to keep everyone this long. I expected to be out of town by now. The original plan was to cut through my apartment complex and wait in the woods for the group to show up. I thought you would get there around the same time since you were all supposed to be at the memorial dinner. I was going to pop out, give my spiel, and collect my money. But then Fiona showed up ahead of everyone—waving around a gun—so I had to rearrange my plans.

"I snuck into the theater to reassess the situation. Unfortunately, Seth had the same idea. We ran into each other, so I tried to explain everything to him one-on-one, but he wasn't happy about the deal I offered. He tried to bash my head in with a shovel. I had to retaliate. It was me or him.

"After heaving him into the elevator and scrubbing away some blood, I ran upstairs to hide. Luckily, I was able to turn on a walkie to listen in on your conversations. Fiona had arranged chairs in the office, so I figured there was a good chance she would dump you there for an interrogation. I wasn't happy about how much you were babbling, but I was confident you would never reveal the full story. And I was right. In any case, I got impatient. I shut down the lights to separate you."

She shoots a megawatt smile at me. "Thanks for the idea, by the way. I had to tell you *no* when you called so you wouldn't escape early, but it turned out to be a good way to get the gun out of the equation. I almost snatched it when Fiona went looking for me earlier, but it was hard with the rest of you running around too. Like rats. Scuttling in every corner."

"Timing is a bitch," I say through gritted teeth. "Your original plan probably would've worked, but why would we give you a cent now? Buying your silence is pointless when Fiona knows we were involved. We already told her the whole story."

"No. You shifted the blame onto Seth. Which is rather convenient considering he can't defend himself. A smart move by the one who is most to blame."

"What are you implying?" Raven asks. "Because I'll let you know right now, turning us against each other isn't going to work."

"Evan, you might want to encourage them to cooperate. Unless you're cool with everyone hearing the unfiltered story. I thought you were only hiding your dirty little secret from Fiona, but I guess you don't trust the others, either."

My fingers flutter near my pocket. I consider lunging toward her, jamming the box cutter between her ribs, but there's too much distance separating us. She would have all the time in the world to reposition her gun and bury a bullet in me.

"You're bluffing," I say, forcing myself to hold still. "How could you possibly know what went down that day?"

"Faith told me herself."

"So you're psychic now? You can speak to the dead?"

"Oh, yeah. You aren't caught up yet. I already gave Fiona the spiel, so I'll run through the bullet points. Faith was unconscious when you found her, not dead. You really should've taken her pulse. Then again, I think you avoided checking on purpose." Her mismatched eyes burn holes in me, her smirk growing. "Isn't that right, Evan?"

My head rushes, the room spinning around me. She knows. I don't understand how, but she knows. I pinch my eyes closed, massaging my temples. I can deny, deny, deny, but she's going to keep pushing until I spill my guts or my money.

It's not like I *wanted* Faith to drop dead. The night she went missing, the whole theater was wasted. Usually, we would sneak a single bottle of liquor past her parents and mix it with the fountain drinks. But since we were alone, we smuggled a few bottles. We took shots. We watched each other tumble past tipsy to wasted to blackout drunk. But I remember everything.

Early on, when we were all bullshitting in the lobby, a twin snuck out the back door by the dumpsters. She was wearing a milky white, button-down shirt with ruffles and strings. Like a kindergarten art project. It screamed *Fiona*. I was too drunk to notice it wasn't the outfit she had been wearing minutes earlier.

I counted out sixty seconds, then crept outside to join her. I called her name while sparking a cigarette that the wind kept trying to extinguish. When she twisted toward me, I was met with perfect, plucked brows instead of bushy ones, a birthmark on the chin instead of the lip. The wrong twin.

I didn't want to be rude—or waste the cigarette—so I strolled over to her. She sat cross-legged on the ground, next to a pile of chunky vomit.

"Are you okay?" I asked, my nose wrinkling.

"Yeah. I think I have a stomach bug. Or drank too much. I don't know. I needed some fresh air. The theater is too stuffy."

She folded her arms and hunched forward, trying to hide the baggie on her lap with her thick brown gloves—but I had already seen the pills. Half of them were crushed into fine dust.

"What are those?" I asked, blowing out a puff of smoke.

"Tylenol. I'm a baby. Can give a mean BJ, but can't swallow pills whole. I usually get the liquid version, but the store was fresh out."

"Ah. That sucks," I said, flicking ash onto the dirt. I didn't bother asking any more questions. She was already lying.

No one needed two dozen pills for a stomach bug. She needed three, max. And if she had trouble swallowing them, she could split them down the middle. Instead, she turned them into a powder she could sneak into a drink. There was no way those pills were for her. So, what the hell was she doing with them?

"You should probably add some vitamins to that mix," I said, dropping the cigarette and grinding it with my heel. "For the baby."

Her eye twitched. "Seth wasn't supposed to tell anyone."

"Don't worry. I'm a vault."

"Right. That's why Raven knows."

"She doesn't count. What I meant was, it won't get back to your sister. It's not my secret. Not my business."

"Yet you're bringing it up to me."

Good point. Normally, I would leave her alone. This was already in the running for our longest conversation to date. But during my two-second peek at the bag, a few pills were rattling around the plastic, whole and untouched. I needed a closer look. Which meant I needed to keep her talking.

"Like you said, no one is supposed to know," I shrugged. "Thought it might be nice to talk about it with someone who does."

"There's nothing to say. We had sex. We didn't use protection. I got pregnant."

"You didn't have five bucks for condoms?"

"It's not that simple."

I stole a step toward her. "If you're telling me Seth refused to wear one, I'll kick his ass for you."

"Believe it or not, I don't let men make decisions for me."

Another step. "Wow. I guess we have something in common, after all."

"Are you done? Because I have—" She screeched to a stop as my fingers grazed her shoulder. "Don't touch me," she hissed, her breath fogging the air. Her gloved hands flung up from her lap as she leaned away, exposing the baggie.

"My bad," I said, skimming the serial numbers, committing them to memory. "Just trying to help."

"Screw your help."

"Wow. Okay. Sorry for caring."

I swung back to the lobby, leaving her shivering out in the cold. Everyone else had relocated to theater three, waiting for the movie to start, so the guest service area was untouched. I snuck around the semi-circle desk, booted up the clunky computer, and plugged in the serial number carved into the pills.

When I read the name of the medication, my heart dropped to my feet. It was the drug the twins had been driven to the hospital over when we were younger. A doctor had prescribed it to them when they wound up with UTIs around the same time, but it turned out they were allergic.

If a single pill put them in the hospital, an amount that large was suicide. But if Faith was planning on taking the drugs herself, why would she smash them into a powder? If she had trouble swallowing pills, why not hang herself, shoot herself, throw herself in front of a speeding car? There were simpler methods. Unless…

They were meant for Fiona.

My whole body tensed, my chest on fire, but I quickly patched myself together. I didn't want anyone wondering what was wrong. It was best to keep the information under wraps. I couldn't warn Fiona her sister was planning on poisoning her. Not without proof. If I misread the situation, she would never speak to me again. She would always choose Faith over me.

I tethered myself to Fiona for the rest of the night. I missed the climax of the movie, the action scenes, the death scenes, the sex scenes. I stared mindlessly at her drink instead, making sure her sister wasn't able to sink her claws into it.

The film was entering its third act when Faith squeezed through the aisle carrying another round of drinks for our row. Before Fiona could steal a sip of hers, I slowly, subtly uncapped the lid. A thick, chalky substance swirled around the liquid. I let Fiona share my straw instead. She was too drunk to argue. She might not have even registered it was mine.

A few minutes after moving her cup to my holder, Faith had gotten up to pee. Everyone surrounding us was either engrossed in the movie or distracted by side conversations. No one was paying attention to me.

I'd like to say what came next was a difficult decision, but it wasn't a decision at all. Swapping cups was a knee-jerk reaction, as instinctive as blinking.

An hour later, Cameron stumbled outside to smoke a joint. He found Faith sprawled in the woods and dragged us out with him to examine the scene. There was a pile of vomit next to her, brown and watery. It must have been morning sickness. She must have been running outside to puke so no one would hear her in the bathroom and put two and two together.

Or maybe she realized she chugged the wrong drink and gagged herself. Her real cup wasn't even spiked, so the difference in taste must've been obvious. Either way, some of the pills were out of her system—and her allergy was less severe than her sister's to begin with. I couldn't be sure she was dead. I swore I saw the rise and fall of her chest, signs she was clinging to life, but I had seen a corpse do the same at a wake once. It could be a trick of the mind.

Either way, in that instant, I made my decision. It was in our best interest for her to die. I didn't want anyone to perform CPR on her or call an ambulance to save her. So I kept my friends at a distance. I warned them not to get any fingerprints on her because the cops might assume they were involved. We all had motives, I reminded them.

If I told them the truth then and there, maybe they would've kept my secret, but I couldn't risk it. I didn't want them to know about the role I played in her death. I trusted them, but that trust only extended so far. I didn't want them to have the hard facts to turn me in.

As far as they knew, we were all in this together. It was Seth's idea to steal the items dropped from her pocketbook. Not mine. He swiped the remaining drugs, the pink-lined pregnancy test, and the catty notes. Then Raven suggested we hide everything underground. That way, we wouldn't get caught carrying evidence on the parking lot cameras.

I mentioned it would be pretty easy to stuff the materials in our pockets and dump them in the ocean, but it was a thirty-mile drive to the beach. No one wanted to hold onto the items a second longer than necessary and our parents were expecting us home soon. Using the capsule felt fair, like we were all taking an equal amount of risk. Besides, it would be easy. We already had the capsule tucked into the earth. It wasn't hard to claw our way back to the container, empty the original items, and replace them with the evidence.

Faith must have been more conscious than I thought while we worked. She must have heard our plan to shove everything in the capsule and passed on the information to her friend. I'm not sure how Perry figured out the exact coordinates, but my guess is she went through my phone. I had the numbers saved deep in my notes app, so far back I forgot they existed. She could've scrolled through the entries or airdropped them to herself while I was snoring beside her in bed. There were other numbers scattered in between grocery lists—phone numbers for billing companies and tracking numbers for deliveries—but she could've sent every possible combination to herself, then checked them in a navigation app. She knew the capsule would be close to the theater. Narrowing down her options wouldn't be hard.

I lock eyes with her now. Like everyone else, she's turned toward me, impatiently awaiting an explanation. The rest of her night went sideways, but she still thinks she can predict how this ends. She expects me to cooperate, fork over the money, and convince my friends to do the same. She knows I'm smart, knows I could work out more lies to protect my secret while convincing them to pay their share. But I've danced around the truth enough for the last ten years. It's time to confess.

I crouch, placing the capsule near my feet to leave my hands free. "Cameron," I say into the walkie. "Can you tell them what drugs Faith bought off of you?"

He clears his throat. "Me? I already gave my side of the story."

"Would you just answer the question?"

"I mean… I don't remember. It was a weird one. I wasn't sure if I could hook her up with it at first because it wasn't weed or molly, like most people want. It was some kind of pill. It could have been Calan? Or Cipro, maybe."

"Ciprofloxacin?" Fiona says, scrunching up her face. "No, she would never take that. We're both allergic to it."

I flash back to the twins in side-by-side hospital beds. Faith was annoyed that their blond, hunky doctor was paying more attention to Fiona, but it was because her reaction to the medication was worse. *Life-threatening,* I overheard a nurse whisper. Faith only had a rash and slight swelling, but they kept her overnight too since they were twins. A reminder they weren't exactly the same but were close enough.

"I don't get it," Fiona says. "Are you telling me she was suicidal? Why would she give herself an allergic reaction?"

I exhale, long and shaky and slow. Here we go.

"She wasn't trying to kill herself," I say. "She was trying to kill you."

At first, there's no reaction. Fiona silently bats her lashes, like her mind is buffering, struggling to compute my words and their order. Then the confusion fades. Her face crumples, like melted wax.

Perry wears the opposite expression, pure stone. She gambled that I would give up my firstborn before exposing the real story. My selfishness would secure her the win. And now she's losing.

"I wasn't one-hundred percent sure what she was going to do with the pills in the beginning," I continue. "But toward the end of the night, when you were really wobbling, she slipped drugs into your drink. I swapped them when she ran to the bathroom, so she drank it instead of you."

Silence. The truth hangs in the air. I'm the one who hurt her. Not Seth. Me.

"It was extreme, sure. I could have reported what I saw to the cops or ratted on her to your parents or said something to you directly, but it didn't feel right. Once a person reaches the point of literal murder there's no going back. It's not like she was a kid who didn't know what she was doing. We were almost eighteen. Old enough to know better. Old enough to get sentenced for real. If I dumped the drink down the sink that day, then she might've tried to kill you in a different way, and I wouldn't have been there to stop it. I didn't want you to die, Fiona. I figured it was better to lose you as a friend than lose you for real."

More silence. Raven's hand is clutching her chest, like it's about to give out on her. Jonah pinches between his eyes like he's holding back tears. Even Perry is respectful enough to bite her tongue. Unless she's busy calculating how to move forward. I threw another wrench into her plans, but she's been flexible. This isn't game-set-match yet.

"Why didn't you tell me once it was over?" Fiona rasps. "Once she was gone and we were searching for her? You saw how miserable I was.

You knew it was killing all of us. Why didn't you pull me aside and tell me if you supposedly cared about me so much?"

There are the obvious reasons. I was worried about getting prison time, maybe even the death penalty. Who knew what would happen once the cops got their hands on me? I ran my mouth worse when I was younger than I do now. I wouldn't exactly come across as sympathetic to a jury.

But it wasn't all about self-preservation. I was trying to protect the Flynns. Their family swore they wanted the truth, but what they really wanted was to feel better. The honest story—about Faith being a homicidal monster—wasn't going to give them peace. It would be easier for everyone if they thought she died an angel, gone too soon. It would hurt, but in a different way. A less traumatizing way.

Fiona can tell me I was wrong until she's blue in the face, but back then, nothing would have changed my mind. I did the right thing.

At least, I thought I did.

CHAPTER 26

FIONA

My vision shrinks to a pinpoint. The theater disappears. Perry. The pistol. All I see is Evan. She stands directly across from me, her chest puffed and chin raised, despite her confession.

"Don't clam up now," I snap at her, my voice cracking. "You always have something witty to say, so go on. Why did you keep this from me?"

She hitches her shoulders. "Knowing your own twin wanted you dead would have gutted you. You would've made excuses about why I was wrong. You would have turned me into the cops the second I confessed. I didn't stand a chance against her, especially when she wasn't around to defend herself."

I shake my head, not wanting to believe it. Sure, we got into scrapes here and there, but any set of siblings would say the same. I have a scar on my knee from when she shoved me during hopscotch. Another on my eyebrow from when she launched a rock at me during recess. And there was the sparkler incident. But those were accidents, average kid behavior. Weren't they?

I think back to our final argument. If you could even call it an argument. She was the only one who raised her voice.

I stumbled into our bedroom while she was in one of her moods. She rifled through our closet in a towel, shoving aside hangers draped with blouses and jeans. It wouldn't have been anything out of the ordinary, except she was on the right-hand side of the closet. My side.

I plopped onto my bed, hugging a pillow. "What are you doing ransacking my clothes?"

"What, I'm not allowed to borrow a single shirt? God, Fiona. I know you like to layer, but you can't wear them all at once."

"That's not what I said. I'm just surprised you want to borrow anything. You hate my style. We aren't even the same size."

"I thought our parents taught us to share."

"Sharing usually requires permission."

She raised her voice to a cartoonish pitch. "Okay. Can I please have permission, *your highness?*"

Without waiting for a response, she ripped more shirts off the rack. A hanger clattered onto the floor.

"What is going on with you?" I asked. "What is that supposed to mean?"

"Think a little. You're the smart one. You should be able to figure it out."

"Did you flunk a test or something? Since when do you care about being smart?"

"I don't, but everyone else does. Mom. Dad. Our teachers. You've always been the favorite and I'm sick of it. Even if I get a B, it's not good enough because you got an A. Even if I worked five days a week, it looks bad because you work six. I hate being compared to you every second of my life. We're not the same person, so why do they have to act like we are? Do other sisters go through this or is it because we're the same age? Because we look alike? Do I need to chop my hair off? Get plastic surgery?"

I held back a comment about how her wearing my clothes would make us look even more similar. Instead, I said, "What are you talking about? No one is comparing us."

"You're so oblivious. Just because they're not saying it out loud doesn't mean they're not thinking it. You're so bad at reading people."

"Okay, well, even if people are comparing us, everyone likes you better than me, so you win."

It was true. She might have rubbed some people wrong, but it's not like I was teeming with friends. She was the one who could handle social situations without anxiety or OCD getting in her way. The one who matched the shape of women in magazines and made out with whatever boy she wanted.

Still, she refused to accept the compliment. "The only way I would be the favorite is if one of us dropped dead," she said, rolling the closet closed with a hard thud.

At the time, I thought she was referring to the way dead people are placed on pedestals, how relatives don't realize how much they love someone until that person is gone. For weeks after she went missing, I secretly worried it was a suicide. I was scared I missed an obvious warning sign and should've involved my parents. The anger brewing within her was easy to see, simmering red and hot, but I never thought it would be directed toward me.

As much as it hurts, what Evan said *does* line up with the diary entries. She might have finally, at long last, been telling the truth.

"What did she tell you about me?" I ask Perry. I rotate toward her, forcing the gun against my forehead. "Why did she hate me so much?"

"She didn't hate you. She hated being a twin. Hated that everyone thought it was the most interesting thing about her. Killing you wasn't her original plan. She was supposed to run away with me."

I think of the travel vlog. The plane tickets to Paris.

"We were about to graduate high school," Perry says. "I had thousands in my bank account, so we decided to take a gap year. Travel the world, starting in Europe and switching towns every few weeks. She never mentioned it to you or your parents because she knew they wouldn't approve. And honestly, I don't think she was ever planning on coming back. She wanted a clean break. To separate herself from your family. Or, more specifically, you.

"But a couple of months before we were set to leave, she got pregnant. She kept it a secret from me in the beginning. I think she was considering an abortion, so it wouldn't interfere with our trip. But then Evan opened her big mouth."

Evan scrunches her nose, primed to protest.

"I know. You don't remember talking to me," Perry says. "I walked in one day when you and Raven were working the ticket booth. I asked where Faith was, and you said *probably pissing again. The baby has been hell on her bladder.* Then you guys laughed about how painful popping out the *demon seed* would be. Real classy."

"Anyway," Perry sing-songs. "When she told me it was true, that she was pregnant, I lost it. I yelled at her about hiding something so huge from me when we were supposed to tell each other everything. I couldn't believe Evan—the girl she constantly bitched about—found out before me. I told her we couldn't travel if she was pregnant, anyway, so I canceled the flights, the hotel rooms, the whole trip. I didn't realize how much it would upset her, that it was the only thing keeping her going."

She squeezes my shoulder. "Since I took away her chance to get away from you, she decided she would get rid of you instead. I wouldn't have approved of it, to be perfectly clear, but I didn't find out until late that night. She called me, in a panic, and explained that Evan and her friends tried to kill her. She was scared they would try again once they realized she was alive, so she begged to stay at my place. I forgot all about our fight. None of it mattered anymore. She was my best friend. I had to help her." She exhales. Hard. "One night in our guest room turned to two, then three, and somewhere along the line, she decided to stay until the baby came. She didn't want to raise the girl herself, but she wanted her to have a good life. I always wanted a daughter, a family member who couldn't leave me like my parents always did—and I was too young and naïve to realize what a big commitment it was—so I agreed to take her, pretend she was mine. That way, we both won."

"If you were such good friends, why did you keep her death a secret?" Evan cuts in, arms crossed. "And why did you wait so long to get revenge? Why come charging in on your white horse after ten years?"

"I couldn't tell the truth because Destiny would get taken away from me. I didn't come to town until now because I didn't need money until now. Revenge alone would've been great, but I wasn't going to risk prison time when I had a kid at home. I'm doing this *for* the kid. I need the cash to support her, to give her the future she deserves." She shifts back to me. "The hair your parents found in the mail was from her, by the way. It's long and beautiful like yours."

She runs her fingers through my ponytail and tugs, forcing my chin toward the ceiling. I stiffen, worried what she's going to do next—but I'm even more worried about what she's already done. Who knows how much damage was inflicted on Destiny after ten years of brainwashing?

"She could be lying," Evan says to me. "There's no proof this kid exists. She told me about her during our dates, but she was never home. And the door to her room was shut. It could've been empty."

"Believe what you want. You're not meeting her either way," Perry snaps, keeping her focus on me. "I invited you here so Evan and her friends would have a good reason to cooperate. *Pay me or I'll blab all your secrets to Fiona.* But now they already know. How do we convince them to cough up money when the secret is out, hmm?"

My knees buckle, my whole body going numb. I take in short, rapid breaths, turning to the group. "I won't tell on you guys," I sputter. "If you give her the money, the cops will never know what happened. You don't have to worry about me. I swear on my sister."

They glimpse at each other, chewing nails and twisting hair.

"They weren't born yesterday," Perry says. "There's no way you're going to keep their secret. As long as you're alive, they aren't forking over any money. Luckily, I already have blood on my hands. I might as well raise the body count. And finish what Faith set out to do ten years ago.

"We can make it look like a murder-suicide. Seth's wife already thinks he's cheating. We can say we saw you sneaking around together, that he missed Faith so much that he settled for the next best thing. But once he went to break it off with you, you snapped and stabbed him. Once you realized what you'd done, you put a gun to your head. It's not like you had much to live for anyway. No one would be surprised."

Perry cocks the gun. "This pistol belongs to you. Your prints are all over it. It's a pretty believable story. This town would eat it up. They already think you're the one who went after Faith. They would easily believe you sent the letter to your own parents. A fitting ending for the sad, guilty twin."

There's nothing left to do. I don't knock her arm and send a bullet flying toward the wall. I don't race across the room and escape. I squeeze my eyes closed and brace for the explosion, ready to be reunited with my sister.

But for the first time since she went missing, that thought doesn't bring me any peace.

CHAPTER 27

EVAN

Time races. One second, the gun is pressed against Fiona's skull. The next, Jonah is rushing Perry. I'd noticed him tiptoeing closer as she gave her little speech and made sure my eyes never darted toward him, giving his position away. I wanted to keep her focused on me. The one she thought was the leader. The one she considered a threat.

Now, his broad shoulders collide with her chest, knocking her backward. She keeps her grip on the pistol as she stumbles, clutching her ribs. "Fiona. Move," he shouts as he lunges forward and tries to wrestle the gun away. Fiona shudders like she's waking from a dream, then scrambles across the room and huddles behind Raven and me for safety.

Perry steadies her arm, aiming her weapon, as Jonah sweeps out his leg, trying to knock her onto her ass—but he's not quick enough.

She fires, sending shockwaves through me. My ears clog like they're stuffed with cotton. My vision clouds with spots. When it clears up, Jonah is writhing on the ground, dark blood spurting from his thigh. A crimson pool forms around his crooked legs.

He winces at the wound, grunting and moaning, as Raven sprints toward him. She drops to her knees and sheds her jacket, wrapping it around his leg to staunch the wound. Blood sneaks onto her fingers, but she doesn't wince.

I glance at Fiona, shivering behind me, panicked from brushing so close to death—but all I can see is her ponytail flying behind her as we played manhunt in the woods. Her sneaking me break room cookies before the boys gobbled them down. Her huddled beneath a cotton blanket, leaving space for me to squeeze in beside her.

What is wrong with me? I should've been the one snapping to action like Jonah, the one bleeding out to save her. Fiona was a victim, then and now. She's the least deserving to die out of everyone trapped in this theater.

I caused this. I need to end it.

"I'll give you your damn money," I blurt out, turning toward Perry, who is panting with rage. "Let everybody else leave."

"You're going to pony up the amount all three of them are supposed to pay?" she snaps. "I don't think you can exactly cover the cost."

"I don't know what you want me to tell you. You picked crappy targets. It's not like the struggling musician or small business owner is going to be able to give you much either. Seth was the only one of us without loans, with a house that isn't one storm away from collapsing, and you took that option off the table."

Her smirk wavers.

"I got half the money from my house sale. I was saving it in case of an emergency, and I'm pretty sure this qualifies as one. I'm living with my family. I don't have to pay for groceries or heat or electricity. I can survive without money in the bank, for at least a while. I'll transfer you every penny in my account. It's the best deal you're going to get."

"How much are we talking?"

"A hundred grand."

Her lips purse, but there's no doubt in my mind she'll take the deal. She's desperate. She can't slaughter us and redo her scheme on a group with more money. We're the only ones she can blackmail because we're the only ones she has dirt on. Plus, judging by the glimmer in her eye, there's a good chance I offered more than she was originally planning on requesting.

"Fine. You've got a deal," she says, waving me over with the gun. "I'll let you cover the cost for your friends. Hopefully, they'll be so thankful they won't run straight to the cops and rat you out. That's why you're doing this, right? Taking the fall to make it look like you have a heart?"

"You're assuming my mind is as sick as yours."

She raises a brow, like *of course it is,* then spins to address the others. "None of you are leaving until the transfer is complete. I need a head start out of town. This should take ten minutes, tops. If you leave the building before we're done, I'll kill your girl Evan here."

I hope the threat holds weight, but now that they know the truth about my role in the murder, they might not care about me making it out alive. It might be easier if I was out of the picture.

Perry directs me toward the concrete stairwell. I take small steps, giving myself time to run through scenarios, brainstorming my smartest move. When we reach the projection room, an oversized duffel bag sags in the corner. She kicks it closer, unzippers a side pouch, and pulls out a tablet.

I plop onto a wobbly metal chair shoved in the corner, hunching forward and fiddling with my thumbs. The whole night, my game plan was to appear strong and unshakable, but that technique isn't going to work on Perry. I let water pool in my eyes. Drop my chin. Slump my shoulders.

It's mostly an act. *Mostly.*

Perry types a code into her tablet, swipes the screen, and pulls up an encrypted website to transfer funds. "Insert your banking information," she says, thrusting it toward me.

"You got it," I say, pecking at the screen with one finger, extra slow. "Can I just ask you one thing? Now that we're alone?"

"I already spilled all my information on the twins. There's nothing left to say."

"I meant about us."

"Well, then." She barks out a laugh. "Let's hear it."

"I'm going to sound pathetic since you have me at gunpoint, but I thought we were pretty cute together. You made it look like we were, at least. If the whole murderer thing doesn't work out, you might want to give Hollywood a shot."

"You're not serious. There's a dead body downstairs. You could be dead soon, too. But you're worried about a dry spell?"

"You don't have to rub it in. Forget I said anything." I drop my eyes and resume typing.

"Evan, please. Don't let me bruise your ego too badly. I wasn't faking every second we were together. Sure, I lied about some personal things, but the sexual tension was there. You're attractive. Funny. Smart. The sarcasm can be a bit much, but you shouldn't have too hard of a time finding someone else. In real life or prison."

"Awesome. Thanks." I fill out the bottom section of the form, scribbling in boxes. "So, any ideas on where you're going? You could start over anywhere."

"I'm not gullible enough to tell you. I don't need the police banging down my door one day."

"I guess you're not gullible enough to bring me with you, either?"

She snorts. "Please be kidding."

"You were right earlier. I have no life. I have no real plans. And I won't have any friends now that they know what I did to Faith. You're going on the run anyway, so letting me tag along wouldn't change much. Having another set of eyes could be helpful."

She clucks her tongue, looking me up and down. "Nah. I don't buy it."

"That I would prefer a life with you over life in a prison cell?"

"Are those the only two ways you see your story ending?"

"It has to be one or the other. Even if Fiona keeps quiet as a *thank you* for saving her life, the rest of them aren't going to stay loyal to me. They probably think I deserve this. I'm the reason they're in this situation. I don't think they actively want me dead, but they wouldn't give a rat's ass about me going to prison. Especially Jonah. We're strangers."

Nothing is stopping them from running to the police and regurgitating everything they learned tonight. Sure, they hid what they thought *might* be construed as evidence, but they could say I tricked them into doing it. They could say they remained silent all these years because they were scared of me retaliating. They could say anything. It would be four against one.

"Okay," Perry says. "Let's say I agree with your idea. How would our arrangement work?"

"Don't ask me. I'm just along for the ride. I can start a new shop under a fake name anywhere. We wouldn't be millionaires, but we would be comfortable."

She holsters her gun, stowing it in the back of her slacks. "Continue."

"The other day, when I spent the night at your place, it was…intense is an understatement. We could feel like that every single day. I'd be relieved to throw this trash life away in exchange for a clean slate."

She bends forward, curling her slender fingers around my armrests. Her cherry-scented lipstick tickles my nose, taunting me. We're only an inch away from a kiss. She brings her lips even closer to whisper, "It's a good pitch. But flattering me isn't going to stop you from sending the money, Evan. I'm not leaving without it."

Without breaking eye contact with her, I smack the SUBMIT button to complete the transfer. A bar crawls across the page, slowly filling as the payment is processed through the system.

"There," I say, thrusting the tablet toward her. "It's sent. You have everything of mine now. And I'm not only talking about the money. You know the worst thing about me, that I killed someone. Or at least, that I tried to kill someone. That I lived with the belief I got away with it for a decade."

She squints, trying to read me.

"No offense, *Brooke*, but you're not exactly normal, either. Not if you pulled off a scheme like this. Maybe we belong together."

The device beeps, signaling the transfer is complete. She glances between the screen and me, a smile playing on her lips. "You really are a mess, aren't you?"

"I thought you liked that about me."

She tilts forward, sealing the space between us, letting our lips brush. Electricity branches through me—and I can picture it. Sprawling out on white sand, rubbing sunscreen onto her porcelain shoulders. Ordering at seaside restaurants, sharing champagne and chocolate-covered strawberries. Hopping from town to town when someone gets suspicious about our history, always on the move, on a never-ending adventure.

I slip my tongue in her mouth, pushing back a strand of her hair with one hand. The other slips the box cutter out of my front pocket. I press the plastic tip against her stomach, as gentle as a dove. Moving slow and steady, I slide my thumb against the lever, lightly shoving up the blade until—fingers clamp down on my wrist.

"Don't insult me," Perry whispers, twisting the bone until it snaps. I yelp, the blade dropping from my wilting fingers. The knife clatters onto the floor, and before I can grope for it with my good arm, she reaches both hands behind me, ramming my chair. I fly backwards. My head cracks against concrete.

"You know what happens when rich parents want you out of their hair?" she asks, towering over me. "They sign you up for every class under the sun. Horseback riding. Ballet. Kickboxing. Self-defense. Firearm training."

She kicks a heel into my ribs, and my knees hitch, curling in a ball. The box cutter is only a few feet away, a lump in the dark. I stretch out my fingers, skimming the handle and skating off.

"I was hoping to keep you all alive tonight," she says, "But thanks to that big mouth of yours, my plans are changing. Again."

I catch the edge of the knife, shifting it closer, but Perry is already moving. She smirks as she aims the gun at my heart—*my most vulnerable place*—and pulls the trigger once, twice, three times.

Nothing happens.

She turns the weapon over in her hands, fiddling with the safety and swearing beneath her breath. She tries to unload the cartridge, to fix the issue.

Fiona must have jammed it by playing with the safety.

Sounds like karma, I think as I latch onto the knife.

I struggle to rock myself onto my feet, cradling my stinging wrist against my chest. But once I'm standing, I don't waste time.

I charge toward Perry and thrust the blade into her stomach. She screams out, stumbling back from me and colliding with a wall. I lean forward with her, refusing to create a gap between us. I twist the blade while it's still lodged in her gut, then yank it out and let the blood flow. I'm not sure whether the wound is big enough to kill her and I'm not going to make the same mistake twice.

I'm not letting her get away like Faith.

Perry clutches the hole with one palm and uses the other to readjust her gun. Before she can retry the trigger, I slash the blade against her neck, splitting her open. A fountain of blood sprinkles me, coating my shirt in red.

Perry skids against the wall, slumping to the ground. Bubbles burst from her ragged, ruptured throat. I wait for the gurgles to cease, for the light in her eyes to dim and her mouth to go slack. When silence descends, I straddle her and fumble in her pocket for her keys.

Footsteps pound the staircase. The others must be headed upstairs. They must have heard her dying screams and mistook them for mine.

I lurch onto my feet and swing open the door. Raven and Fiona stagger to a stop in the middle of the hall, taking in my crooked wrist, my bloodied face. They crane their heads, like they can't make sense of the scene in front of them.

Neither of them ask questions. Not *what happened?* Not *are you okay?* They're waiting for me to break the tension, to explain my splattered clothes are some sort of misunderstanding. I could lie and claim the murder was self-defense, but I'm not sure they would believe a word.

"164B," I say, extending the key to Fiona. "That's her apartment number. She's in the complex behind the woods. She might have the kid there."

She nods slowly, slinking toward me. My bloody fingers brush hers, smearing rust-colored streaks onto her skin. When our eyes meet, I swallow, bracing for the worst. A warning to stay away from her family. A threat to have me locked up by morning.

Instead, she plucks the key from my palm and whispers, "Thank you."

And that's when I collapse into sobs.

CHAPTER 28

FIONA

The blood drizzling down the front of Evan, darkening her clothes to purple, is too much to process. It feels like staring at an actress squirted with condiments, not an old friend who committed murder. My mind can't comprehend the enormity of what she's done for me. Or herself. It doesn't matter, really. All that matters is that horrible woman can never touch my niece again.

I tuck the apartment key in my pocket and toss Raven the employee set. She's shaking from top to bottom, her eyes beet-red, but she's the only one who can help. Jonah is downstairs, bleeding. Evan is on the floor, sobbing. And everyone else is dead.

"The silver key opens the freezer where I left Cameron," I say. "And make sure you call an ambulance for Jonah. He should have his cell phone with him."

"The police are already on their way," Raven says. "EMS should show up with them. But they're going to want our statements."

I'm not sure whether they're planning on telling the cops the truth about Evan or whether they'll continue protecting her. I don't have time to ask. The cops might scold me for fleeing an active crime scene, but waiting around for them isn't an option. I need to find Destiny.

"I'm sure you'll do the right thing," I say, then bolt into the break room. I climb out the emergency exit and fly down the staircase, metal clanging beneath my feet. It deposits me near the sidewalk, on the wrong side of the building. There aren't any back roads connecting the theater to the apartment complex. It's faster to go on foot than drive down winding streets pockmarked with traffic lights.

I squeeze between the clothing shop and the theater, slipping on an ice patch. My knee crashes against the pavement, tearing my leggings, but the adrenaline drowns out the pain. I scrabble to my feet and keep going.

Once the slippery ground turns solid, I break into a run, weaving through the trees, scratching my cheeks on branches and tripping over tree roots. At the end of the forest, I cut through a snow-dusted backyard, scanning apartment numbers.

When I locate the building, I climb three flights of stairs, peel down the hallway, and pound on the last door along the strip. I wait several beats, my ear squished against the door to listen for footsteps or creaks, but it's eerily quiet. If the girl is home alone, I don't want to scare her by bursting into the apartment. But I don't want to waste precious time if she's injured either. Perry could have left her unconscious in there.

I fumble in my pocket for the key. It nearly slips out of my hand, warm and slick with blood. I wipe it on my pant leg, twist it in the lock, and step through the threshold.

The apartment has a few plants and paintings, but it feels more like a showroom than a home where a mother and child live. There aren't any toys clumped on the rug or pictures magnetized to the fridge. I think back to what Evan said, about her never seeing the girl when she visited. Destiny might be another lie.

I pass a sparkling white bathroom without any soaps or makeup products on the counter, then a master bedroom with sheets that are perfectly tucked. Suitcases wait by the door, ready to go.

I approach a bedroom labeled with a KEEP OUT PLEASE AND THANK YOU sign covered in stickers. The letters are written in a loopy, flourishing font. Just like the journal entries. It's hard to believe my niece scrawled those words, unknowingly writing exactly like her mother.

Unless it was Perry.

I suck in a breath, unsure what's going to be waiting on the other side. Crushing disappointment or a new family member.

I rap on the door three times, just in case, then turn the knob slowly. Unlike the rest of the apartment, this room is brightly decorated. Lopsided posters cling to the walls. Stuffed animals pepper the floors. A miniature cactus perches on the windowsill.

And in the corner of the room, on a purple bedspread, a little girl is sitting with her knees to her chest, earbuds in her ears. She starts when she sees me, but she doesn't scuttle away or scream for help. I should be relieved she's so calm, but it's such an odd reaction. I can't help but worry she takes after Perry, who tried to murder me—or my sister, who tried to murder me—that something is broken inside her.

"Are you Destiny?" I ask without budging from the doorway.

She nods, popping out an earbud. "You look like me."

My stomach flips. I give myself a second to look at her, really look at her. The birthmark on her chin is in the same exact spot it sat on Faith. It's like staring at a vision from the past.

Fortunately, there aren't any visible cuts or bruises or cigarette burns on her. She looks perfectly healthy. Her skin is dewy. Her hair is silky. She even has braces with colored rubber bands, green and red, for the holidays.

"You look more like your mother," I say, holding back the tears. I don't want to freak her out.

She cocks her head, but she doesn't accept the compliment. She might not even think of it as a compliment. She might not want anything to do with this mother she's never met, this woman who was supposed to raise her but dropped off the planet instead. It's not Faith's fault she died, but kids can't always grasp that fact. Neither can adults. There are still days when I'm pissed at Faith for abandoning us. Today especially.

Destiny stares, waiting for more, but I'm not sure where to lead the conversation. I don't know how much *she* knows. "Did Perry tell you anything about what was going on, about why you moved to this town?" I ask.

"She said I have family in the neighborhood, that they were going to lend us money. Is that you?"

"Yes. It is. It's nice to finally meet you. I didn't learn about you until recently or I would've made sure to come over sooner."

She twirls a strand of dark, wavy hair. "I didn't know about the adoption until a few weeks ago either. Mom was pretty vague about it. She didn't want to tell me too much about you."

"That's okay. I can answer whatever questions you have. Me, and my mom and dad—your grandparents—are going to help you get through this. We want you to be happy. We won't let anything bad happen, okay? Perry is gone. She can't hurt you anymore. You're safe."

Her face drops. "Gone? You mean, dead?"

I freeze, wishing I could snatch the words and stuff them back down my throat. It wasn't my place to break the news to her. The police should've sat her down to explain the gory details.

"It just happened," I say, wincing. "I'm so sorry."

Her head rattles like she's about to deny it, to ask for proof, to insist it can't be true. Then she crumples into tears. She buries her head in between her thighs, her shoulders heaving.

I risk a step forward, resting a hand on her leg. She jerks away, banging her knee against the wall.

"Leave me alone," she murmurs, smushing herself into the corner. "Get out of my room. I don't even know you. Get away from me. Get out."

I spin around, my cheeks burning with regret. I should've guessed she wouldn't take the news well. I'm not sure how much she knows about what Perry has been doing, but even if she discovers the full truth—about her murdering Seth and shooting Jonah—there's still going to be a piece of her that loves and misses her 'mother.'

It's the same with me and Faith. She doesn't deserve my pity, not when I know how happy she would've been if our roles were reversed, if I died and she lived. But a part of me is always going to miss her. Hating her doesn't make losing her any easier. Hearts aren't that clever.

CHAPTER 29

EVAN

I stride into the funeral parlor, bookended by my parents. My father cups the shoulder above my cast. My mother intertwines her fingers with my good hand. They've been acting off-the-charts clingy after learning about my near-death experience at the theater. They haven't pried themselves from my hip in days. But I have to do this alone.

"I'll meet up with you in a little while," I whisper, breaking apart from them. They stop to chat with another couple while I cross the hall.

A sign perched beside the entrance says IN LOVING MEMORY OF SETH ADAMS. I suck in a deep breath and enter a room with rows of mourners, stacks of prayer cards, and thick, lavish flower arrangements. His body isn't fit for viewing, so there's a closed mahogany casket at the head of the room with more sprays, vibrant reds, blues, and purples.

I pass Raven, who is admiring snapshots tacked to a corkboard. Then Cameron, slouched on a chair in his oversized suit and loose tie. Patel, the officer who handled the missing person case, is there too, his hands clasped in prayer.

I stiffen on instinct, but he has no reason to arrest me. He's well aware I killed Perry, but everyone in the theater that night claimed it was in self-defense. The cops, lazy as always, were happy to accept the story as the truth.

I have to give them some credit, though. Not only did they fire Officer BJ for leaving us hanging at an active crime scene, but they were able to hack into Perry's tablet and retrieve the money sent to her—by me and Faith's parents. Every penny is back in my account, and in the eyes of the public, I'm an innocent victim.

Everyone believes Perry and her father kidnapped Faith, stole the baby straight from her womb, and murdered her in cold blood. No one realizes Cameron sold her drugs. Or Seth knocked her up. Or Raven cat-fought her. Or I poisoned her.

Since those key details have been missing from the papers, people aren't exactly sure why Perry targeted our group, but they don't care, either. They're comfortable believing an outsider rode into town and committed unspeakable crimes. It's easier for them to sleep soundly at night knowing their neighbors are good people who would never dare cause them harm.

I proceed toward the head of the room, waiting in a staggered line to give my condolences. Seth's kids are swallowed by monster-sized chairs, their eyes red with tear tracks staining their cheeks. I wasn't sure whether they were old enough to understand his death, but I guess it's not too hard to wrap their minds around the fact their daddy is never coming back home.

Seth's wife isn't faring much better. She greets each mourner with a slack, expressionless stare. Like the numbness has made a home in her.

I can't blame her. She knows more about Seth's murder than the police chief. Fiona told her the bullet points under doctor-patient confidentiality. She didn't have much of a choice in the matter. Angel had a million questions about why he snuck out to meet us in the middle of the night. She didn't buy our lie, that we were reminiscing at the place where we originally met. If we kept her in the dark, she would've hounded the police to find out more. Besides, Fiona thought it was important for her to know Destiny was his biological daughter.

So far, Angel hasn't told anyone our dirty little secret. In fact, when the dust settles, she's planning on setting up playdates between her sons and Destiny. There's an age gap, but she wants them to know each other as more than strangers at school.

When it's my turn to approach her, I say, "I'm so sorry for your loss. I can't imagine what you're going through. I'm Evan, by the way. I was friends with your husband in high school."

"I know who you are."

I wait. This could go either way. She could be grateful I killed the woman who killed her husband. Or she could blame me for dragging him to the theater where his life was cut short.

"Seth never talked about you," she says. "A few days ago, I wouldn't have been able to pick you and your friends out of a lineup. But when I was looking through boxes of photos for the collages, I found a bunch with you all in them. He looked happy. I'm thankful you were a part of that happiness."

"He was a good guy. I wish I could've done something to save him."

"I blame myself, too. What if I didn't fall asleep so early that night? What if I woke for a glass of water and realized his car was missing? I'll tell you what I've been telling myself. You aren't psychic. You couldn't have seen this coming. Some things are outside of our control."

I nod, but it's more complicated for me. If I admitted to my role in the murder ten years earlier—or ten hours earlier—then he would be alive. His kids wouldn't be forced to grow up without a father.

I push down the guilt, kiss Angel on the cheek, and give her kids the sorry for your loss spiel they must be bored of hearing by now. Then I slip a condolence card into the gilded stand in the corner and start toward the exit. Usually, I speedrun these things. I show my face, pay my respects, then book it to the parking lot. But with Seth, it feels wrong to leave until the whole three hours are up.

I sweep the room for an empty seat. My eyes stick when they reach Fiona, hunched over a podium, jotting her name onto the address book. Either she's walking in now, or she's already on her way out the door. I wander over in case it's the latter.

"Hey," I say, tucking hair behind my ear. "Can we talk?"

She gives a half-hearted shrug as she finishes scribbling her information. I lead her through a side door, connected to an employee parking lot. The sun is burning bright today, but she hovers close to the exit, hugging her chest.

"I wasn't sure if you would come," I say. "Seth didn't exactly treat you the greatest. I wouldn't have blamed you for bailing on this."

"It wouldn't feel right to miss it. He wasn't my favorite person, but I'm close with his wife. She's my therapist, remember?"

"Right. I might need to borrow her number."

She blinks. "You've never tried therapy? After everything you've gone through?"

"If I did, I would've asked for a refund by now. I'm not exactly a shining example of a good person."

"You're not a bad person, either, Evan."

"God. Don't do that."

"Do what?"

"Forgive me," I groan. "I haven't even apologized yet."

"I know you're sorry about my sister."

"It's not only that. I want to say sorry for ditching you, too. I shouldn't have dropped out of your life without an explanation. And ever since I got back to town, I haven't been any better. I don't know. I don't have a good excuse for how I've been treating you. Maybe part of me resented everything I did for you. Being stuck living with it all these years wasn't easy. Not that I have a right to complain."

"I get it. It must have been hard sacrificing so much for me and feeling like you weren't able to tell me. Or anyone else. But I appreciate you talking to me now. I know how hard it is for you to speak from the heart, without smirking or getting all sarcastic."

"There we go. That's what I wanted to hear." I crook my finger. "Come on, throw a few more punches. I deserve them."

"I don't want to hurt you. How I behaved the other night... I made mistakes, too. I never should have—"

I raise a hand, cutting her off. "If I don't have to apologize, neither do you. You've always been a better person than me."

She nips her lip, looking up at me through her lashes. Like when we were younger. Before I pushed her away.

"But enough of the sappy crap. If you *insist* on forgiving me, at least let me earn it. Let me buy you coffee. Cook you dinner. Give you some shoulder massages. It'll add up over time."

"That would require staying in town, wouldn't it? I mean, if you want to make up for *every* single thing."

"It's going to be a while before I'm back on my feet, either way."

She nods, but she doesn't say a word.

"I get if hanging with me is too weird, though. We don't have to snap back to being friends. Maybe it's better if I stay out of your way. Whatever you want. It's up to you. I'm flexible."

"I don't think I can give you an answer right now," she says. "But I'll consider it."

After everything I put her through, I can't really ask for more than that.

CHAPTER 30

FIONA

I stare down a six-foot hole at my second funeral this week. I didn't even have time to toss my black slacks in the wash. Cat hair clings to the fabric, and a coffee stain is splashed on the collar. But no one expects me to be put together on the day my sister is being buried.

The police found her remains in Perry's childhood yard, planted beneath a flowerbed. They were able to identify her without my help, so they encouraged me to stay away from what was left of her. *You don't want to remember her like this,* Patel told me. *You won't be able to wash your mind clean of the image.* I already had enough I wished I could forget, so I took his advice.

Her service passes in a blur. Choir music plays. A priest recites blessings. Roses are sprinkled onto the coffin. And she's gone.

Once the service ends, the family and friends gathered around me break into clusters. A few of them excuse themselves, veering toward their cars, promising to meet us at the diner where we scheduled lunch. It shouldn't cost too much, considering there are only two dozen of us. I'm relieved my parents planned such a small occasion, an intimate goodbye to Faith.

My mother lingers in her spot beside the headstone, a tissue clutched in hand. We stand shoulder-to-shoulder, staring at nothing, thinking of everything. The wind whistles as she whispers, "It shouldn't have gone on so long."

I shift toward her, silent. There's no point in trying to say the right thing. There is no right thing. It's all different shades of wrong.

"The memorial dinners," she says, pulling her eyes from the grave and settling them on me. "We should've stopped throwing them years ago. I was so concerned with Faith coming home… I didn't see what they did to you."

"No. Mom. You don't have to—"

"The town talked terribly about you. And you had to relive those rumors year after year. No one had the chance to forget because we forced them to remember. It was unfair to you."

She squeezes my palm with her free hand. I squeeze back.

"There are so many things we should've done differently," she continues. "It's our fault you were trapped in the theater with that…That woman. We put so much pressure on you, with the anniversary dinners and with the business. If there are too many bad memories, you don't have to go back to work. We understand if you want to make other plans for your life."

"I'm never going to quit the theater," I say, and am surprised to realize I mean it. The two worst days of my life took place in that building, but so did some of the best. "I hate to break it to you, but you're not getting new management anytime soon."

My father roams over at the tail-end of the conversation, chuckling. "Thank goodness. I'm glad you're sticking with us, pumpkin. I'm still having trouble running those new registers, so I don't know how we'd survive without you. And *you*," he says as Jonah limps over on a single crutch. "Thank you for taking care of our little girl."

"Are you kidding?" he says, resting the heel of his cast on the grass. "She made it out without getting shot. She's the real badass." He winces, his voice dropping. "Can I say that in front of a church?"

"After what you've been through," my father says, "You've earned the right to say whatever the fuck you want."

The three of them swap hugs, then my parents part hand-in-hand, leaving us alone on the cemetery hill. A breeze tussles the hair tumbling down my shoulders, but the cresting sun keeps me warm. Snow might fall again soon, but for now, everything has melted.

"You look good," Jonah says, slapping my arm. "But you must feel like crap."

"I did most of my crying before this. I'm actually okay."

He readjusts his crutch. "What about the kid? Did the adoption go through yet?"

"Apparently, it takes forever for the paperwork to get processed and approved. But they're letting her stay with us in the meantime, so it doesn't make much of a difference. They've got her room all set up. She mostly locks herself in there, keeps to herself."

"Where is she now?" he asks, scanning the cemetery. "I'm excited to meet her. She's going to call me Uncle Jonah, right?"

"I'll be lucky if she calls me Aunt Fiona." I nod toward the minivan parked against the curb. A rear window is unrolled, revealing the top of her dark head of hair. "She's waiting in the car, watching movies. Everyone thinks her 'mother' killed Faith, so today is weird for her, too."

"Poor kid. I hope your parents know what they're getting into raising her."

"What do you mean? She's family."

"Faith was family, too."

His phone vibrates, and he fumbles to shut it off, nearly dropping his crutch. "Crap," he mumbles. "It's nine already? I hate to leave without you, but I have physical therapy. The sooner this cast comes off, the sooner you can put me back to work."

"Go ahead," I say, giving a tightlipped smile. "I need a second by myself anyway."

He nods and hobbles down the sidewalk. As he disappears into a two-door car, I step closer to the grave, circling around the ditch until reaching the tombstone at the head. It's an elaborate structure, with two granite vases built into the base. Carnations are bursting out of them, bunches of yellows and pinks. The centerpiece is carved with LOVING SISTER, FRIEND, AND DAUGHTER.

I expected my parents to ask for advice on the arrangements, but they put together everything before I could volunteer to help.

Apparently, they weren't as optimistic as they acted in front of me. They had her casket and tombstone picked out ten years ago, waiting to be used. We were all in purgatory, awaiting an answer, permission to move on with the rest of our lives.

"I guess this is finally goodbye," I whisper, running my fingers along the stone's curved edges. "I'm going to miss you, Faith."

It's funny. She thought death would separate us, but she's always going to be a part of me. She didn't get what she wanted in the end, after all.

SEVEN MONTHS LATER

EVAN

I cruise down the road with my windows yawning, passing a group of girls selling lemonade, fifty cents per cup. Further down, a man strolls along the sidewalk with a wagging chihuahua. Boys streak by on matching blue bicycles, shouting and laughing. It's weird how much more you see—of a town, of a person—when you finally start paying attention.

"This is the one." Fiona slaps my arm from the passenger seat. "Turn it up. That's the song."

I fiddle with controls on my dashboard, raising the volume. Cameron's voice reverberates through the speakers, crooning out a rock song called RESURRECTION. His new band is playing on a local station. It's only broadcasted to a few hundred people, but it's a start.

I've been working as his PR person, helping him mock up posters with the same programs I use to advertise for my e-shop. After his three-month stint at rehab, he's been much more open to the idea of plastering his face across social media. He understands that he needs to market himself to go viral. And he knows nothing worse can happen to him than what we've already been through.

Raven's salon has been kicking ass, too. She hired me to clean up her website and keep her portfolio updated from week to week. I offered to work pro bono for them both, but they weren't having it. The extra money is nice, but I'm mostly happy they don't hate my guts.

It's surprisingly nice having old friends within walking distance. Cameron invites me to his gigs every weekend, and Raven and Jonah let me play the third wheel on their dates. They make a cute couple, but it's hard to keep up with them. Especially since I've been following Fiona's lead and cutting down on the alcohol. My new therapist thought it would be good for me.

"I can't lie. This song is amazing," Fiona says, drumming her thighs. "I'm impressed."

I nod. "Agreed. Even if we didn't know him, I would be into it."

"I'm proud of him. And you for helping him."

"Ehh, he did all the hard work. I just pushed him along."

"Look at you, being all modest."

She glances at me for a split second too long, like she's considering going in for a kiss—then she snaps her eyes back to the road. I'm lucky enough she's given me a second chance as a friend. If this turns into a relationship, it'll be an unexpected bonus.

"Should we stop at the corner store for some cupcakes or wine coolers or something?" I ask, glancing at the foil-wrapped cookies in the backseat. "I burnt half the batch, so they went straight to the trash. The rest are technically edible, but not everyone likes them too crunchy, so we should—"

"Stop. If you're trying to impress my parents, you already won. Sometimes, it feels like they like you better than me."

"I'm thrilled to hear it, but the kid is a different story. You know Destiny has it out for me. I'm trying to change her mind about me before she gets old enough to slit my throat as payback."

Her eyes taper. "Don't talk like that. She's family, Evan."

"Sorry. Sorry. I'll shut my mouth."

I tighten my grip on the steering wheel. I don't want to cause any more drama. Especially since their lives are finally starting to settle down. According to the break room gossip at Mom's school, Destiny is a social butterfly. She's already made a bunch of friends her age, but she had a rocky start with Fiona. Which is understandable. It's not like they were instantly going to feel like family because they share some DNA. Bit by bit, the tension has been fading. Fiona has been playing historian, answering every question the kid has about her mother since she knew Faith better than anyone. Or at least, she thought she did. It's probably best for Destiny to get to know the watered-down version of her mother, anyway, not the one willing to commit murder.

We pull up to the two-story, picket-fenced house at six on the dot, parking beside my parents' bulky brown car. They're probably already inside, swapping stories with the Flynns. Ever since our brush with death at the theater, they've become the best of friends, bonding over the trauma we've put them through.

Plus, they've been working hard to set us up. My parents want me to settle down with someone nice and safe after dating a woman who aimed a gun at me and pulled the trigger. And the Flynns don't understand why Fiona is so hesitant about me since they've been spared the full story. To them, I'm a close friend, an ex-employee, a semi-successful business owner. Not the reason their other daughter is dead.

When we ring the bell, her mother encases me in a bear hug. Her father pulls me aside to chat about my business. Meanwhile, my own parents are snacking from a cheese plate, browsing through an eclectic movie collection to pick something to watch after dinner. A comedy, hopefully.

Destiny is locked in her bedroom, chipping away at homework, which is a relief. Putting on a happy face for the Flynns is taxing enough. Small-talking with the kid is another thing entirely. Of course, she can't stay cooped up in her room forever.

When the oven dings, Mrs. Flynn assigns chores. She calls Fiona to help carve the chicken and asks me to grab Destiny to set the table.

"We don't need to bother her," I say, heading for the silverware drawer. "I can set it myself."

Mrs. Flynn shakes her head. "Nonsense. You're our guest. Besides, it's important she learns responsibility."

"Okay, okay. If you insist."

I slink toward the twins' old room, knocking on the door hard enough to crack it open. Destiny is sprawled out on her canopied bed, underneath moon-shaped shelving. She completely changed the design, swapping out the pastel color palette to shades of purples so dark they verge on black. With a sagging beanbag chair and furry rug, it could pass for an average kid's room. But the little touches break the illusion—the true crime novels on the bookshelf, the scribbled, fanged drawings on her desk.

"Hey," she says, removing her earbuds. So much for homework. "What do you need?"

"Dinner is almost ready. They wanted me to bully you into setting the table."

"All right. Tell them I'll be out in a minute."

"Cool." I start to leave, then hear Fiona in my head, warning me to at least try to get along with her. "What are you listening to? Anything good? I've been on the lookout for some new bands."

"You wouldn't know it."

"Try me."

"It's mostly orchestral. It's a movie soundtrack."

"Nice. That sounds pretty—"

"From *It's Always Bloody*."

I frown. "Oh. I still haven't watched it. Isn't it rated R? Seems a little gruesome for a fifth-grader."

"I've seen scarier things in real life."

She pops her earbuds back in. Conversation over.

I shuffle back to the kitchen, my stomach in knots. Unlike everyone else, Destiny doesn't consider me a small-town hero for murdering another murderer. Why would she, when the woman was her mother? Fiona might have forgiven me, but the kid isn't going to let the past go anytime soon.

I try not to talk too much crap to Fiona, but sometimes, Destiny gives me serial killer vibes. She tackled another girl on the playground and fractured her ankle, then laughed about it over dinner. She set multiple fires in the backyard, one that nearly burned down her whole treehouse. And whenever she's on her laptop, she's watching horror films and murder docs instead of cartoons like other kids her age.

I can't stop thinking about the *nature versus nurture* argument. A killer raised her and another killer birthed her, so either way, she's in trouble. There's something dark stirring inside her, but her family hasn't wanted to acknowledge it. They chalk up her mood swings to a kid being a kid. *She's been through so much at such a young age,* they say, *she's making the best of a bad situation.*

I'm not ignorant. I understand kids can heal from trauma and be better than the environment in which they were raised. That's therapy 101. Chances are, Fiona is right. I'm overreacting. With a little bit of time and a shit-ton of counseling, the girl is going to turn out perfectly fine.

Still, in the middle of dinner, when she refills my drink without asking, my throat is too tight to thank her. The birthmark on her chin and the dark hair tumbling down her shoulders is uncanny. She looks like the spitting image of Faith. Faith who crushed pills into a powder. Faith who slipped poison into a cup.

I swirl my straw around the glass, on the lookout for floating white specks. It would be poetic, getting revenge on me for murdering her adoptive mother by using the same trick as her biological one.

Fiona must read my mind because she rolls her eyes, her mouth a tight line. After everything I've done to her, all the lies and betrayals, this is our most frequent fight. Not liking Destiny. Not trusting Destiny.

I don't want to spark another argument. So I tilt my head back and gulp.

END

HOLLY RIORDAN is a senior staff writer for Thought Catalog and Collective World. She has amassed close to a billion views on articles about modern relationships, astrology, and mental health. Follow her on Instagram and Twitter @HollyyRio

THOUGHT CATALOG Books

Thought Catalog Books is a publishing imprint of Thought Catalog, a digital magazine for thoughtful storytelling, and is owned and operated by The Thought & Expression Co. Inc., an independent media group based in the United States of America. Founded in 2010, we are committed to helping people become better communicators and listeners to engender a more exciting, attentive, and imaginative world. The Thought Catalog Books imprint connects Thought Catalog's digital-native roots with our love of traditional book publishing. The books we publish are designed as beloved art pieces. We publish work we love. Pioneering an author-first and holistic approach to book publishing, Thought Catalog Books has created numerous best-selling print books, audiobooks, and eBooks that are being translated in over 30 languages.

ThoughtCatalog.com | **Thoughtful Storytelling**
ShopCatalog.com | **Shop Books + Curated Products**

MORE FROM THOUGHT CATALOG BOOKS

Forget Her
—*Holly Riordan*

Severe(d): A Creepy Poetry Collection
—*Holly Riordan*

The Poet's Girl, A Novel of Emily Hale & T.S. Eliot
—*Sara Fitzgerald*

Hot Tea & Mercy
—*Rae Lashea*

THOUGHT CATALOG Books
THOUGHTCATALOG.COM